Leonardo Sciascia was born
where he still spends part of t
that focuses his work and, in a
the political, social and spirit
only to a degree.

LEONARDO SCIASCIA

The Day of the Owl

Equal Danger

with an afterword by Frank Kermode

Paladin
An Imprint of HarperCollins*Publishers*

Paladin
An Imprint of HarperCollins*Publishers*
77–85 Fulham Palace Road,
Hammersmith, London W6 8JB

Published by Paladin
in association with Carcanet 1987
9 8 7 6 5 4 3 2

First published in Great Britain by
Carcanet Press Ltd 1984

Il Giorno dela Civetta copyright © Giulio Einaudi Editore 1961
English translation copyright © Jonathan Cape Ltd 1963
Il Contesto copyright © Giulio Einaudi Editore 1971
English translation copyright © Jonathan Cape Ltd 1973

ISBN 0 586 08600 5

Set in Ehrhardt

Printed in Great Britain by
HarperCollinsManufacturing Glasgow

THE DAY OF THE OWL

translated from the Italian by
ARCHIBALD COLQUHOUN
& ARTHUR OLIVER

THE bus was just about to leave, amid rumbles and sudden hiccups and rattles. The square was silent in the grey of dawn; wisps of cloud swirled round the belfry of the church. The only sound, apart from the rumbling of the bus, was a voice, wheedling, ironic, of a fritter-seller; fritters, hot fritters. The conductor slammed the door, and with a clank of scrap-metal the bus moved off. His last glance round the square caught sight of a man in a dark suit running towards the bus.

'Hold it a minute,' said the conductor to the driver, opening the door with the bus still in motion. Two ear-splitting shots rang out. For a second the man in the dark suit, who was just about to jump on the running-board, hung suspended in mid-air as if some invisible hand were hauling him up by the hair. Then his brief-case dropped from his hand and very slowly he slumped down on top of it.

The conductor swore; his face was the colour of sulphur; he was shaking. The fritter-seller, who was only three yards from the fallen man, sidled off with a crab-like motion towards the door of the church. In the bus no one moved; the driver sat, as if turned to stone, his right hand on the brake, his left on the steering-wheel. The conductor looked round the passengers' faces, which were blank as the blinds.

'They've killed him,' he said; he took off his cap, swore again, and began frantically running his fingers through his hair.

'The carabinieri,' said the driver, 'we must get the carabinieri.'

9

He got up and opened the other door. 'I'll go,' he said to the conductor.

The conductor looked at the dead man and then at the passengers. These included some women, old women who brought heavy sacks of white cloth and baskets full of eggs every morning; their clothes smelled of forage, manure and wood smoke; usually they grumbled and swore, now they sat mute, their faces as if disinterred from the silence of centuries.

'Who is it?' asked the conductor, pointing at the body.

No one answered. The conductor cursed. Among passengers of that route he was famous for his highly skilled blaspheming. The company had already threatened to fire him, since he never bothered to control himself even when there were nuns or priests on the bus. He was from the province of Syracuse and had had little to do with violent death: a soft province, Syracuse. So now he swore all the more furiously.

The carabinieri arrived; the sergeant-major, with a black stubble and in a black temper from being woken, stirred the passengers' apathy like an alarm-clock: in the wake of the conductor they began to get out through the door left open by the driver.

With seeming nonchalance, looking around as if they were trying to gauge the proper distance from which to admire the belfry, they drifted off towards the sides of the square and, after a last look around, scuttled into alley-ways.

The sergeant-major and his men did not notice this gradual exodus. Now about fifty people were around the dead man: men from a public works training centre who were only too delighted to have found such an absorbing topic of conversation to while away their eight hours of idleness. The sergeant-major ordered his men to clear the square and get the passengers back on to the bus. The carabinieri began pushing sightseers back towards the streets leading off the square, asking passengers to take their seats on the bus again. When the square was empty, so was the bus. Only the driver and the conductor remained.

'What?' said the sergeant-major to the driver. 'No passengers today?'

'Yes, some,' replied the driver with an absent-minded look.

'Some,' said the sergeant-major, 'means four, five or six ... I've never seen this bus leave with an empty seat.'

'How should I know?' said the driver, exhausted from straining his memory. 'How should I know? I said "some" just like that. More than five or six though. Maybe more; maybe the bus was full. I never look to see who's there. I just get into my seat and off we go. The road's the only thing I look at; that's what I'm paid for ... to look at the road.'

The sergeant-major rubbed his chin with a hand taut with irritation. 'I get it,' he said, 'you just look at the road.' He rounded savagely on the conductor. 'But you, you tear off the tickets, take money, give change. You count the people and look at their faces ... and if you don't want me to make you remember 'em in the guard-room, you're going to tell me now who was on that bus! At least ten names ... You've been on this run for the last three years, and for the last three years I've seen you every evening in the Café Italia. You know this town better than I do ... '

'Nobody could know the town better than you do,' said the conductor with a smile, as though shrugging off a compliment.

'All right, then,' said the sergeant-major, sneering, 'first me, then you ... But I wasn't on the bus or I'd remember every passenger one by one. So it's up to you. Ten names at least.'

'I can't remember,' said the conductor, 'by my mother's soul I can't remember. Just now I can't remember a thing. It all seems a dream.'

'I'll wake you up,' raged the sergeant-major, 'I'll wake you up with a couple of years inside ... ' He broke off to go and meet the police magistrate who had just arrived. While making his report on the identity of the dead man and the flight of the passengers, the sergeant-major looked at the bus. As he looked, he had an impression that something was not quite right or was missing, as when something in our daily routine is unexpectedly missing, which the senses perceive from force of habit but the mind does not quite apprehend; even so its absence provokes an empty feeling of discomfort, a vague exasperation as from a flickering light-bulb. Then, suddenly, what we are looking for dawns on us.

'There's something missing,' said the sergeant-major to Carabiniere Sposito, who being a qualified accountant was a pillar of the Carabinieri Station of S., 'there's something or someone missing.'

'The fritter-seller,' said Carabiniere Sposito.

'The fritter-seller, by God!' The sergeant-major exulted, thinking: 'An accountant's diploma means something.'

A carabiniere was sent off at the double to pick up the

fritter-seller. He knew where to find the man, who, after the departure of the first bus, usually went to sell his wares at the entrance of the elementary schools. Ten minutes later the sergeant-major had the vender of fritters in front of him. The man's expression was that of a man roused from innocent slumber.

'Was he there?' the sergeant-major asked the conductor.

'He was,' answered the conductor gazing at his shoe.

'Well now,' said the sergeant-major with paternal kindness, 'this morning, as usual, you came to sell your fritters here ... As usual, at the first bus for Palermo ... '

'I've my licence,' said the fritter-seller.

'I know,' said the sergeant-major, raising his eyes to heaven, imploring patience. 'I know and I'm not thinking about your licence. I want to know only one thing, and, if you tell me, you can go off at once and sell your fritters to the kids: who fired the shots?'

'Why,' asked the fritter-seller, astonished and inquisitive, 'has there been shooting?'

* * *

'Yes, at half past six. From the corner of Via Cavour. A double dose of *lupara** probably from a twelve-bore, maybe from a sawn-off shotgun ... Nobody on the bus saw a thing. A hell of a job to find out who *was* on the bus. When I got there they had all made off. A man who sells fritters remembered – after a couple of hours – seeing something like a sack of coal. He's made a vow of

*Lupara literally 'wolf-shot'. A cartridge loaded with five or seven ball-bearings used for mafia killings. (Tr.)

half a peck of chick-peas to Santa Fara because by a miracle he didn't get some of the lead, he says, standing as near as he was to the target ... The conductor didn't even see the sack of coal ... The passengers, those sitting on the right-hand side, say the windows were so steamy they looked like frosted glass. Maybe true ... Yes, head of a co-operative building company, a small one which seems never to have taken on contracts for more than twenty million lire ... small building lots, workers' houses, drains, secondary roads ... Salvatore Colasberna, Co-la-sbe-rna. Used to be a bricklayer. Ten years ago he formed the company with two of his brothers and four or five local bricklayers; he was in charge of the work, though a surveyor figured as director, and used to keep the accounts. They got along as best they could. He and his associates were content with a small profit, as though they were working for wages ... No, it seems they didn't do the sort of job that gets washed away by the first shower of rain ... I've seen a farm building, brand new, caved in like a cardboard box because a cow rubbed against it ... No, built by the Smiroldi company, big building contractors. A farm building smashed by a cow! ... Colasberna, they tell me, used to do a solid job. There's the Via Madonna di Fatima here, made by his outfit, which hasn't sunk a centimetre, in spite of all the trucks that use it; while other streets, made by much bigger contractors, look like a camel's back after only a year ... Had he a criminal record? Yes, in nineteen forty ... here we are, in nineteen forty, the third of November, nineteen forty ... He was travelling on a bus – he doesn't seem to have much luck with buses – and people were discussing the war we had just declared on Greece;

someone said: "We'll suck it dry in a fortnight" – he meant Greece. Colasberna said: "What is *it*? An egg?" There was a Blackshirt on the bus who reported him ... What? ... Sorry, you asked me if he had a criminal record and I, with the file in front of me, say he had ... All right, then, he hadn't a criminal record ... Me? ... A Fascist? When I see fasces I touch wood ... Yes, sir. Yours to command.'

He replaced the telephone on its hook with the delicacy of exasperation and wiped his forehead with his handkerchief. 'This one's been a partisan,' he said. 'I would have the luck to hit on someone who's been a partisan!'

* * *

The two surviving Colasberna brothers and the other members of the Santa Fara Co-operative Building Society were waiting for the captain to arrive. They were all sitting in a row, dressed in black; the brothers had black woollen shawls over their shoulders, and bloodshot eyes; they were unshaven in sign of mourning. Motionless they sat in the waiting-room of the Carabinieri Station of S., their eyes riveted to a coloured target painted on the wall with the ironic wording: UNLOAD FIREARMS HERE. They felt an overwhelming shame at being in such a place and at having to wait. Compared to shame, death is nothing.

Sitting apart from them, perched on the edge of her chair, was a young woman. She had come in after them and wanted to see the sergeant-major, so she told the orderly. The reply was that the sergeant-major was busy and the captain was on his way. 'I'll wait,' she said, and sat on the edge of her chair, fidgeting with her fingers so that it made the others nervy to look at her. They knew her by sight; she was the wife of a tree-pruner from another village who had come from near-by B. to settle down in S. after the war, married here, and now in this poverty-stricken place – what with his wife's dowry and his job – was considered well-off.

'She's had a row with her husband and has come to make a charge,' thought the members of the Santa Fara Co-operative Society, and the thought helped take their minds off that burning shame of theirs.

There came a sound of a car pulling up in the court-yard, and of the engine cutting off, then the click of heels down the passage. Into the waiting-room came the captain, for whom the warrant-officer opened the door of his own office with a salute so stiff and a head held so high that he seemed to be inspecting the ceiling. The captain was young, tall and fair-skinned. At his first words the Santa Fara members thought, with a mixture of relief and scorn, 'A mainlander.' Mainlanders are decent enough but just don't understand things.

Again they sat down in a row in front of the sergeant-major's desk. The captain sat in the desk-chair with the sergeant-major standing beside him, and on the other side, crouched over the typewriter, sat Carabiniere Sposito. Sposito had a baby face, but the brothers Colasberna and their associates were in holy terror of his presence, the terror of a merciless inquisition, of the black seed of the written word. 'White soil, black seed. Beware of the man who sows it. He never forgets,' says the proverb.

The captain offered his condolences and apologized for

summoning them to the barracks and for keeping them waiting. Again they thought: 'A mainlander; they're polite, mainlanders,' but they still kept a wary eye on Carabiniere Sposito whose hands were lightly poised over the keyboard of the typewriter, tense and silent as a hunter lying in wait for a hare in the moonlight, his finger on the trigger.

'It's odd,' said the captain, as though continuing an interrupted discussion, 'how people in this part of the world let themselves go in anonymous letters. No one talks, but luckily for us – I mean us carabinieri, of course – everyone writes. They may forget to sign, but they do write. After every murder, every hold-up, there are a dozen anonymous letters on my desk. Even after a family row or a fraudulent bankruptcy they write. And as for my men's love-affairs ... ' He smiled at his sergeant-major, and the Santa Fara members thought he might be alluding to the fact that Carabiniere Savarino was having an affair with the daughter of Palazzolo the tobacconist, as was known in the whole town where an early posting for Savarino was expected.

'As for the Colasberna case,' went on the captain, 'I've already had five anonymous letters; quite a crop for something that only happened the day before yesterday – and there'll be more to come. One nameless correspondent says that Colasberna was killed out of jealousy and gives the name of the jealous husband ... '

'Nonsense,' said Giuseppe Colasberna.

'I agree,' said the captain and went on: 'According to another he was killed by mistake, because he happened to resemble a man called Perricone, who – my anonymous informer says – deserves what's soon coming to him.'

'That might be,' said Giuseppe Colasberna.

'No, it mightn't,' said the captain, 'because the Perricone mentioned in the letter got a passport a couple of weeks ago and right now happens to be in Liège, Belgium. You didn't know that, maybe; certainly the writer of the letter didn't; but the fact could hardly have escaped the notice of anyone intending to bump him off ... I won't waste your time with other even more ridiculous information, but there is one aspect of the case to which I would ask you to give serious thought ... In my opinion, it might be the right track. I mean your own work, competition, contracts. That's where we should start.'

Another quick glance of consultation. 'That can't be,' said Giuseppe Colasberna.

'Oh, yes, it can,' said the captain, 'and I'll tell you exactly how and why. Apart from your particular case, I've a great deal of inside information on the contracting business, only hearsay, unfortunately, but if I had proof ... Well now, let's just suppose that in this district, in this province, there are ten contracting firms operating. Each firm has its own machinery and materials, that lie by the roadside or on the building site at night. Machines are delicate things. All you have to do is remove a piece, even a single bolt, and it will take hours or days to get it running again. As for the materials, fuel oil, tar, timber, it's easy enough to lift those or burn them on the spot. True, there is often a hut near the machinery and materials where some workmen sleep, but that's just it; they sleep. Well now, there are other people – and you know who I mean – who never sleep. Wouldn't it be natural to turn to these people – these people who never

18

sleep – for protection? Especially when protection has been offered you at once and, if you've been unwise enough to refuse it, something has happened to make you decide to accept it ... Of course, there are the stubborn, the people who say no they don't want it, and wouldn't accept it even with a knife at their throats. From what I can see, you're stubborn ... or perhaps only Salvatore was ...'

'This is all new to us,' said Giuseppe Colasberna, and the others, with taut faces, nodded assent.

'Maybe it is, maybe it isn't,' said the captain, 'but I haven't finished yet. Now, let's say that nine out of ten contractors accept or ask for protection. It would be a poor sort of association – and you know what association I refer to – if it were to limit itself to the functions and pay of night-watchmen. The protection offered by the association is on a much vaster scale. It obtains private contracts for you, I mean for the firms which toe the line and accept protection. It gives you valuable tips if you want to submit a tender for public works, it supports you when the final inspection comes up, it saves trouble with your workmen ... Obviously, if nine companies out of ten have accepted protection, thus forming a kind of union, the tenth which refuses is a black sheep. It can't do much harm, of course, but its very existence is a challenge and a bad example. So, by fair means or foul, it must be forced to come into the fold or be wiped out once and for all.'

Giuseppe Colasberna said: 'This is the first I've ever heard of all this,' and his brother and partners made signs of approval.

'Now, let's suppose,' went on the captain as though he

had not heard, 'that your company, the Santa Fara, is the black sheep of the district, the one that won't play ball, that submits honest tenders and competes for contracts without protection. Sometimes, especially with the system of maximum and minimum prices, it succeeds in making the winning offer simply because it has made an honest estimate ... One fine day, a person "worthy of respect", as you would say, comes to have a little talk with Salvatore Colasberna; what he says might mean anything and nothing, allusive, blurred as the back of a piece of embroidery, a tangle of knots and threads with the pattern on the other side ... Colasberna cannot or will not look at the other side and the man "worthy of respect" takes umbrage. The association moves into action; as a first warning, a small dump goes up in smoke, or something like that. Then comes a second warning; late one evening, round about eleven, as you are on your way home, a bullet just misses you ... '

The partners of the Santa Fara avoided the captain's eyes. They stared at their hands, looked up at the portrait of the Commander-in-Chief of the Carabinieri, at that of the President of the Republic and at the crucifix hanging on the wall. After a long pause, the captain struck just where they were most sensitive.

'I seem to remember something of the kind happening to your brother six months ago,' he said, 'just as he was going home, round about eleven ... Didn't it?'

'Er ... I ... I never heard about it,' stammered Giuseppe.

'They won't talk,' broke in the warrant-officer, 'even if they're picked off one by one, they still won't talk. They'd sooner get themselves killed ... '

The captain interrupted him with a gesture. 'Listen,' he said, 'there's a woman waiting out there ... '

'I'll go at once,' said the sergeant-major, rather crest-fallen.

'There's no more for me to say to you,' went on the captain. 'I've already said a good deal and you have nothing to tell me. Before you go I want each one of you to write his name and surname, place and date of birth, and address on this sheet of paper.'

'I write very slowly,' said Giuseppe, and the others affirmed that they also wrote slowly and with difficulty.

'No matter,' said the captain, 'there's plenty of time.' He lit a cigarette and watched the efforts of the partners on the sheet of paper. They wrote as if the pen were as heavy as a pneumatic drill: and because of their awkwardness and shaking hands, it vibrated like one too. When they had finished, he rang for the orderly, who came in with the sergeant-major.

'Show these gentlemen out,' ordered the captain.

'Christ, he knows how to treat people,' thought the partners, and in their joy at having been almost spared (the 'almost' referred to those specimens of their handwriting the captain had wanted) and at having been called gentlemen by an officer of Carabinieri, they went out quite forgetful of their mourning and longing to run and skip like boys just let out of school.

Meanwhile the captain was comparing their handwriting with that of the anonymous letter. He was sure that one of them had written it and, in spite of its clumsy slope and disguise, it did not need an expert to tell by comparing it to that of the personal details on the other sheet of paper in front of him that the writer was

Giuseppe Colasberna. The clue provided by the anonymous letter was a sure one.

The sergeant-major could not understand why the captain was bothering to study that handwriting.

'It's like squeezing tripe: nothing comes out,' he said, meaning the Colasberna brothers, their partners, the town in general and Sicily as a whole.

'No, something,' replied the captain.

'Well, as long as you're happy,' thought the sergeant-major, mentally using the personal "tu". In his inner thoughts he would use it with General Lombardi himself.

'What about that woman now?' asked the captain, getting up to leave again.

'It's about her husband,' answered the sergeant-major. 'He went off into the country the day before yesterday to do some pruning and is not back yet. He must have been invited to some farmhouse party, you know, a fat lamb and lots of wine, then he probably went to sleep it off in a haystack, dead drunk … He'll turn up this evening, I'll bet my life.'

'The day before yesterday … If I were you I'd start looking for him,' said the captain.

'Yes, sir,' said the sergeant-major.

* * *

'I don't like him,' said the man in black, looking as if his teeth were on edge from eating unripe plums; his sun-baked face, alive with a peculiar intelligence, was wry with disgust. 'I don't like him at all.'

'But you didn't like the other one, the one before him,

either. Do we have to change 'em every couple of weeks?' said, with a smile, a well-dressed fair man who was sitting beside him. Both were Sicilians and differed only in physique and manners.

They were in a café in Rome, a pink, silent room with mirrors, chandeliers like great clusters of flowers and a shapely brunette cloakroom girl who looked as if she could be peeled out of her black dress like a fruit.

She shouldn't be made merely to take it off, thought both the fair man and the dark man alike, but it should be removed stitch by stitch.

'I took a dislike to that other fellow because of the fuss he made about firearm licences,' said the dark man.

'And before the firearm licences there was someone else you disliked because of the internment camp.'

'Is an internment camp a laughing matter?'

'No, no laughing matter at all, I know; but, for one reason or another, you never manage to get on with any of them.'

'But this is different. The presence of a man like him in our part of the world ought to upset you more than it does me. He was a partisan; with all the hotbed of communists we have down there, they had to send us an ex-partisan as well. No wonder our interests are going to pieces ... '

'But what evidence have you that he protects the communists?'

'I'll give you just one example. You know how badly the sulphur mines are doing at the moment. I curse the day I ever went into partnership with Scarantino in that mine. What little capital I had, my life's blood, is being sucked dry by that mine. We're ruined.'

'So you're ruined, then,' said the fair man, ironically incredulous.

'Well, if I'm not utterly ruined, I owe it to you. To you and the government which, one must admit, really has been taking measures over the sulphur crisis ... '

'Such measures that with the money it pays out you could pay your workers regularly and adequately without them ever going down the mine; and perhaps that would be the best solution.'

'Anyway, things are going badly. And, of course, they are going badly for everybody. Why should I be the only one to pay? The workers must pay their share as well ... They've had no wages for two weeks ... '

'Three months,' corrected the other man with a smile.

'I don't remember exactly ... Anyway, they went and held a protest meeting outside my house ... such foul language and catcalls ... they deserve to be shot ... Well, I went to complain to him and d'you know what he said to me? "Have you eaten today?" "Yes, I have," I said. "Yesterday, too?" he asked. "Yesterday, too," I said. "Is your family starving?" he asked. "No, thank the Lord," I replied. "And these people who came and made a row outside your house, have they eaten today?" I was on the point of saying: "What the hell do I care whether they have eaten or not?" but from politeness I replied: "I don't know." He said, "You ought to find out." "I've come to you," I told him, "because they are outside my house and threatening me. My wife and daughters can't even go out to go to Mass." "Oh," he said, "we'll see that they get to Mass all right. That's what we're here for ... You don't pay your workmen but we see that your wife and daughters get to Mass." I'm telling you, the look on his face made my fingers itch and you know how hot-blooded I am ... '

'Now, now, now,' said the fair man in crescendo, his tone reproving the urge to violence and at the same time enjoining discretion.

'Oh, nowadays my nerves are as steady as a winch-rope. I'm not what I used to be thirty years ago. But I say: has a policeman ever dared to talk so to a man of honour before? He's a communist. Only communists talk like that.'

'Not only communists, unfortunately. We have people in the party who talk just the same ... If you knew the struggle we have, every day ... every hour ... '

'I know. They're all the same to me, communists, the lot of them.'

'They're not communists,' said the fair man, gloomily thoughtful.

'Well, if they aren't communists, why doesn't the Pope give them a little plain talk? That'd fix them.'

'It's not quite so simple ... but enough of that. To return to our little matter, what's the name of this ... communist?'

'Bellodi, I think. He commands the Carabinieri Company in C. and in three months he's already become a nuisance. Now he's poking his nose into local contracting companies ... Commendatore Zarcone is counting on you too. He said to me only the other day: "Let's hope our Honourable Member gets him sent back north to eat polenta!" '

'Dear old Zarcone!' said the Honourable Member. 'How is he?'

'He could be doing better,' said the dark man with meaning.

'We'll see that he does,' promised the Honourable Member.

* * *

Captain Bellodi, commanding the Carabinieri of C., sat facing the 'informer' of S. He had sent for him, with the usual precautions, to find out what the man thought about the Colasberna killing. Usually when something serious happened in the town the informer showed up of his own accord. He had been a sheep rustler just after the war but now, as far as was known, was merely a go-between for usurers. He informed partly by vocation and partly because he deluded himself that by so doing he could carry on his activity with impunity. This activity he considered honest and sensible compared with that of armed robbery, befitting the father of a family, and his past as a sheep-stealer he wrote off as an error of youth. Now, without a lira of capital, simply by handling the money of others, he managed to support a wife and three children and was even able to set some aside to be invested later in a little business: for to stand measuring out cloth behind the counter of a little shop was his life-long dream.

But his easy and lucrative living was connected with his youthful error and the fact that he was an ex-convict: for the gentry who entrusted their money to him, honest men quite above suspicion, supporters of the social order and pillars of the Church, relied on his reputation to prevent their victims lapsing in their payments and to ensure no trouble about secrecy. Indeed, such was the fear that the go-between inspired ('I've left my jacket at the Ucciardone prison,' he used to say as a joke or a threat, meaning that if he killed someone he would go back and fetch it, though as a matter of fact the very thought of prison made him shudder), that debtors paid one hundred per cent interest and dead on time. Rare extensions were granted by applying a cumulative rate of interest, whose net result was that anyone who had obtained a loan, say, to buy the mule necessary to work the few acres of land he owned, found himself after a couple of years minus both mule and land.

Had it not been for his fear, the informer would have reckoned himself happy and an honest man both morally and financially. But terror lurked within him like a rabid dog, growling, panting, slobbering, sometimes suddenly howling in its sleep. For incessant gnawing at the liver and sudden painful stabs at the heart, like a live rabbit's in a dog's mouth, doctors had made diagnosis after diagnosis and prescribed him enough medicines to fill his dressing-table drawer; of his terror the doctors knew nothing.

He was sitting in front of the captain, turned slightly sideways so as not to look him in the face, and nervously twisting his cap, while all the time the dog inside him bit, growled, bit again. The evening was icy cold and the tiny electric stove in the captain's office gave out so little warmth that it made the vast, bare room seem even colder. Even the old-fashioned whitish enamelled tiles with which it was paved looked like ice. Still, the man was sweating; a cold death-shroud enveloped him, chill over the fiery laceration of the *lupara* slugs which were already rending his flesh.

From the moment he had heard of Colasberna's death,

the informer had begun thinking out his story. At each detail he added, each little touch, like a painter standing back from his canvas to judge the effect of a brush-stroke, he would say to himself: 'Perfect. Not another thing needed,' but kept on adding and retouching. And he was still feverishly adding and retouching even as he told it to the captain. But the captain knew, from a voluminous dossier on the police informer, Calogero Dibella, alias *Parrinieddu* or 'Little Priest', that of the two *cosche* or local mafia groups (*cosca*, they had explained to him, meant the thick cluster of artichoke leaves) Dibella was closer to, if not actually a member of, the one which had certain if unprovable connections with public works. As S. was a coastal town, the other *cosca*, younger and more enterprising, mainly concerned itself with the contraband of American cigarettes. He thus foresaw the informer's lie; but in any case it would be useful to watch the man's reactions while telling it.

He listened without interrupting, occasionally adding to Dibella's discomfiture with a distracted nod. In the meanwhile he thought of those other informers buried under a thin layer of soil and dried leaves high in folds of the Apennines. Wretched dregs, soaked in fear and vice; yet they had gambled with death, staking their lives on the razor's edge of a lie between partisans and fascists. The only human emotion they had was the tormenting agony of their own cowardice. From fear of death they faced death every day; until finally it struck, final, permanent, unequivocal death, not the double-cross, the double death of every hour.

The informer of S. was risking his life; sooner or later one *cosca* or the other, either with a double-barrel of *lupara* or a burst from a submachine gun (the two *cosche* also differed in their choice of weapons), would fix him. But between mafia and carabinieri, the two sides between which he played his game of chance, death could come to him only from one side. On this side there was no death; there was only this fair, clean-shaven man in his smart uniform, who lisped, never raised his voice, or treated him with scorn. Yet he was just as much the law as was that gruesome death. To the informer the law was not a rational thing born of reason, but something depending on a man, on the thoughts and the mood of this man here, on the cut he gave himself shaving or a good cup of coffee he has just drunk. To him the law was utterly irrational, created on the spot by those in command, the municipal guard, the sergeant, the chief of police or the magistrate, whoever happened to be administering it. The informer had never, could never have, believed that the law was definitely codified and the same for all; for him between rich and poor, between wise and ignorant, stood the guardians of the law who only used the strong arm on the poor; the rich they protected and defended. It was like a barbed wire entanglement, a wall. The thief who had done time, was involved with the mafia, negotiated extortionate loans and played the informer asked only to find a hole in the wall, a gap in the barbed wire. If he did, he would soon raise enough capital to open his little shop; his elder son he would put into a seminary, either to become a priest or leave before ordination to become, better than a priest, a lawyer. Once over the wall the law would no longer hold terrors. How wonderful it would be to look back on those still behind the wall, behind the barbed wire.

So, tortured by fear, he tried to find some consolation by fondly picturing his future peace, a peace founded on poverty and injustice. But for him the fatal bullet was already cast.

Captain Bellodi, on the contrary, an Emilian from Parma, was by family tradition and personal conviction a republican, a soldier who followed what used to be called 'the career of arms' in a police force, with the dedication of a man who has played his part in a revolution and has seen law created by it. This law, the law of the Republic, which safeguarded liberty and justice, he served and enforced. If he still wore a uniform which he had first put on by chance, if he had not left the service to become a lawyer, the career to which he had been destined, it was because the task of serving and enforcing the law of the Republic was becoming more arduous every day.

The informer would have been astounded to know that the man he was facing, a carabiniere and an officer too, regarded the authority vested in him as a surgeon regards the knife: an instrument to be used with care, precision and certainty; a man convinced that law rests on the idea of justice and that any action taken by the law should be governed by justice. His was a difficult and ungrateful profession; but the informer only saw him as a happy man, happy in the joy of being able to abuse his powers, a joy the more intense the more suffering can be inflicted on others.

Like a shopkeeper displaying his lengths of cheap cotton to country housewives, *Parrinieddu* unwound his roll of lies. His nickname of Little Priest was due to the easy eloquence and hypocrisy he exuded. But, as a result of the officer's silence, his fluency began to leave him, his words began to sound tearful or strident, and the pattern he was weaving became incoherent, incredible.

'Don't you think –' the captain quietly asked him after a while, in a tone of friendly confidence – 'don't you think it might be more useful to explore other possibilities?' The double-s of the Emilian accent left the word incomplete and vague and for a moment distracted the informer from his flow.

Parrinieddu did not reply.

'Don't you think that there's a chance that Colasberna was done away with for, let us say, a question of interest? For not having accepted certain proposals? For having continued, in spite of threats, to land all he could in the way of contracts?'

Captain Bellodi's predecessors had been in the habit of questioning the informer in threatening tones with explicit alternatives of either internment by the police or a charge of usury. This, instead of frightening *Parrinieddu*, had given him a certain sense of security. The link was clear: the police were forcing him to some betrayal and he just had to produce enough information to keep them quiet and himself out of trouble. But with someone treating him kindly and taking him into his confidence, things were different. So he answered the captain's question with a disjointed motion of the hands and head: yes, it was possible.

'And,' continued the captain in the same tone, 'do you happen to know of anyone who takes an interest in such matters? I don't mean those who work on contracts; I mean those who don't, who concern themselves with helping, with protecting ... It would be enough for me to know the name of the man who, some months ago,

31

made certain proposals to Colasberna; proposals, mark you, only proposals ... '

'I know nothing,' said the informer and, encouraged by the captain's gentle manner, his spy's instinct soared like a lark trilling its joy at being able to hurt. 'I know nothing,' he repeated, 'but, taking a shot in the dark, I'd say that the proposals were made either by Ciccio La Rosa or by Saro Pizzuco ... ' But already that giddy flight of joy had turned into a headlong drop, a stone plummeting down into the very centre of his being, his fear.

*   *   *

'Another question in the House,' said His Excellency. ' "Is the Minister aware of the serious acts of violence which have recently taken place in Sicily and what steps does he intend to take ... ?" etc. etc. The communists, as usual. It seems that they are referring to the murder of that contractor ... What was his name?'

'Colasberna, Excellency.'

'Colasberna ... A communist, it seems ... '

'A socialist, Excellency.'

'You will make that distinction. You are stubborn, my friend, allow me to tell you. Communist or socialist, what's the difference?'

'At the present juncture ... '

'For heaven's sake, no explanations. Even I read the papers sometimes, you know ... '

'I would never take the liberty of ... '

'Good. Now, to avoid this ... '

'Colasberna.'

'This Colasberna becoming a martyr in the communist ... sorry, I mean socialist cause, we must find out who killed him. Pretty damn quickly, too, so that the Minister can reply that Colasberna was the victim of a question of interest, or had been after somebody's wife and politics had nothing to do with it.'

'The investigation is going well. It is clearly a mafia crime, but nothing to do with politics. Captain Bellodi ... '

'Who is this Bellodi?'

'He commands the Carabinieri in C. He's been in Sicily some months now ... '

'Right. Now here's the point: I've been wanting to talk to you for some while about Bellodi. This fellow, my dear friend, has a fixation about the mafia. One of those Northerners with a head full of prejudices who begin to see the mafia in everything before they even get off the ferry-boat. If he says that Colasberna was killed by the mafia, we're sunk. I don't know whether you read what a journalist wrote some weeks ago about the kidnapping of that landowner ... What was his name?'

'Mendolia.'

'That's it, Mendolia. He said things to make your hair stand on end. That the mafia exists, that it is a powerful organization, that it controls everything: flocks, fruit and vegetables, public works and Greek vases ... That about Greek vases is priceless ... like a comic postcard. What I say is this: let's have a little sense of responsibility ... Do you believe in the mafia?'

'Well, er ... '

'And you?'

'No, I don't.'

'Good man! We two, both Sicilians, don't believe in

the mafia. That ought to mean something to you, who evidently do. But I can understand you. You aren't Sicilian and prejudices die hard. In time you will be convinced that it is all a build-up. But, meanwhile, now for heaven's sake keep an eye on the investigations of this man Bellodi ... And you, who don't believe in the mafia, try to get something done. Send someone, someone who knows how to handle things. We don't want any trouble with Bellodi, but ... *Ima summis mutare*. Do you understand Latin? Not Horace's: mine, I mean.'

*　*　*

Paolo Nicolosi, tree-pruner by trade, born at B. on December 14th, 1920, now domiciled and resident in S., at No. 97 Via Cavour, had been missing for five days. On the fourth day his wife had gone back to see the sergeant-major, who, this time, began to take things seriously. His report lay on Captain Bellodi's desk and 'No. 97 Via Cavour' was underlined in red. The captain was pacing up and down the room smoking furiously; he was waiting to hear from the Records Office and from the Magistrature if Paolo Nicolosi had a criminal record or there were any outstanding charges against him.

Colasberna had been shot from the corner of Via Cavour and Piazza Garibaldi. Having fired the shots, the murderer would hardly have come forward into the square where there was a bus with about fifty people on board and a fritter-seller only two paces from the dead man. It was more logical to assume that he had made his get-away down Via Cavour. The time had been six thirty in the morning and the report stated that Nicolosi was to have gone to prune trees at the Fondachello farm, about an hour away on foot. Perhaps, when the killer was running down the street, Nicolosi had come out and recognized him. But how many other people had seen him? The murderer could have counted on Nicolosi's silence, as on that of the fritter-seller and all the others, had he been either a resident or someone well-known in the town; but certainly, in a crime of this sort, he must have been a hired assassin from elsewhere. We learn from America.

No flights of fancy, the major had warned him. All right, then, no flights of fancy. But Sicily is all a realm of fantasy and what can anyone do there without imagination? Nothing but plain facts, then, which were these: a man called Colasberna had been killed just as he was getting on a bus for Palermo in Piazza Garibaldi at six thirty in the morning. The murderer had shot him from the corner of Via Cavour and Piazza Garibaldi and made his escape down Via Cavour. On the same day, at the same time, a man who lived in the same Via Cavour was leaving home, or just about to. According to his wife, she had been expecting him back in the evening, at about Angelus time as usual, she said, but he had never turned up then, nor for the next five days. At the Fondachello farm they say that they've not seen him; they were expecting him that day but he never appeared. He had vanished, together with his mule and his implements, between the door of his house and the Fondachello farm, some four or five miles apart. He had vanished without a trace.

If Nicolosi turned out to have a criminal record or to be involved in some way with the underworld, then he might possibly have gone into hiding; or maybe someone had settled a grudge and covered up all trace of him. But if he hadn't; if there were no reason for him to make any premeditated disappearance; if he were not a man to have any direct or indirect accounts to settle with the underworld; then his disappearance could be definitely, without any flight of fancy, connected with the murder of Colasberna.

The captain did not at that moment take into account a chance of Nicolosi's disappearance being in some way connected with his wife; of it being, in other words, one of those crimes of passion, so useful alike to mafia and police. Ever since the time when, in the sudden silence of the orchestra pit, during *Cavalleria Rusticana*, the cry of '*Hanno ammazzato cumpari Turiddu!*' ('They've killed Turiddu!') first chilled the spines of opera enthusiasts, criminal statistics and number symbols of the lottery in Sicily have had closer links between cuckoldom and violent death. A crime of passion is solved at once: so it is an asset to the police; it is also punished lightly: so it is an asset to the mafia. Nature imitates art; Turiddu Macca, having been killed on the stage by Mascagni's music and Compare Alfio's knife, began to figure on tourist maps – and autopsy tables – of Sicily. Sometimes, though, either by knife or by *lupara* (luckily no longer by music) the Alfios get the worst of it. At that moment Captain Bellodi did not take this into account; a distraction that was to bring him a minor reprimand.

Negative reports on Paolo Nicolosi were brought back by Sergeants D'Antona and Pitrone from the Magistrature and the Records Office – no charges outstanding, no previous convictions. The captain was satisfied, but impatient; impatient to hurry over to S. and talk with Nicolosi's wife, with some of the missing man's friends, with the sergeant-major; to question the people at Fondachello and then, should circumstances warrant, have a word with the two men named by the informer, La Rosa and Pizzuco.

It was already midday. He ordered his car and hurried downstairs, feeling like singing from mounting excitement, and actually humming as he made his way to the canteen. There he ate a couple of sandwiches and drank a hot coffee, a coffee made specially for him by the carabiniere-barman, with the right amount of coffee and all the skill of a Neapolitan trying to get on the right side of his superior.

The day was cold and bright, the country limpid: trees, fields and rocks gave an impression of gelid fragility as though a gust of wind or an impact would shatter them with a tinkle of breaking glass. The air, too, vibrated like glass to the engine of the little Fiat 600. Overhead large black crows flew around as if in a glass maze, suddenly wheeling, dropping or circling up vertically as though between invisible walls. The road was deserted. In the back seat Sergeant D'Antona held out of the window the muzzle of his sten-gun, his finger on the trigger. Only a month before on this road the bus from S. to C. had been held up and all the passengers robbed. The bandits, all minors, were already in San Francesco Prison.

The sergeant, watching the road uneasily, thought of his income and his expenses, of pay and wife, pay and television set, pay and sick children. The carabiniere-driver thought about a film, *Europe by Night*, which he

37

had seen the evening before, and of his surprise at Cocinelle being a man, a man indeed! Behind this thought, which was more vision than thought, lay a worry, deep down and hidden lest the captain guess it, at not having eaten in barracks and if they would be in time to get anything with the Carabinieri of S. But that captain – what a man! – did guess and told the two of them, sergeant and driver, that they would have to scrounge something for themselves at S. and that he was sorry for not having thought of it before leaving. The driver blushed and thought, not for the first time: 'He's a kind man, but he reads my mind.' The sergeant said that he was not hungry and could go without eating till next day.

At S. the sergeant-major, who had not been warned, came out with his mouth full, his face red with surprise and mortification. He'd had to leave a plate of roast mutton; cold, it would be disgusting; heated up, worse; mutton must be eaten hot, swimming in fat and savoury with pepper. Oh, well, it's a penance; let's hear the news.

News there was. The sergeant-major nodded his approval; though, to tell the truth, not altogether convinced of a link between the shooting of Colasberna and Nicolosi's disappearance. He sent for the widow, a couple of Nicolosi's friends and the man's brother-in-law. 'Widow' was the word he used as he sent the carabiniere to fetch her, for he had no doubt the man was dead. A quiet-living man like Nicolosi only vanishes for so long for that one simple reason. Meanwhile, he invited the captain for a bite; the captain declined, saying that he had already eaten.

'So you've eaten, have you!' thought the sergeant-major, his resentment chill as the fat on his mutton chops by now.

She was pretty, the widow; with dark brown hair and jet black eyes, fine features, and a serene expression, but a vaguely mischievous smile on her lips. She was not shy. Her dialect was comprehensible so the captain did not need the sergeant-major to act as interpreter; he himself asked the woman the meaning of certain words and sometimes she found the right Italian equivalent or explained by a phrase in dialect. The captain had known many Sicilians, during his partisan period and, later, among the carabinieri. He had also read Giovanni Meli with Francesco Lanza's notes and Ignazio Buttitta with the facing translation by Quasimodo.

That day her husband had been up just before six. She had heard him get up, in the dark, not wanting to wake her. He had been a very considerate man – 'had been', just like that – for evidently she shared the sergeant-major's opinion. But she woke up as she did every morning; and, as usual, told him that the coffee was ready in the sideboard – all it needed was heating up; then she had got back to sleep; not quite asleep, though, but dozing. She heard her husband moving about in the kitchen, then go downstairs to open the street door of the stable. In five or ten minutes, by the time he had got the mule ready, she had again dropped off to sleep. A clink of metal woke her; it was her husband, come up again to fetch his cigarettes and, fumbling on the bedside table in the dark, had knocked over a little silver Sacred Heart, given to her by an aunt who was Mother Superior at the Immacolata Convent. Almost wide awake, she asked her husband what was the matter. 'Nothing,' was

39

his reply, 'go to sleep. I've forgotten my cigarettes.' 'Put the light on,' she said, wide awake now. He said there was no need, then asked her whether she had been woken by two shots fired near by, or by him knocking over the Sacred Heart. That was just like him, she said, capable of blaming himself all day for having woken her. He really had loved her.

'And did you hear the two shots?'

'No. In my sleep I hear every sound in the house, my husband's movements, but outside there might be the fireworks for Santa Rosalia and I'd not wake.'

'What happened next?'

'I put on the light, the little light beside me, sat up in bed and asked him what had happened, what the two shots had been. My husband said: "I don't know, but running down the street I saw ... "'

'Who?' The captain rapped in sudden excitement, leaning across the desk towards the woman. Sudden alarm distorted her features; for a moment she looked ugly. The captain leaned back again in his chair and, in a quiet voice, again asked: 'Who?'

'He said a name I don't remember, or perhaps a nickname. Now I come to think of it, it might have been a nickname.'

She used the word *ingiuria* and for the first time the captain needed the sergeant-major's talents as interpreter.

'Nickname,' said the sergeant-major, 'almost everybody here has one, some so offensive that they really are "injuries".'

'It might have been an *ingiuria*,' said the captain, 'but it might also have been some odd surname sounding like an *ingiuria*. Had you ever heard your husband use the name or *ingiuria* before ... ? Try to remember. It's very important.'

'I'm not sure I'd ever heard it before.'

'Try to remember ... and in the meanwhile tell me what else he said or did.'

'He said nothing else. He just left.'

For some minutes, ever since the woman had shown sudden alarm, the sergeant-major's face had been frozen into an expression of baleful incredulity. That, according to him, had been the moment to put on the screw, to frighten her enough to force it out of her, that name or nickname. Sure as God, she had it stamped on her memory. The captain, on the other hand, was being kinder than ever.

'Who does he think he is? Arsène Lupin?' thought the sergeant-major, whose reading days were so far behind him that he mistook burglar for policeman.

'Try to remember that *ingiuria*,' said the captain, 'and in the meanwhile the sergeant-major will be kind enough to offer us some coffee.'

'Coffee too,' thought the sergeant-major. 'It's bad enough not to give her a proper go over, but coffee ... !'

'Yes, sir,' was all he said.

The captain began to talk about Sicily, at its loveliest when most rugged and barren; and how intelligent the Sicilians were. An archaeologist had told him how swift and deft the peasants were during excavations, much more than specialized workmen from the North. It's not true, he said, that Sicilians are lazy or lack initiative.

The coffee came and he was still talking about Sicily and Sicilians. The woman drank hers with little sips, showing some refinement for a pruner's wife. The captain was now passing Sicilian literature in review from Verga to *The Leopard*, dwelling on a particular aspect of literature, *ingiurie*; how they often gave an accurate picture of a whole character in a single word. The woman understood little of this, nor did the sergeant-major; but some things not understood by the mind are understood by the heart; and in their Sicilian hearts the captain's words rustled like music.

'How well he talks,' thought the woman and the sergeant-major. 'Yes, he can talk all right. Better than Terracini,'* whom, apart from his ideas of course, he considered the greatest orator he had ever heard at any of the political meetings which he had to attend as a matter of duty.

'There are *ingiurie* which reveal a person's physical characteristic features or defects,' said the captain, 'and others which reflect his moral character. Still others refer to a particular happening or episode. Then there are hereditary *ingiurie* which include a whole family and can also be found on the maps of the register of landed property ... But let us proceed in order. Of the *ingiurie* which deal with characteristic features or defects, the most banal are: "one-eye", "limper", "lop-sided", "left-handed" ... Was the *ingiuria* your husband said like any of those?'

'No,' said the woman, shaking her head.

'Then there's likenesses – to animals, trees, objects ... For example, "cat" for a man who has grey eyes, or something that makes him look like a cat. I knew a man nicknamed *Lu chiuppu*, "poplar", owing to his height

*A prominent communist senator.

42

and a sort of quiver he had – that was how I had it explained. Objects ... let's see, nicknames due to a likeness to something ... '

'I know a man nicknamed "bottle",' said the sergeant-major, 'and he really is the shape of a bottle.'

"If I may,' said Carabiniere Sposito, who had sat so still he had become almost invisible in the room, 'if I may, I can tell you a few *ingiurie* which are names of objects. "Lantern", for one whose eyes pop out like lanterns; "stewed pear", for one rotten with disease; *vircuocu* – "apricot" – I don't know why, perhaps for a blank look; "Divine Host" for someone with a white round face like a Host ... '

The sergeant-major gave a meaning cough; he did not allow jokes about persons or things in any way connected with religion. Sposito stopped.

The captain looked inquiringly at the woman. She shook her head once or twice. The sergeant-major made a sudden violent movement, his eyes like watery slits between their lids, leaning forward to look at her. Suddenly, as if the word had been brought up by a sudden hiccup, she said: '*Zicchinetta*.'

'*Zecchinetta*,' promptly translated Sposito, 'a game of chance: it's played with Sicilian cards ... '

The sergeant-major gave him a glare; now they had the name, the time for philology was past; whether the word meant a game of cards or a saint in paradise was unimportant (and his instinct for the chase roused the sound of hunting horns in his head, making the saint in paradise bump a nose against Sicilian cards).

The captain, on the contrary, had felt a sudden, sombre sense of discouragement; of disillusion, helplessness. That name or *ingiuria* or whatever it was, was finally out; but it had only come out at the second when the sergeant-major had suddenly seemed to become for her a terrifying threat of inquisition, of condemnation. Maybe she had remembered the name from the very moment her husband had uttered it and not forgotten it at all. Or else her sudden desperate fear had brought it back. Anyway, without the sergeant-major, without that ominous transformation of his from a fat, jovial man to the incarnation of menace, they might never have got the name out of her.

'Give me time for a shave,' said the sergeant-major, 'and I'll soon find out whether this *Zicchinetta* is a local or not. My barber knows everyone.'

'All right,' said the captain wearily; and the sergeant-major asked himself: 'What's up with the man?' Disillusionment, with the captain, had brought on a stab of homesickness; the ray of sun which slanted down on to the table through golden specks of dust, shone for him on throngs of girls on bicycles on the roads of Emilia, on a filigree of trees against a white sky, and on a big house where town gave way to country, a house mellow in evening light and in his memory. He repeated to himself the words of a poet from those parts – 'where thou art missing from our hallowed evening custom' – words written by a poet for a dead brother. In self-pity for his exile, in his disillusionment, Captain Bellodi felt a faint premonition of death.

The woman gave him an apprehensive look, the ray of sunshine falling on the table between them, separating them in a remoteness which, for him, had a sense of unreality and, for her, an obsessive nightmare quality.

44

'What sort of a man was your husband?' asked the captain; and as he put the question he found it natural to use the past tense.

The woman, in her daze, did not understand.

'I would like to know about his character, his habits, his friends.'

'He was a good man: work, home, was his life. On days he wasn't working he'd spend an hour or two at the smallholders' club. On Sundays he'd take me to the cinema. He had few friends, all very respectable, the mayor's brother, a municipal guard ... '

'Had he ever any quarrels, rows about interest, enemies?'

'Never. Everyone liked him. He wasn't a local and strangers are all right here.'

'Oh, of course, he wasn't a local! How did you meet him, then?'

'At a wedding. A relation of mine married a girl from his village, and I went to the wedding with my brother. He saw me there; and, when my relation came back from his honeymoon, he asked him to apply to my father to marry me. My father made inquiries, then spoke to me. He said: "He's a decent young fellow, with a very good job." "I don't even know what he looks like," I said. "I wanted to meet him first." He came one Sunday, not as engaged, but as a friend; he hardly opened his mouth, just looked at me all the time as if bewitched. Spellbound, my relation said; as if I'd put a spell on him. He was only joking, of course. I decided to marry him.'

'And did you love him?'

'Of course; we were married.'

The sergeant-major came back, reeking of barber's

cheap eau-de-Cologne. 'Nothing,' he said, then moved behind the woman's back and mimicked frantically towards the captain to get rid of her, that there was red-hot news, amazing news about the woman. '*Zicchinetta* be damned,' his head-high, rotating hand seemed to say.

The woman was shown out. Breathlessly the sergeant-major poured out the news that she had a lover, a man called Passerello, a dues-collector from the electric light company. Reliable information, from Don Ciccio the barber.

The captain showed no surprise. Instead, he asked about *Zicchinetta*, thus reversing the good old custom of giving priority to the passionate elements of a crime, if they exist.

'Don Ciccio,' said the sergeant-major, 'states categorically that there is no one in the town with that name or *ingiuria*; and in such matters Don Ciccio is infallible ... If he says poor Nicolosi was a cuckold, then the fact's signed and sealed. So let's get hold of this Passerello and put the squeeze on him ... '

'No,' said the captain, 'we'll take a little trip instead, and pay a visit to your colleague at B.'

'I get it,' said the sergeant-major, rather put out.

They drove along the coast to B. in silence, the calm sea reflecting the muted tones of the sky. They found the sergeant-major in his office; conspicuous on his desk was a dossier concerning one Diego Marchica, known as *Zicchinetta*, released from prison only a month or so before thanks to an amnesty. The dossier was in such a conspicuous position because of some new information about gambling, and *zecchinetta* in particular, a game

46

that Marchica was wont to play at the sportsman's club, losing largish sums and settling them on the spot, almost impossible for an unemployed farmhand to do unless he had secret – and certainly illicit – sources of income.

Born in 1917, Marchica had begun his career in 1935: housebreaking; convicted 1938; arson. Those whose evidence had convicted him for theft had had their sheaves of grain burned on the threshing-floor: acquitted for lack of evidence. August 1943: armed robbery; retention of military weapons; criminal association. Tried by the Americans: acquitted (with what justification was not clear). 1946: membership of an armed band; captured during a shooting incident with the carabinieri: convicted. 1951: murder; insufficient evidence; acquitted. 1955: attempted murder during a brawl; convicted. The 1951 murder charge was interesting. It was a murder committed on behalf of a third party, according to the confessions of his accomplices to the carabinieri, confessions which of course melted like snow during the preliminary proceedings. The two men who had confessed displayed bruises, abrasions and excoriations to doctors and judge, all due, of course, to torture by the carabinieri. It was odd that Marchica, the only one not to talk, should have no single bruise to show to the judge. A sergeant and two carabinieri were put on trial for obtaining confessions extorted by violence, and found innocent. This meant that the confessions should have been considered spontaneous. But the case was never reopened, or maybe the file was on its rounds in the labyrinth of the law.

The notes described Marchica as a very shrewd and

cunning criminal, a reliable hired assassin, but capable, when gambling or in his cups, of sudden outbursts of rage, as indicated by the charge of attempted murder during a brawl. In the file there was also a report on a political meeting held by the Honourable Member Livigni. This gentleman, encircled by the flower of the local mafia, on his right the local grey eminence, Don Calogero Guicciardo, and on his left Marchica, had appeared on the centre balcony of the Alvarez palazzo. At a certain point in his speech he had said, verbatim: 'I am accused of being associated with members of the mafia and so with the mafia itself. But I assure you that I have never yet been able to find out what the mafia is or even if it exists. I give you my word with the clear conscience of a good Catholic and a citizen, that I have never met one member of the mafia.' Whereupon, from the direction of Via La Lumia, at the end of the piazza where the communists usually congregated during an opposition meeting, a loud voice demanded: 'And those characters up there with you, what are they? Seminarists?' A wave of laughter swept through the crowd, while the Honourable Member, ignoring the question, plunged into a peroration about his programme for agricultural reform.

This report was included in Marchica's dossier as a warning of the protection which he might have in the event of his arrest. The sergeant-major of B. knew his job.

* * *

'There's something afoot,' said the old man, 'something I don't like. The police are up to something.'

'They're shadow-boxing,' said the young man.

'Don't get the idea all police are stupid. Some could take the shoes off the likes of you and you'd be walking barefoot before you realized ... In '35, I remember, there was a sergeant here with the nose of a bloodhound, he even looked like one. When something happened, off he'd go on the trail and get you like a newly-weaned hare. What a nose he had, that son of a ... ! He was born a policeman, as one is born a priest or a cuckold. Don't you believe that a man wears horns because a woman puts them there or becomes a priest because, at a certain moment, he gets a vocation; they're born to it. And a man doesn't become a policeman because he needs a job or reads a recruiting poster; he becomes one because he was born one. Mark you, I'm only talking about real police; some, poor things, are as good as gold; but I don't call them police. A decent man like that sergeant-major who was here during the war – what was his name? – the one who got on so well with the Americans, nobody could call him a policeman. He'd do us favours; and we'd return them, with cases of pasta and demijohns of oil. A gentleman. Not a born policeman, but not stupid either ... We are inclined to call policemen all those with that flame emblem and V.E. on their caps ... '

'They've no V.E. any more ... '

'Nor they do; I always forget we've no king now ... But among them there are stupid ones, good ones and then real police, born so. It's the same with priests. Could you call Padre Frazzo a priest? The best one can say of him is that he's a good father to his children. But, take Padre Spina, there's a born priest for you.'

'And what about the cuckolds?'

'I'm just coming to them. Suppose a man finds his wife has been betraying him and makes a shambles; he's no born cuckold. But if he pretends not to notice or resigns himself, then he is ... Now I'll tell you what a born policeman is like. He arrives in town; you begin to make up to him, do him favours, ingratiate yourself. If he's married, you even take your wife to call; your wives become friends, you become friends; people see you and think you are all friends together. You kid yourself that he thinks you're a nice person, considerate, a loyal friend; but for him, you're always what his office files say you are. If you've ever been fined, then in his eyes, all the time, even when he's drinking coffee in your parlour, you're a man who's been fined. If you happen to break the law, a trifle, even if only you and he know and not even God Almighty has seen you, he'll fine you just like that. So if it's anything more serious ... In '27, I remember, there was a sergeant-major of carabiniere who practically lived in my house. Not a day passed without his wife and children paying us a visit. We were such friends that his youngest son, a kid of three, used to call my wife "aunt". One day he turned up in my house with a warrant for my arrest. It was his duty, I know; they were difficult times – there was Mori – but the way he treated me ... just as if we'd never met, never known one another ... And the way he treated my wife when she went to the barracks for news. He was like a rabid dog. Whoever takes up with a copper can say goodbye to his wine and cigars, so they say. With that sergeant-major I certainly said goodbye to a good deal of mine, the amount he drank and smoked.'

'In '27,' said the young man, 'during fascism, things

were different. Mussolini named members of Parliament and mayors. Did just what he liked. Nowadays it's the people who elect.'

'The people,' said the old man, sneering, 'the people were cuckolds then and they still are. The only difference is that fascism hung only one flag on the people's horns and democracy lets everyone hang one on his own horns and choose his own colour. We're back to the old argument. Not only men, but entire nations are born cuckolds, cuckolds from olden times, generation after generation ... '

'I don't consider myself a cuckold,' said the young man.

'Nor do I. But we, my dear boy, walk on the horns of others; like dancers ... ' and the old man got up and did a few tripping dance steps, mimicking the balance and rhythm of one hopping from the tip of one horn to another.

The young man laughed; it was a pleasure to hear the other talk. The cold astute violence for which he had been famous in his youth, the calculated risk, the presence of mind, the swiftness of hand, all the qualities, in short, which had caused him to be regarded with such respect and dread, sometimes seemed to ebb from him like the sea from the shore, leaving empty shells of wisdom on the sands of the years. 'He becomes a real philosopher at times,' thought the young man, mistaking philosophy for a sort of play of mirrors in which a long memory and a brief future reflect twilit thoughts and vague distorted images of reality. At other times the older man would reveal how hard and merciless he had been; and it was strange that when he was delivering his severest and most realistic judgments on the world, his

51

speech was literally strewn with the words 'horns' and 'cuckold', often with different meanings and nuances, but always to express scorn.

'The people, democracy,' said the old man, sitting down again, slightly out of breath after his demonstration of how to walk on people's horns, 'are fine inventions; things dreamed up at a desk by people who know how to shove one word up the backside of another, and strings of words up the backside of humanity, with all due respect ... With all due respect to humanity, I mean. Humanity's a forest of horns, thicker than the woods of Ficuzza when they really were woods. And d'you know who the people are who have fun walking on its horns? Firstly – bear this well in mind – priests. Secondly: politicians; and the more they say they're with the people, out for the people's welfare, the more they trample on their horns. Thirdly: people like you and me ... It's true that there is the risk of putting a foot wrong and being gored, for me as for priests and politicians; but even if a horn rips into my guts, it's still a horn; and anybody who wears one on his head is a cuckold. The satisfaction of it, by God, the satisfaction! I'm done, a goner, but you, you're nothing but cuckolds ... !

'By the way, speaking of cuckolds, I wonder about that *Parrinieddu* ... with all this coming and going of police .. he has a hand in it I suspect ... he must have. Yesterday, when I ran into him, his face changed colour; he pretended not to see me and vanished up an alley. I say to myself: "I've let you play the spy because you've a living to earn, I know; but you must do it with discretion, not set yourself against Mother Church" '; and by Mother Church he meant his own inviolable self and the sacred knot of friendships which he represented and protected.

Continuing to address himself to *Parrinieddu* as though the man were present, he said with icy solemnity: 'And if you set yourself against Mother Church, my friend, what can I do about it? Nothing. I can only tell you that in your friends' hearts you're a dead man.'

They were silent a while, as though reciting a requiem for the man who was dead in their hearts. Then the old man said: 'Diego ought to go away for a little holiday, I think. I seem to remember he has a sister in Genoa ... '

* * *

Diego Marchica was arrested at 9.30 in the evening at the sportsman's club. The sergeant-major of B. had intended to kill two birds with one stone but caught only one. He had hoped to catch gamblers red-handed playing *zecchinetta* and to run Diego in, but all the players, including Diego, had been engaged in an innocent game of *briscola*; evidently a lookout had tipped them off about the arrival of the carabinieri. However, *briscola* or no, Diego, at first indignant, then submissive, was hauled off to the barracks amid the comments of bystanders. Those which reached the ears of Diego and the carabinieri were of surprise and commiseration ('What's he done? Just minding his own business, wasn't he? Not interfering with anyone, was he?'); but, *sotto voce*, almost inaudibly, they expressed almost unanimous hopes that Diego would spend the rest of his life behind the bars he was so used to.

While Diego was being arrested at B., at S. *Parrinieddu* became the number which, in the art of foretelling lottery numbers, is assigned to the victim of a violent death; the only form, apart from his immortal soul, in which he was to survive.

The last twenty-four hours of the life of Calogero Dibella, known as *Parrinieddu*, were spent in a kind of dream, of crossing a boundless forest, thick as a bramble-bush and so lofty and dense that it shuts out the light. For the first time in his career as an informer he had given the carabinieri a thread to pull which, if they went about it the right way, could unravel a tissue of friendships and interests interwoven with his own existence. Usually his information only concerned people outside these friendships and interests; youths who saw a hold-up at the cinema one night and went out next day and held up a bus; small-time crooks, in fact, isolated and without protection. But this time things were different. It was true that he had given two names, of which one, La Rosa's, had nothing to do with the case; the other, though, was the right thread, a certainty. And ever since he had mentioned that name he had known no peace; his body was a terror-soaked sponge, absorbing even a gnawing liver and agonizing stabs at the heart.

Pizzuco, who had invited him to a bitter vermouth at the Café Gulino, as so often in the past, was astounded at *Parrinieddu's* refusal and abrupt flight; though not particularly bright, he wondered about it for the rest of the day. *Parrinieddu*, for his part, was so rattled that he spent the day attributing sinister meanings to that offer of a bitter vermouth, bitter betrayal, bitter death, over-looking the well-known fact that Pizzuco suffered from

54

what the doctors called cirrhosis due to his fondness for Averna's bitter vermouth – a beverage which made him proclaim his faith as Separatist and ex-soldier of the Volunteer Army for Sicilian Independence; though according to police records he had merely been a minor accomplice of the bandit Giuliano.

Many others noticed *Parrinieddu*'s peculiar behaviour, his apprehensive walk like someone with a mastiff at his heels; those who feared him and wished to avoid him noticed it most. Then had come that meeting with the man he feared most, a man capable of knowing – or guessing – what had been said in confidence between office walls. He had pretended not to see him, turned a corner at once; but the other had seen him, and followed him with his impassive gaze from beneath heavily-lidded eyes.

Since that meeting, the informer's last twenty-four hours had been all anguished frenzy. Longing for flight, which he knew to be impossible, alternated with visions of himself as a corpse. Flight was in the prolonged whistle of a train, in the countryside unfolding from the train window, towns rolling slowly by full of bright flowers and women at windows; then, suddenly, along came a tunnel, the word death hammered by the rhythm of the train, and death's black waters closing over him.

Without realizing it, by three days of anxiety, of false steps, of visible apprehension and nervousness, he had dug his own grave. Now he thought he'd be shot down, 'like a dog'; but he thought death was coming to him because of his betrayal, that it was known or suspected, and not because his terror had turned to madness and he had become the living image of treachery. The two names he had let slip were only in the memory of Captain Bellodi who, not wishing to have another corpse on his hands, had every intention of protecting the informer; but *Parrinieddu*, his nerves ragged from anxiety, saw his information floating round like chaff. Beyond hope, at dawn of what was to be his last day, he wrote the captain two names on a flimsy sheet of airmail paper, and the words: 'I'm dead', then, as if finishing off a letter, ended 'With regards, Calogero Dibella'. He posted the letter while the town was still deserted; all that day he spent either wandering about the streets, or rushing home a dozen times, determined to shut himself up there, then coming out as many times to get himself killed once and for all; just when he had finally made up his mind to hide, two unerring pistol shots got him on his own doorstep.

The captain read the letter only after hearing of the death. After giving instructions to the sergeant-major of B. to arrest Marchica, Captain Bellodi, tired out, returned to C. and went straight to his quarters. When told of Dibella's death, he went down to the office; and there was the letter in the afternoon's post. It gave him a great shock.

The man had left this life with one final denunciation, the most accurate and explosive one he had ever made. The two names were in the middle of the page and, beneath, almost at the foot, that desperate message, the 'regards' and the signature. It was not the importance of the denunciation which made such an impression on the captain, but the agony, the despair which had provoked it. Those 'regards' made him feel brotherly compassion and anguished distress, the compassion and distress of one who under appearances classified, defined and rejected, suddenly discovers the naked tragic human heart. By his death, by his last farewell, the informer had come into a closer, more human relationship; this might be unpleasant, vexatious; but in the feelings and thoughts of the man who shared them they brought a response of sympathy, of spiritual sympathy.

Suddenly this state of mind gave way to rage. The captain felt a wave of resentment at the narrow limits in which the law compelled him to act; like his subordinates he found himself longing for exceptional powers, exceptional liberty of action; a longing he had always condemned in them. A few months' suspension in Sicily of constitutional guarantees, and the evil could be uprooted for ever. Then he remembered Mori's repression of the mafia under fascism and rejected this alternative. But his anger smouldered on, his Northerner's anger against the whole of Sicily, the only region in the whole of Italy actually to have been given liberty during the fascist dictatorship, the liberty of safety of life and property. How many other liberties this liberty of theirs had cost, the Sicilians did not know or want to know. In the dock at the assizes they had seen all the *Dons* and *zii*, the election riggers and even those Commanders of the Order of the Crown of Italy, the doctors and lawyers who intrigued with or protected the underworld. Weak or corrupt magistrates had been dismissed; complaisant officials removed. For peasant, smallholder, shepherd and sulphur-miner, dictatorship had spoken this language of freedom.

'And perhaps that's why there are so many fascists in Sicily,' thought the captain. 'They never saw fascism as buffoonery or, like us, lived out its full tragic consequences after September 8th; but it's not only that. It's because in the condition they were in, one liberty was enough, they would not have known what to do with any others.' But this was not an objective opinion.

As he pursued these thoughts, at times clear and at others confused, for he lacked knowledge, he was already on his way through the night to S., a night which the cold white headlights made even vaster and more mysterious, an endless vault of splendid crystals and of glittering apparitions.

The sergeant-major of S. had had a terrible day, and was about to wade through an even worse night, with silent insidious waters of sleep waiting to drown him at any moment. From the neighbouring town he had brought in Marchica who, to tell the truth, had caused no trouble and, indeed, seemed half asleep like a puppy at its mother's dugs: he had gone peacefully into the guard-room and, even before the door was closed behind him, thrown himself, like a sack of bones, on the plank bed.

And, as if Marchica were not enough, the last straw for the sergeant-major had been another corpse. It was enough to drive the most placid of men crazy; but the sergeant-major, with his pangs of hunger and his weariness, just felt sleepy. Then just as he was slipping off for a cup of coffee he was stopped on the very threshold of the bar by the voice of the captain, who had arrived that minute, which showed what an unlucky star he had, at least in his relations with his superiors. Instead, the captain joined him in a coffee, and insisted on paying for both, in spite of the barman saying what a pleasure it was for the bar to offer a coffee impersonally to the *Signor Capitano* and the *Signor Maresciallo*, thus making the sergeant-major's ill humour foam silently like a glass of beer. 'Now he'll think I come in here and drink free,' he was thinking. But the captain had quite other worries.

The body of *Parrinieddu*, covered by a bluish cloth, still lay on the pavement. The carabiniere picket raised the cloth; the body was contracted in the dark womb of death as though in prenatal sleep. 'I'm dead,' he had written, and here he was dead by his own doorstep. Through the closed windows came the moans of his wife, and the murmur of neighbours hurried in to comfort her. The captain looked at the body for a moment, then made a sign for it to be covered again. The sight of the dead always disturbed him, particularly this one. Followed by the sergeant-major, he went back to barracks.

His plan was this: to arrest forthwith the two mentioned in *Parrinieddu*'s farewell message and interrogate, separately and almost simultaneously, under conditions and in a way which he had already carefully worked out, both of them and the third man already under arrest. The sergeant-major considered the arrest of Rosario Pizzuco an easy matter, that is to say, without troublesome consequences. But, with the second name, the one that the informer had only had the courage to write when dead, he had visions of successive calamities rolling down from one step to another like a rubber ball, till finally they bounced up into the face of Sergeant-Major Arturo Ferlisi, commanding the Carabiniere Station of S.; not for much longer, the way things were going. In his bewilderment he took upon himself to point out respectfully the consequences to the captain. The captain had already weighed them up. There was nothing for it, then, but to tie up the donkey where its owner wanted it; Sergeant-Major Ferlisi felt he was tying it up amid a lot of crockery and that the effect of its kick would be something to remember for the rest of his days.

* * *

'I just can't understand, it's unthinkable; a man like Don Mariano Arena, upright, devoted to family and parish, old too, and with so many infirmities and crosses to bear ... And they arrest him like a common criminal while, if you'll forgive my saying so, there are so many real ones walking around under our very noses, or rather yours. But I do know how much you personally try to do and I appreciate your work highly, even though it's not for me to give it its full due.'

'Thank you, but we all do our best.'

'No, let me have my say ... When in the middle of the night they knock up an honoured household, yes, honoured, and pull out of bed a poor creature who's also aged and decrepit, and drag him off to jail like a common criminal, causing anguish and consternation to an entire family; no, no, it's not only inhuman, it's rank injustice ... '

'But there are well-founded suspicions that ... '

'Founded? Where and how? Say someone goes out of his mind and sends you a note with my name on it; then you come along here, at dead of night, and, old as I am, without regard for my past record as a citizen, drag me off to jail as if I were anyone ... '

60

'Well, to tell the truth, there *are* some stains on Arena's record ... '

'Stains? Listen to me, my friend, let me talk as a Sicilian and as a man in my position, if that offers any guarantee. The famous Mori wasted blood and tears in these parts ... That was one of the sides of fascism on which it's better not to dwell; and, mark you, I'm no detractor of fascism; some newspapers, in fact, even go as far as to call me one myself ... And was there no good in fascism? Indeed there was, and how ... Now this rabble who call liberty the mud they sling about to besmirch the finest people and the purest sentiments ... But don't let's go into that ... Mori, as I was saying, was a scourge of God here; he swept up all and sundry, guilty and innocent, honest and dishonest, according to his own whims and his spies ... It was a catastrophe for the whole of Sicily, my friend ... And now you come and talk to me of stains. What stains? If you knew Don Mariano Arena as I do, you'd not talk of stains. He's a man, let me tell you, of whom there are few of his kind about. I'm not referring to the integrity of his faith, which to you, rightly or wrongly, may be a matter of indifference; but to his honesty, his love for others, his wisdom ... An exceptional man, I assure you. All the more so when one considers that he is uneducated, uncultured ... but you know how more important a pure heart is than any culture ... Now the arrest of a man like that as a common criminal, and I'm speaking with all sincerity, takes me right back to Mori's times ... '

'But public opinion says that he is a head of the mafia ... '

'Public opinion! What is this public opinion? Rumours in the air, rumours which spread calumny, defamation, cheap vengeance. Anyway, what *is* the mafia? Just another rumour. Everyone says it exists, but where no one knows ... Rumours, will-o'-the-wisp rumours echoing in empty heads, believe me. D'you know what Vittorio Emanuele Orlando used to say? I'll quote you his very words and, far in time as we are from his ideas, when repeated by us they take on even more authority. He used to say –'

'But, from what I have been able to gather from certain phenomena, the mafia *does* exist.'

'You grieve me, my boy, you grieve me. Both as a Sicilian and as the reasonable man I claim to be ... What I unworthily represent, of course, has nothing to do with it ... But both the Sicilian I am and the reasonable man I claim to be rebel against this injustice to Sicily, this insult to reason ... And mind you, I have always spelt the word reason with a small "r" ... Is it really possible to conceive of the existence of a criminal association so vast, so well-organized, so secret and so powerful that it can dominate not only half Sicily, but the entire United States of America? With a head here in Sicily interviewed by reporters and then, poor fellow, vilified by the press in the blackest terms? ... D'you know him? I do. A good man, an exemplary father, an untiring worker. He's got rich, certainly he has, but by his own efforts. And he, too, had his troubles with Mori ... Certain men inspire respect: for their qualities, their savoir-faire, their frankness, their flair for cordial relations, for friendship. Then what you call public opinion, the wind of calumny, gets up at once and says: "These are the heads of the mafia." Now here's something you don't know: these men, the men whom public opinion calls the heads of the mafia, have one quality in common, a quality I would like to find in every man, one which is enough to redeem anyone in the eyes of God – a sense of justice ... naturally, instinctively ... And it's this sense of justice which makes them inspire respect ... '

'That's just the point. The administration of justice is the prerogative of the State; one cannot allow ... '

'I am speaking of the sense of justice, not the admini-stration of justice ... Anyway, suppose we two were squabbling about a piece of land, a will, or a debt; and along comes a third party and settles things between us; then in a sense that third party is administering justice. But you know what might have happened if we had continued litigation before *your* justice, don't you? Years would have passed and finally maybe, from impatience or anger, one or both of us might have resorted to violence ... In short, I don't consider that a man of peace, a peacemaker, is usurping the administration of justice which, of course, is the legitimate prerogative of the State ... '

'Well, if you put things in those terms ... '

'What other terms can I put them in? In the terms of that colleague of yours who wrote a book on the mafia, which if you'll allow me to say so, was so fantastic that I'd never have expected such nonsense from a responsible person ... '

'I found the book very instructive.'

'If you mean you learned something new, all right; but whether the things described in the book really exist is another matter ... Now let's look at it from another point of view. Has there ever been a trial during which it has emerged that there is a criminal association called the mafia and that this association has been definitely responsible for or actually committed a crime? Has any document or witness any proof at all which has ever come to light establishing a sure connection between a crime and the so-called mafia? In the absence of such proof, and if we admit that the mafia exists, I'd say it was a secret association for mutual aid, no more and no less than freemasonry. Why don't you put down some crimes to the freemasons? There's the same amount of proof that the freemasons go in for criminal activity as there is that the mafia does.'

'I believe ... '

'You just believe me. Take my word for it and, in the position I unworthily hold, God knows if I could deceive you, even if I would ... What I say is this: when you, with the authority vested in you, direct – how shall I put it? – your attention to persons indicated by public opinion as belonging to the mafia merely on the grounds of suspicion, with no concrete evidence that the mafia exists or that any single individual belongs to it, then, in the eyes of God, you are committing unjust persecution. This brings us to the case of Don Mariano Arena ... And, incidentally, of this officer of carabinieri who arrested him without thinking twice, with an irresponsibility unworthy, if I may say so, of the uniform he wears. Let us say with Suetonius: *"ne principum quidem virorum insectatione abstinuit ..."* In plain language, this means Don Mariano is revered and respected by the whole town, is a bosom friend of mine and – believe me, I know how to choose my friends – he's also highly thought

of by the Honourable Member Livigni and by the
Minister Mancuso.'

* * *

The twenty-four hours of preliminary arrest had
already expired for Marchica and were falling due for
Arena and Pizzuco too. At nine o'clock sharp Marchica
started pounding on the guard-room door to insist on his
rights, of which he was well aware, and was told by the
sergeant-major that the Public Prosecutor had extended
his detention for another twenty-four hours. Marchica,
more or less reassured as to the form, resigned himself
to the substance, or the plank bed on which he lay down
again with a certain relief. The sergeant-major left him,
mulling over the fact that Marchica had started agitating
exactly at nine o'clock when he had no watch, as this,
together with his wallet, tie, belt and shoe-laces, were in
a drawer of the office.

At ten o'clock the sergeant-major woke Marchica
again and returned his belongings. Marchica thought he
was about to be released; the combination of sleep,
worry and stubble on his face broke into a triumphant
grin. But outside the barracks was a car into which the
sergeant-major shoved him. There was already one
carabiniere in the back and another one followed
Marchica, who found himself squeezed tight between
two carabinieri in the back seat of a Fiat 600. He at once
invoked the highway code, and the sergeant-major,
already seated beside the driver, was so taken by surprise
that he merely changed the subject with an amiable:
'Anyway, you're all thin.'

At C., Pizzuco and Arena were already in the cells of

the Carabinieri Company H.Q. The captain had thought that if he let them stew in their own juice for twenty-four hours, they would be riper for interrogation; a day and a night of discomfort were bound to have their effect on all three men.

He began with Marchica.

Company H.Q. was in an old convent, rectangular, each side with two rows of rooms divided by a corridor, one row with the windows facing inwards on to a courtyard, the other outwards on to the streets. To this unharmonious building the Sicilian statesman Francesco Crispi, and his even more harassed ministry, had added another, ugly and shapeless, which attempted to reproduce, in smaller proportion, the original layout. The result was something like a child's copy of an engineer's design. In place of the courtyard there was a kind of shaft; and the two buildings were connected by a maze of passages and staircases which made it difficult to find one's way about until one knew them really well. It had, though, the advantage of providing larger rooms than the old building. The first floor was used as offices and the second as the C.O.'s quarters.

The C.O.'s office had a large window opening on to the shaft; opposite, with an equally large window, was his lieutenant's office, the two windows being so close that, by leaning out, papers could be passed from one to the other.

The desk was arranged for Marchica to sit facing the window, with the office door on his right.

'Were you born at B.?' began the captain.

'Yes, I was,' replied Marchica in a tone of resignation.

'And have you always lived there?'

'Not always. I've been in the army and done a few years in prison.'

'I suppose you know many people in B.?'

'It's my home-town. But you know how it is, sometimes one's away for a couple of years; then one suddenly finds the boys grown up, the old people older. And as for the women ... You leave 'em as little girls playing with nuts in the street and, when you come back, find 'em with babies clinging to their skirts and maybe misshapen bodies ...'

'But those of our own age, who have always lived near us and played with us as kids, we recognize them at once, don't we?'

'Sure,' said Marchica, beginning to worry more about the captain's unruffled, conversational manner than the trend of his questions.

The captain was silent a moment as though absorbed in his own thoughts; and Marchica looked out of the window at the lieutenant's office opposite, empty and brightly lit. The captain had been careful to light only the table-lamp in his own office and it was turned down towards a little side-table where the sergeant was writing; thus Marchica had a perfect view of the other office.

'Then you must have known a man called Paolo Nicolosi ...'

'No,' said Marchica hastily.

'You must have,' said the captain. 'Maybe you don't remember him for the moment, as he left B. some years ago. I'll try to refresh your memory. Nicolosi used to live in Via Giusti which is a turning off Via Monti where you, if I'm not mistaken, have always lived ... His father was

67

a smallholder but worked as a tree-pruner; the son, now married and living in S., carries on the same job ... '

'Now you mention all this, I do seem to remember ... '

'Good ... After all, some things, some people; it's not so difficult to remember, particularly if they're associated with a happy period of one's life: childhood, for instance ... '

'We used to play together, I remember. But he was younger. And when I went to prison for the first time – unjustly, as truly as God is in the Sacrament – he was still a boy; I've never seen him since ... '

'What's he like? His face, I mean, his build ... ?'

'About my height, with fair hair and bluish eyes ... '

'A little moustache,' said the captain with conviction. 'He had one before ... '

'Before when?'

'Before ... before he shaved it off.'

'So you must have seen him when he had a moustache, then after he'd shaved it off.'

'Maybe I'm getting mixed up ... Now I come to think of it, I'm sure I am ... '

'No, you're not,' the captain reassured him, 'your memory's excellent. He wore a moustache until he got married, then he shaved it off. Maybe his wife didn't like it ... You must have met him at B., then. I don't know whether Nicolosi has been to B. lately, since you were let out under the amnesty, but it seems likely ... Or maybe you met him at S.?'

'I haven't been to S. for years.'

'That's odd,' said the captain, as though faced by an unexpected problem, 'very odd; for it was Nicolosi himself who said he'd met you at S. and I can't see any reason for him to lie about it ...'

Marchica was floundering. The captain looked at him, gauging his bewilderment; to and fro under the midday August sun ranged Marchica's mind like a dog, exploring every possibility, every uncertainty and presentiment with the instinct of a hunted beast.

Suddenly the door of the office opened and Marchica automatically looked round to see who it was. In the doorway was the sergeant-major of S., who saluted and said: 'He's made up his mind.' Behind him, holding up his trousers, dishevelled and unshaven, stood Pizzuco. At a sign from the captain, the sergeant-major quickly closed the door and withdrew. Marchica was overwhelmed with dismay. There was no doubt about it, Pizzuco, after the flogging he had undergone, was going to spill the beans (actually Pizzuco had been dragged out of bed that minute, with nerves shattered by bad dreams, not by torture). Then under the naked light in the office opposite, Marchica saw Pizzuco, the lieutenant, and the sergeant-major enter, the lieutenant sit down and at once put a short question to Pizzuco. Pizzuco began talking away and the sergeant-major writing furiously. Actually the lieutenant had merely asked him about his means of livelihood; and Pizzuco was pouring out the edifying story of his honest and blameless existence based on indefatigable toil, all of which was being taken down by Sergeant-Major Ferlisi's nimble pen. But Marchica, in his inner ear, heard Pizzuco's voice revealing a story which, at the very best, meant a twenty-seven-year sentence for him, twenty-seven long years in the Ucciardone from which not even God could save him.

69

'What reason could there be to lie about it?' went on the captain. 'I don't mean you, I mean Nicolosi. What reason could he have had, to say something that's, after all, so petty, so unimportant?'

'He can't say it,' said Marchica firmly.

'And why not?'

'Because ... because he can't.'

'Perhaps it's because you think, rightly and with good reason, that Nicolosi's already dead ... '

'Dead or alive, it's all the same to me.'

'Well, no, you're right, you know. Nicolosi *is* dead.'

Visible relief showed on Marchica's face, a sign that, without the captain's confirmation, he would still have had some doubts whether Nicolosi was really dead or not. Therefore he was not the man who had killed Nicolosi.

(In the other office Pizzuco was muttering: 'You bastard, you yellow rat, you son of a sow. Four strokes of the cat and you spew up everything. You'll pay for it, though; either at my hands or someone else's, you'll pay!')

'Yes,' said the captain, 'Nicolosi is dead, but sometimes the dead talk, you know ... '

'Only at a spiritualist's table,' said Diego scornfully.

'No. They can talk by the simple method of writing something before they die. And Nicolosi, after meeting you, had the excellent idea of writing your name and nickname on a piece of paper: Diego Marchica known as *Zicchinetta*. He then added the time and place and the very plausible opinion that the presence of *Zicchinetta* at S. at that hour was connected with the killing of Colasberna ... Quite a letter, in fact ... which, seeing that Nicolosi is dead, will carry more weight with the

70

judges than any evidence he could have given alive ...
What a blunder you made! Nicolosi left the note with
his wife with instructions only to hand it over to us if
anything happened to him. If you'd let him live, I'm
certain he would never have dared give evidence, let
alone come forward and report what he had seen. It was
a fatal mistake, killing him ... '

In the opposite office Pizzuco had finished his
harangue; the sergeant-major put his sheaf of papers in
order, and came over to make him sign the sheets, one at
a time. Then the sergeant-major left the room and
appeared a moment later in the captain's office with some
sheets of paper under his arm. Marchica was sweating
blood.

'I don't know what you think of Rosario Pizzuco?'
said the captain.

'A sponge-full of slander,' said Diego.

'I'd never have believed it, but I agree with you. I
understand that, for you Sicilians, "slander" is the word
used for revealing actions that should never be revealed,
though they deserve the proper punishment of the law ...
I agree with you. Pizzuco has committed that kind of
"slander". Do you want to hear it? ... Read it out,' he
said to the sergeant, handing him the sheets which had
been brought in by the sergeant-major.

The forged statement, which had been very carefully
thought out, declared that, of his own free will ('flogging', thought Diego, 'flogging'), Rosario Pizzuco confessed to having met Marchica some time previously and
told him confidentially of insults that he had received
from Colasberna. Marchica had offered to avenge him;
but he, being Rosario Pizzuco, a man of sound moral

71

principles, allergic to any kind of violence and quite alien to vindictive feelings, had rejected the offer. Marchica had insisted, even blaming Pizzuco for his undignified attitude of forbearance in regard to Colasberna, adding that he, Marchica, also had personal motives for resentment against the same man, about a job or some money refused him by Colasberna, Pizzuco didn't quite remember which; and that, one of these days, he was going to *astutare* or 'snuff' Colasberna, meaning that he was going to snuff out his life as one snuffs a candle. This proposal he would doubtless have put into effect. But a day or two after Colasberna's murder, Pizzuco had gone to B. on a land deal, met Marchica by chance, and been told in confidence, without his even asking, an appalling story of a double murder. Marchica's exact words had been: 'I set off to snuff out one and found that I had to snuff out two,' which, in Marchica's underworld jargon, meant quite definitely that he had committed two murders: Colasberna, and the other, Pizzuco suspected, Nicolosi, whose disappearance was arousing comment. Pizzuco had been appalled at this dangerous revelation and gone home very upset. Of course, he had not mentioned the matter to a living soul, as, knowing Marchica's violent character, he'd feared for his own life. Asked why Marchica had confided such a dangerous secret to him, Pizzuco had replied that perhaps Marchica, who had been away from the district for a long time, thought he could take Pizzuco into his confidence owing to certain experiences in common – though only superficially so, added Pizzuco; both, during the confused period of the Separatist Movement, having served with the EVIS, the Volunteer

72

Army for Sicilian Independence, Pizzuco for the purest of idealistic motives, Marchica for his own criminal ends. To the further question whether it was possible to discern the hand of other persons, of instigators, that is, behind Marchica, Pizzuco had replied that he did not know but that, in his own opinion, this was quite out of the question; he simply attributed the crimes to the violent character and the overwhelming criminal urge to prey on others' lives and property of which Marchica had always given ample proof.

It was a masterly piece of forgery, a living portrait of men like Marchica and Pizzuco, and had been concocted by three sergeant-majors in collaboration. The wiliest touch was the last statement attributed to Pizzuco: the downright exclusion of complicity by a third party. To bring in the name of Mariano Arena would have struck a false note, and been too improbable; the whole card-castle would have come tumbling down under Marchica's suspicious analysis. But the technique of throwing all blame downwards, that is on to Marchica; the categorical denial of any on his own part; the rejection of any suggestion of a third party; all this made Marchica agonizingly certain that the statement was authentic. Not for one moment, in fact, did he doubt the voice of the sergeant which was now supplying the sound-track to that mute scene which he had watched through the window before.

Demoralized, blinded by a rage which, had he been able to lay hands on Pizzuco, would have meant the end of the latter's career of crime, he sat for a long while in silence. Then he said that, if that was the way things were, all he could do was what Samson did. 'Samson died,' he said, 'and so did all his companions' ('*Mori Sansuni cu tuttu lu cumpagnuni*'), by which he meant that he was going to put the facts narrated by that filthy son of a bitch in their proper light.

He had met Pizzuco for the first time in many years during the first week of December of the previous year at B. Pizzuco had suggested he should bump off Colasberna, who had mortally insulted him; the price, three hundred thousand lire. Marchica, who had only been out of prison for a month or so and wanted to enjoy a little freedom in peace, had said that he didn't feel like the job. Then, being broke, when Pizzuco insisted and flashed before his eyes the prospect of a cash payment on account and the rest on completion, promising him a job as an overseer into the bargain, he had yielded. Only because he was broke, mind you. Terrible being broke. So he and Pizzuco studied a plan of action; Pizzuco even promised to abet him by leaving the murder weapon for him in a house of Pizzuco's in the country where Marchica was to go the night before the killing. From this house, which was not far from town, Marchica was to follow an agreed route and take up a position at the corner of Via Cavour at the time the first bus left for Palermo, since Colasberna used to catch that bus every Saturday. Having pulled off the job, Marchica was to make a rapid get-away down Via Cavour and return to the house in the country, whence Pizzuco was to pick him up later with a car and drive him back to B.

A few days before the killing Marchica went to S. to reconnoitre and make sure that he could recognize Colasberna. On this occasion Pizzuco fixed the date for the murder.

On the sixteenth of January at six thirty a.m., following in every detail the plan devised by Pizzuco, Marchica killed Salvatore Colasberna. However, there had been one snag: while Marchica was running off down Via Cavour he had bumped into his fellow-townsman, Paolo Nicolosi, who evidently recognized him, since he called him by name. Marchica had been alarmed by this and when, shortly afterwards, Pizzuco came to pick him up at the house, he told him of the encounter. Pizzuco was thrown into a high state of alarm and began swearing; then, calming down, he said, 'Don't you worry, we'll fix it.' Pizzuco had then taken him in a small van to the Granci neighbourhood, just under a kilometre from B.; first, though, he had paid him one hundred and fifty thousand lire which, with the payment on account, made up the agreed three hundred thousand, and cleared the deal.

A day or so later Pizzuco came to B. and told Marchica that he need not worry about Nicolosi any more, as the latter, in Pizzuco's exact words, 'was only good for giving sugar dolls to children', a reference to a local custom, whereby, on All Souls' Day, children receive gifts of sugar dolls. From this expression Marchica was sure that Nicolosi had been eliminated.

Asked whether Pizzuco, when commissioning him to kill Colasberna, might have been acting on behalf of others, Marchica answered that he did not know, but he, personally, did not think so. Asked whether Pizzuco's remark: 'We'll fix it' did not imply the participation or help of others unknown to Marchica but accomplices of Pizzuco, Marchica repeated that he did not think so, and even went on to say that he could not really remember whether Pizzuco had said: 'We'll fix it' or 'I'll fix it.' Asked if he had any idea where or how Nicolosi had been killed, he said he had none.

As he talked, Diego Marchica grew calmer. He nodded at the captain's reading of his confession, and signed it with satisfaction. Having fixed that swine Pizzuco – and incidentally himself – and having had the good manners not to involve others who were not swine, he felt at peace with his conscience and resigned to his fate. Maybe he was meant to spend the rest of his days in prison but, apart from the fact that he was used to it by now and for him it was rather like getting back home after a tiring journey, was not life itself rather a prison?

Life was all tribulation: lack of money, the temptation to play *zecchinetta*, the sergeant-major's searching eye, other people's good advice; and, work above all, the hell of having to do a day's work – work which degrades one to animal level. Enough of it all; better sleep on it. And indeed sleep, dark, amorphous, was again taking possession of all his thoughts.

The captain sent him off to sleep at the S. Francesco prison, in solitary; thus postponing until after the preliminary proceedings the rousing reception that Diego was bound to receive from his fellow jail-birds.

Now came Pizzuco's turn. It was already very late.

In other circumstances, Pizzuco would have aroused pity; stiff from chill and his arthritis, his eyes and nose dripping with a streaming cold, bewildered by what had happened to him, he was rolling his watery eyes in a blank stare, mouthing words as if unable to find his voice.

The captain had the sergeant read him Marchica's

confession. Pizzuco swore by the Holy Sacrament, before Christ on the Cross, on the souls of his mother, wife and son Giuseppe, that Marchica's was the blackest of slanders, and called down on him, until the seventh generation, the just vengeance of heaven where, apart from the other dead relatives already listed, he had an uncle praying for him, a canon who had died under suspicion, well-chosen word, of sanctity. In spite of his chill and misery, he was a brilliant speaker. His speech was thick with imagery, hyperbole and symbolism, couched in an Italianized Sicilian, sometimes more effective, sometimes more incomprehensible than pure dialect. The captain gave him his head for a while, then coldly observed:

'So you don't even know this Marchica?' – for that was what Pizzuco had seemed to be driving at during his long preamble.

'Oh, so far as that goes, I know him, Signor Capitano; though I'd better have been killed before I ever met him. I know him, and I know what he's like ... But we've never been at all close, and as for depriving a human being of life, heaven forbid! ... Never, Signor Capitano, never! For Rosario Pizzuco the life of a human being, any human being, is set on the high altar of a church; it's sacred, Signor Capitano, sacred ... '

'So you do know this Marchica, then?'

'I know him. Can I deny it? I know him, but it's as though I didn't. I know what sort of a man he is and have always steered clear of him.'

'And how d'you explain this confession of his?'

'Who can explain it? Maybe he's gone mad, maybe he wants to ruin me ... Who can tell what goes on in the

77

mind of a man like that? ... His mind is like one of those sour pomegranates; every thought a grain of malice, enough to set the teeth of a man like me on edge with fright ... He's capable of killing out of hand just because someone doesn't say good morning or he takes a dislike to the way he laughs ... A born criminal ... '

'I see that you know his character very well.'

'I should think so, too. He's always crossing my path ... '

'How many times has he crossed your path of late? Try to remember.'

'Let's see ... I met him when he had just come out of prison; that's once ... Then I met him at B., his home-town; that's twice ... Then he came to S. and that was the third time ... Three times, Signor Capitano, three times.'

'And what did you talk about?'

'Nothing, Signor Capitano, nothing. Matters so trifling one forgets them at once, like writing on the waters of a well ... I congratulated him on being free again and thought: what a waste of an amnesty. I said I hoped he'd enjoy his liberty and thought: he'll soon be inside again; and we talked of the harvest, the weather, his friends, mere nothings.'

'According to you then, there's not a grain of truth in what Marchica says ... But, leaving Marchica out of it for the moment, we know with absolute certainty that about three months ago – I can give you the exact date if you want – you had a conversation with Salvatore Colasberna during which you made him certain offers, offers which Colasberna turned down, about ... '

'Advice, Signor Capitano, advice: just disinterested advice for friendship's sake ... '

'If you are in a position to give advice, you must be well-informed.'

'Well-informed? I pick things up here and there. My work gets me around. Today I hear one thing, tomorrow another ... '

'What had you heard that prompted you to give advice to Colasberna?'

'That his business was doing badly. I advised him to seek protection, help ... '

'From whom?'

'Oh, from friends, banks; by trying to get into the right political current ... '

'And which, according to you, is the right political current?'

'The government's, I'd say: who's in power lays down the law, and whoever wants to be in with the law should go along with the party in power.'

'So you had no definite advice to give Colasberna?'

'No, none, Signor Capitano.'

'Shall we say you just gave him some general advice, purely for friendship's sake?'

'Just so.'

'But you weren't all that friends with Colasberna.'

'Well, we knew each other ... '

'Do you always go out of your way to give advice to people you hardly know?'

'That's the way I am. If I see anyone in trouble, I'm always ready to give him a hand.'

'Did you ever give a hand to Paolo Nicolosi?'

'What's that got to do with it?'

'Having given a hand to Colasberna, it seems only natural to give one to Nicolosi.'

The telephone on the desk rang. As the captain listened to the message, he studied Pizzuco, who was now calmer and more sure of himself; even his nose had stopped dri͏ͬping.

Replacing the receiver, he said: 'Now let's start all over again.'

'All over again?'

'Yes. That call was from S. to tell me that the weapon which killed Colasberna has been found. D'you want to know where? ... No, don't blame your brother-in-law ... He was just going to carry out your instructions when the carabinieri arrived and arrested him. Late this evening he went into the country, got the sawn-off shotgun and was just going to get rid of it when the carabinieri showed up ... An unfortunate coincidence ... You know what your brother-in-law's like; he thought that all was up; he said he'd had instructions from you to hide the gun in the Gramoli *chiarchiaro* – on your orders, he said.' Turning to the sergeant, he asked: 'What is a *chiarchiaro*?'

'A stony part,' said the sergeant, 'a place full of caves, holes in the ground, ravines.'

'I thought as much,' said the captain, 'and I have an idea which may, or may not, be a good one. Might we find Nicolosi's body in the *chiarchiaro* too?' And he turned to Pizzuco with a frosty smile. 'What do you think of my idea?' he asked.

'It might be a good one,' said Pizzuco impassively.

'Well, if you approve, I feel quite safe,' said the captain; and he rang up the carabiniere station of S. to order a search made in the Gramoli *chiarchiaro*.

While he was telephoning, Pizzuco was hastily examining the best line to take. By the time the captain said: 'Now you can either confirm Marchica's story by confessing you gave him instructions to kill Colasberna and that you yourself killed Nicolosi; or you can exculpate Marchica by confessing that you killed both Colasberna and Nicolosi,' Pizzuco had already chosen a third alternative which was oddly like the forged statement that had made Marchica confess. It differed from it only on one point, in fact. The sergeant-majors who had elaborated the forged confession knew their business all right. They had the psychology of a man like Pizzuco weighed up with scientific precision. No wonder Diego Marchica had fallen like a capon into the pot.

Pizzuco now said that about three months previously he had met Colasberna and, out of the goodness of his heart, even though they had not been particular friends, had given him some advice on how to run his building concern. But instead of the expressions of gratitude which Pizzuco had expected, Colasberna had told him, in unrepeatable terms, to mind his own business and thank the Lord that he, Colasberna, had not made Pizzuco pick all his teeth up from the ground; those had been his exact words, meaning, of course, that he had not knocked them out for him. Pizzuco, a man of peace, who only got into unpleasant situations owing to his incurable kindness of heart, had been deeply grieved by this reaction of Colasberna's; he happened to mention it casually to Marchica, and the latter had offered to take vengeance, even without any reward on Pizzuco's part, as he too had a personal grudge against Colasberna. Pizzuco, horrified, had categorically rejected this offer. But some days later, Marchica came to S. and asked to be allowed to stay at a house in the country belonging to Pizzuco's wife in the Poggio district, near S. It was to be only for one night, as he had important business to do in S., a town which boasted no hotel. Marchica also asked him for the loan of a shotgun, as he'd heard that hares abounded in those parts and he wanted to do a bit of shooting early in the morning. Pizzuco gave him the key of the house, and told him he would find an old, a very old, shotgun there; it wasn't much good, but it might serve his purpose. Being of a trusting nature and always ready to do a good turn, he had had no inkling of the criminal plot Marchica was hatching. Not even after he had heard of Colasberna's death had his suspicions been aroused. Only when the carabinieri came to his house to arrest him had it dawned on him what a terrible predicament Marchica, taking advantage of his good faith, had plunged him into. So he gave his brother-in-law instructions to get rid of the gun which, it was clear by now, had been used by Marchica for illicit purposes. This had seemed to him the best course, for, owing to Marchica's vindictive nature, he had not dared reveal to the police the circumstances of which he was the victim.

* * *

'Oh, Excellency!' exclaimed His Excellency, leaping out of bed with an agility surprising in one of his age and decorum.

The ringing of the telephone had, with nagging persistency, infiltrated through sleep to his consciousness, and he had reached for the instrument with the sensation that his hand was detached from his body. As faint sounds and distant voices reached his ear, he switched on the light; this meant that his wife would have no more that night of the sleep which always came sparingly to her restless body.

Suddenly the faint sounds and distant voices fused into one single voice, still distant but irritated and inflexible; and His Excellency found himself out of bed, barefoot in his pyjamas, bowing and smiling as though bows and smiles were sliding down the mouthpiece.

His wife gave him a disgusted look and, before turning her splendid bare shoulders to him, muttered: 'He can't see you; there's no need to wag your tail.' Indeed, a tail was all His Excellency needed at that moment to express his devotion.

Again he said: 'Excellency!' then: 'but, Excellency ... no, Excellency ... yes, Excellency ... very well, Excellency,' and after saying 'Excellency' some hundred times, he stood there, telephone in hand, grunting comments about the mother of an Excellency who rang from Rome at two a.m. to upset his life. He looked at his wife's back. Wasn't she upsetting it enough already? He put the telephone down on its rest, then picked it up at once and dialled a number. His wife turned on him like a scalded cat: 'Tomorrow night I'm sleeping in the guest-room,' she snapped.

Now he was saying in the same irritated and inflexible tone he had listened to a few minutes before: 'I'm sorry, my friend, but I've just been woken up myself. I'm awake and you're awake and you'll kindly do me the favour of waking whoever you have to wake ... I've just had a call from Rome; I'm not saying from who, but you can guess ... That Bellodi – I told you, remember? – has stirred up scandal on a national scale ... National, I tell you ... One of those scandals that, when someone like you or I is involuntarily involved, means there's hell to pay, my friend, blackest hell ... D'you know what a Rome newspaper came out with this evening? ... No? Well, you're lucky. I had to hear it from the party concerned and, believe me, he was in a fury ... There was a half-page, blown-up photograph of ... you know who ... standing next to Don Mariano Arena ... What d'you think of that! A photo montage? Not on your life. A genuine photograph. You say you don't care? ... That's not a very bright reaction ... Yes, I know as well as you do that it's not our fault if His Excellency is ingenuous enough, let's call it that, to be photographed with Don Mariano ... Yes, I'm listening ... '

His wife bounded out of bed, ravishing in her nudity. Like a famous actress, in bed she wore only Chanel Number 5; thus arousing His Excellency's sensuality and dulling that bureaucratic ardour of his which had rendered such service in the days of the Salo Republic. Wrapped in an eiderdown and an aura of scorn, she swept out, followed by His Excellency's anxious glance.

'Very well, then,' he said, after listening for a couple of minutes, 'this is what we'll do: in the course of the night you'll either nail down this Don Mariano for me with proof that even God Almighty couldn't touch; or else, also in the course of the night, you'll turn him loose and the press can be told that he was merely held for questioning ... What! The Public Prosecutor is following the investigations and agrees with Bellodi? ... Hell, what a mess! ... Well, do something ... Yes, of course I realize ... But d'you know what he told me only a moment ago? ... You know who ... He told me that Don Mariano Arena is an honest citizen and that one of us here, either me or you, is playing the communists' game ... How ever did this Bellodi get here? Why the devil did they send a man like that to an area like this? What's needed here, my friend, is discretion; a good nose, presence of mind, steady nerves, that's what's needed ... And they send down someone with St Vitus's dance ... But, for goodness' sake! that I don't question for a moment ... I have the utmost respect for the Service, I honour it ... Well, do whatever you want ... ' and he slammed down the receiver.

Now he had to calm his wife, a thornier problem than the thorniest ever set by his job.

*   *   *

Dawn was infusing the countryside; it seemed to rise from the tender green wheat, from the rocks and dripping trees, and mount imperceptibly towards a blank sky. The *chiarchiaro* of Gramoli, incongruous in green uplands, looked like a huge, black-holed sponge soaking up the light flooding the landscape. Captain Bellodi had reached that point of exhaustion and sleeplessness which produces a series of incandescent fantasies: hunger does the same; at a certain intensity it fades into a kind of lucid starvation which rejects any idea of food. The captain thought: 'This is where God throws in the sponge,' associating the sight of the *chiarchiaro* with the struggle and defeat of God in the human heart.

Partly joking, and partly because he knew the captain to be interested in popular sayings, the sergeant said:

> *'E lu cuccu ci dissi a li cuccuotti:*
> *A lu chiarchiaru nni vidiemmu tutti.'*

The captain asked what it meant, his curiosity instantly aroused.

The sergeant translated: 'An owl said to its owlets: we'll all meet in the end at the *chiarchiaro*,' adding that perhaps this meant we shall all meet again in death, the *chiarchiaro* having in some way, who knew why, become associated with the idea of death. The captain knew why very well; and in his feverish imagination he saw a host of night birds in the *chiarchiaro*, an aimless flapping of wings in the pallid light of dawn. No image, he thought, could ever convey more fearsomely the impression of death.

They had left their car on the road and were now approaching the *chiarchiaro* down a narrow, muddy path. Carabinieri could be seen moving about the *chiarchiaro* and a peasant or two helping them.

Suddenly the path ended at a farmhouse; and they had to cross some fields of wheat to reach the sergeant-major of S., who could now be made out quite clearly, gesticulating as he directed operations.

When they were within earshot, the sergeant-major called with an exultation out of keeping with the discovery of a corpse: 'He's here all right, sir! It'll be a job to get 'im up, but he's here!' But this was his work, and the finding of a murdered man was grounds in this case for satisfaction and rejoicing.

It was there, the body; at the bottom of a thirty-foot cleft which had been sounded with a rope and stone as plumbline. The light of electric torches, filtering through

86

bushes growing on the sides of the cleft, barely showed the bottom. But upwards wafted, unmistakably, the stench of putrefaction. To the great relief of the carabinieri, who were afraid the job would fall to one of them, a peasant had volunteered to go down tied to a rope and attach the body to other ropes so that it could be hauled up with comparative ease. A lot of rope was needed and they were waiting for the return of a carabiniere who had gone to fetch it from the village.

The captain went back across the fields to the farmhouse where the path began. It seemed deserted. But, going round to the side facing away from the *chiarchiaro*, a dog suddenly sprang towards him to the limit of its rope; it hung there, nearly choked, by its collar, barking furiously. It was a handsome brown mongrel with little violet half-moons over its yellow eyes. An old man came out of the cowshed to quieten it. 'Down, *Barruggieddu*, down!' he said, and then to the captain: 'I kiss your hands.'

The captain went over to the dog to stroke it.

'No,' said the old man in alarm, 'don't touch 'im, he's wicked! He'll let a stranger touch 'im and be reassured, and then bite 'im ... He's a little devil.'

'What d'you call him?' asked the captain, wondering about the strange name the old man had used.

'*Barruggieddu*,' said the old man.

'What does that mean?'

'Someone who's bad,' said the old man.

'I've never heard that one before,' the sergeant said; then in dialect asked the old man for an explanation. The old man said that perhaps the right name was *Barriccieddu* or maybe *Bargieddu* but, in any case, it meant 'evil', the evil of a man in a position of command. At one time the *Barruggieddi* or *Bargieddi* had lorded it over the townships and sent people to the gallows for their own cruel pleasure.

'I've got it,' said the captain. 'It means the Bargello – the chief of police.'

Embarrassed, the old man was mute.

The captain had wanted to ask him whether, a few days previously, he had noticed anyone going towards the *chiarchiaro* or had seen anything suspicious in those parts; but he realized that there was nothing to be got out of a man who considered a chief of police as evil as his own dog. Perhaps he wasn't so far wrong, thought the captain; for centuries the *bargelli* had bitten men like him, bitten after reassuring, as the old man had said. What had the *bargelli* been but tools of invading tyrants?

He took leave of the old man and set off down the path for the road. Straining at its rope, the dog barked its final menace. '*Bargello*,' thought the captain, '*bargello* like me, with my short length of rope, my collar, my mania,' and he felt more akin to the dog called *Barruggieddu* than to the historic *bargelli* of not so very long ago. 'Hound of the law,' he thought of himself; and then he went on to think of the 'hounds of the Lord', who were the Dominicans, and of the Inquisition, a word which conjured up a dark empty crypt and stirred gloomy echoes of history. He found himself wondering with anguish whether he, too, the fanatical hound of the law, had not already crossed the threshold of that crypt. Thoughts, thoughts born and melting in feverish self-destroying yearning for sleep.

88

He returned to C. and, before going to his quarters for a short rest, called in at the Public Prosecutor's office to report on the progress of his investigations and to extend the detention of Arena whom he wanted to interrogate in the afternoon after marshalling and assessing all his facts.

In the Palace of Justice, journalists were camping out on stairs and corridors. They were on him like a swarm of bees and the photographers' flashes exploded painfully into his arid-feeling eyeballs.

'How's the investigation going? ... Is Don Mariano Arena responsible for the murders or is there someone more important behind him? ... Have Marchica and Pizzuco confessed? ... Will their temporary arrest be extended or are there warrants out? ... D'you know anything about a tie-up between Don Mariano and Minister Mancuso? ... Is it true that the Honourable Member Livigni came to your office yesterday?'

'No, it isn't,' he replied to the last question.

'But politicians have intervened on behalf of Don Mariano, haven't they? Is it true that Minister Mancuso telephoned from Rome?'

'As far as I know,' he said in a loud voice, 'there has not been – nor can there be – any political intervention. As far as any connections between one of the detainees and certain politicians are concerned, all I know is what you've written yourselves. If such connections exist – and I don't wish to cast aspersions on your professional honesty – I have not, so far, had to take them into consideration or investigate them. Should these connections, in the course of my inquiries, become such as to draw the attention of the law, you can be sure that neither the Public Prosecutor nor myself will fail to do our duty ... '

This declaration was presented by an evening paper in a six-column headline as: 'Minister Mancuso also involved in Bellodi investigation.'

Evening papers come out, of course, by midday; and, by what in the South is lunch-time, the telephone wires were burning with the yells of those involved; yells which burst on the eardrums, sensitive enough at the best of times, of certain persons trying to drown their sorrows in the wines of Salaparuta or Vittoria.

* * *

'The problem is this: the carabinieri have three links of a chain in their hands. The first is Marchica, that they've grasped so firmly that it's like a ring for tying up mules set in a farmhouse wall.'

'Diego's not the sort to talk. He's got the guts of the devil.'

'Leave his guts out of this. The trouble with you is that you don't realize that a man who may be capable of killing ten, a thousand, a hundred thousand people, can also be a coward ... Diego, allow me to say so, has talked. So Pizzuco's link is now attached to his ... There are now two alternatives: if Pizzuco talks, there's the third link, Mariano's, joined to his; if he doesn't, he's still linked to Diego, but not very strongly, and a good lawyer could loosen that link without much trouble ... and in that case ... the chain comes to an end and Mariano is free.'

'Pizzuco won't talk.'

'I'm not so sure of that, my dear fellow. I always look on the blacker side of things, so let's suppose that Pizzuco does talk. If so, Mariano's for it. At a guess I'd say that at this moment the carabinieri are trying to weld Pizzuco's link to Mariano's. If it holds, two things can happen: either the chain ends with Mariano, or Mariano, old and ill as he is, decides to tell his beads ... In that case, my friend, the chain gets longer and longer, so long, in fact, that I and the minister and God Almighty get caught up in it ... A calamity, my good fellow, a calamity ... '

'You're talking like a skeleton at a feast ... Heavens alive, don't you know what kind of man Don Mariano is? Silent as the grave.'

'Yes, when he was young; now he's old with one foot in that grave of his. The flesh is weak, as Garibaldi said in his will, afraid that, in a moment of weakness, he might confess his sins to a priest, sins that must have been spiny as prickly pears. What I'm getting at is this: in a moment of weakness Mariano may break down and confess his sins, which, between ourselves, are not exactly few ... I had his dossier in my hands in 1927, it was thicker than that' – he pointed to one of Bentini's tomes – 'a kind of criminal encyclopedia ... a for arson, b for battery, c for corruption ... the lot. Fortunately the dossier vanished ... No, don't look at me like that; I'd no hand in it. Other friends, bigger fry than me, did the three-card trick with that dossier. From this office to that, from that to the other, until it vanished under the very nose of the Public Prosecutor, a terror, I recall. He flew right off the handle, I remember, threats right and left, and those who were under the deepest suspicion were those who had nothing to do with it, poor things. Then the Public Prosecutor was transferred elsewhere and the storm passed. The truth of the matter is this: Attorney-Generals, Public Prosecutors, judges, officers, chiefs of police, corporals of carabinieri, they all pass ... '

'Corporals! I like that!'

'There's nothing to laugh at, my good fellow. I hope with all my heart that your face never gets impressed on the memory of a corporal ... Anyhow, even corporals pass and we stay ... a jolt or two, an occasional scare, but we're still here.'

'But Don Mariano ... ?'

'Don Mariano, too, has had his little jolt, his little scare.'

'But he's still inside. What he must be going through ... '

'He's not suffering physically at all. If you imagine that they are keeping him tied on top of two drawers or giving him electric shocks, forget it. All that sort of thing's in the past; nowadays even carabinieri have to obey the law ... '

'The law be damned! Only three months ago ... '

'Forget it; we're talking about Don Mariano. Nobody would dare lay a finger on him, a man who's respected, enjoys protection, a man who can afford to pay for defence lawyers like De Marsico, Porzio and Delitala, the lot ... Certainly he'll have a bit of hardship to put up with. The guard-room isn't exactly a grand hotel: its plank bed is hard, its bucket stinks and he'll miss his coffee. Poor old fellow, he used to drink a strong double every half-hour ... But in a few days they'll let him out, shining with innocence like the Archangel Gabriel. And his life will settle down again and his affairs will go on prospering ... '

'A moment ago you were being alarmist, making me give up hope; now ... '

'A moment ago it was heads; now it's tails. I say tails should come up and things go well; but it just might come up heads.'

'We must see it's tails.'

'Well, then, listen carefully to my advice. We must pull the first ring out of that wall, we must get Diego freed.'

'Only if he wasn't the one to commit the disgrace ... '

'Even if he was, get him out. Let the investigation go ahead – it's in the hands of those two polenta-eaters anyway and no one can stop it. Let it go ahead, let it finish, let it all come before the Examining Magistrate and, meanwhile, prepare for Diego such a cast-iron alibi that anybody who tries to bite it will break his teeth.'

'How d'you mean?'

'I mean that on the day Colasberna was killed, and at the very same hour, Diego was a thousand miles from the scene of the crime, and in the company of highly respectable persons without a police record among them, honest men whose word no judge'd have the right to doubt.'

'But if he's confessed ... ?'

'If he's confessed, he must take back all he's said: declare that either under physical or moral torture – there are moral tortures too – he made statements to the carabinieri which do not correspond to the truth. The proof that these statements are quite untrue, sheer fantasy, is that certain persons of the utmost integrity bear witness to the material impossibility of Diego having committed the crime. Only saints possess the gift of bi-location and I doubt whether any judge would credit Diego with sanctity ... Now just take a look at this newspaper, this little item of news: "In the S. murder cases, one line of inquiry has been neglected by the carabinieri ... " '

*   *   *

Captain Bellodi was reading about the line of inquiry which the Sicilian paper – usually extremely cautious and not at all addicted to criticisms of the 'forces of law and order' – had accused him of neglecting. This line, of course, was 'passion'; which might, to one conversant with the facts so far revealed by the inquiry, explain one of the crimes, but, in doing so, leave the other two in utter mystery. Perhaps the journalist, when visiting S., had gone to Don Ciccio the barber for a shave and been excited by that story of an affair between Nicolosi's wife and Passerello. In short, as a good journalist and Sicilian, what he said was: *cherchez la femme*. The captain's opinion was that police in Sicily should be given strict instructions not to *cherchez la femme*; for she was always found in the end, much to the detriment of justice.

In Sicily, thought Captain Bellodi, the *crime passionnel* is not the result of genuine passion, a passion of the heart, but of a sort of intellectual passion, an almost juridical concern for forms; juridical in the sense of the abstractions to which law is reduced at various levels of our legal system until they reach that formal transparency in which 'merit', that is, the human element, no longer

94

counts. Once this is eliminated, law simply reflects itself. A character by the name of Ciampi in Pirandello's *Cap of Bells*, for instance, talked as though he had the entire High Court of Appeal in plenary session in his mouth, so carefully did he eviscerate and reconstitute form, never even touching on 'merit'. Bellodi had come across a Ciampi in the early days of his service at C. Just like Pirandello's character, he had turned up in his office, not in search of an author (he already had a most illustrious one) but of a subtle recorder of his evidence; so, fearing the sergeant might be unable to grasp his intricate arabesques, he had insisted on speaking to an officer.

All this, thought the captain, is the result of the fact that the only institution in the Sicilian conscience that really counts, is the family; counts, that is to say, more as a dramatic juridical contract or bond than as a natural association based on affection. The family is the Sicilian's State. The State, as it is for us, is extraneous to them, merely a *de facto* entity based on force; an entity imposing taxes, military service, war, police. Within the family institution the Sicilian can cross the frontier of his own natural tragic solitude and fit into a communal life where relationships are governed by hair-splitting contractual ties. To ask him to cross the frontier between family and State would be too much. In imagination he may be carried away by the idea of the State and may even rise to being Prime Minister; but the precise and definite code of his rights and duties will remain within the family, whence the step towards victorious solitude is shorter.

While waiting for Arena to be brought to his office,

Captain Bellodi pondered these matters, in which literature offered his short experience sometimes the right, and sometimes the wrong, card. And his thoughts were just moving on to the mafia, and how it fitted into this pattern he had just been tracing, when the sergeant showed in Don Mariano Arena.

Before appearing in front of the captain, Don Mariano had demanded a barber and been given a refreshing shave by a carabiniere. Now he was stroking his face and luxuriating in the absence of a sandpapery beard which had caused him more worry than his own thoughts during the past two days.

The captain said: 'Please sit down.' Don Mariano sat down, gazing at the captain steadily from under his heavy lids: an inexpressive stare suddenly interrupted by a movement of the head, as if some mechanism had flicked the pupils upwards and inwards.

The captain asked him whether he had ever had any connection with Calogero Dibella, known as *Parrinieddu*.

Don Mariano asked what he meant by connection: simple acquaintance, friendship or common interests?

'Take your choice,' said the captain.

'Truth is one. There's no choice: simple acquaintance.'

'And what was your opinion of him?'

'He seemed sensible enough. A youthful slip or two; but lately he seemed to be going straight.'

'Did he work?'

'You know about that better than I do.'

'I want to hear about it from you.'

'If you mean work with a spade, which was what his father brought him up to, Dibella worked as hard as you or I ... Maybe he worked with his brains.'

'And how d'you think he used his brains?'

'I don't know and I don't want to.'

'Why not?'

'Because I'm not interested: Dibella went his way and I mine.'

'Why d'you talk of him in the past tense?'

'Because he's been killed ... I heard an hour before you sent the carabinieri to my home.'

'It was Dibella himself, as a matter of fact, who sent the carabinieri to your home.'

'You're trying to muddle me.'

'No. I'll show you what Dibella wrote a few hours before his death,' and he showed Don Mariano a photostat copy of the letter.

Don Mariano took it and studied it at arm's length. He saw better from a distance, he said.

'What d'you think of it?' asked the captain.

'Nothing,' said Don Mariano, handing back the photograph.

'Nothing?'

'Less than nothing.'

'Doesn't it look like an accusation?'

'Accusation?' said Don Mariano in amazement. 'To me it doesn't look like anything. Just a piece of paper with my name on it.'

'There's another name as well.'

'Yes: Rosario Pizzuco.'

'D'you know him?'

'I know the whole town.'

'But Pizzuco in particular?'

'Not in particular. Like many others.'

'Did you have business dealings with Pizzuco?'

'Let me ask you a question. What kind of business d'you think I do?'

'Most kinds.'

'I'm not in business. I live on my income.'

'From where?'

'Land.'

'How many hectares d'you own?'

'Twenty-two *salme* and ... let's call it ninety hectares.'

'Do they pay well?'

'Not always; it depends on the year.'

'On average, what does a hectare of your land yield?'

'Much of my land is left to grass, for pasture ... I can't tell you how much a hectare of fallow land yields. I can tell you how much the sheep on it bring in ... Roughly half a million lire ... The rest is in wheat, beans, almonds and oil, depending on the year ... '

'How many hectares are under cultivation?'

'Fifty or sixty.'

'Then I can tell you how much a hectare yields: not less than a million lire.'

'You're joking!'

'No, it's you that's joking ... You tell me that, apart from your land, you have no other source of income and no interests in industry or commerce ... And I believe you. So I have to suppose that those fifty-four millions which you deposited in various banks last year, not withdrawn from previous deposits in other banks, represent the income from your land. A million per hectare ... I must confess, though, that it astounded an agricultural expert I consulted; according to him no land in these parts yields a net income of over a hundred thousand lire per hectare. D'you think he's mistaken?'

'No, he's not,' said Don Mariano, looking glum.

'We started off on the wrong foot, then ... Let's go back again. What are your sources of income?'

'No, we're not going back, not at all. I do what I like with my own money, move it about as I like ... I can say, though, that I don't always keep it in the bank. Sometimes I make loans to friends, without promissory notes, on trust ... Last year all the money I lent was repaid: so I made those deposits in banks ... '

'Where there were already other deposits, in your name and your daughter's ... '

'It's a father's duty to think of his children's future.'

'Very proper. And you have assured your daughter a life of ease ... But I'm not so sure your daughter would approve of the way you provided her with it ... I know that at the moment she's at a finishing-school in Lausanne – a very expensive, very famous one ... I expect, when you next see her, you'll find her very changed; more refined, pitying what you despise, respecting what you don't.'

'Leave my daughter out of this,' cried Don Mariano, with a spasm of rage. Then he relaxed, as if reassured, and said: 'My daughter's like me.'

'Like you? I hope not; and what's more, you're doing all you can so that she won't be, so that she'll be different ... And when your own daughter's so different that you can no longer recognize her, you'll have paid, in a way, the price of wealth acquired by violence and fraud.'

'You're sermonizing.'

'You're right: you go to church for a sermon, and here you expect to find a policeman: you're right ... So let's

99

talk about your daughter from the point of view of what she costs you in hard cash, and of the money you've accumulated in her name. A great deal, a very great deal of money, of, shall we say, doubtful origin ... Look at these: they are photostat copies of the accounts in your own and your daughter's name at various banks. As you can see, we didn't just check at local branches: we went as far as Palermo ... A great deal, a very great deal of money: can you explain its origin?'

'Can you?' asked Don Mariano impassively.

'I'm going to try. Because it's in the money you so mysteriously accumulate that lie the motives for the crimes I'm investigating; these motives have to be more or less illustrated in my report on you for instigation to murder. I'm going to try ... but in any case you'll have to give an explanation to the income-tax authorities, as we'll be handing over all these data to them.'

Don Mariano shrugged his shoulders.

'We also have a copy of your income-tax returns and of your file at the Inland Revenue Office: you returned an income ... '

'The same as mine,' interrupted the sergeant.

' ... and your taxes came to ... '

'Slightly less than mine,' said the sergeant.

'You see,' said the captain, 'you have quite a bit of explaining to do.'

Don Mariano shrugged again.

'This is the moment when one ought to put on the screw,' thought the captain. 'It's no good trying to catch a man like this with the penal code. There'll never be enough evidence; the silence of both the honest and dishonest will always protect him. It's useless as well as dangerous to consider the chance of a suspension of constitutional rights. A new Mori would immediately become a political-electoral instrument; not of the government, but of a faction of the government: the Mancuso-Livigni one or the Sciortino-Caruso one. We ought to do here what they do in America: grab them for tax-evasion. But not only people like Mariano Arena; and not only in Sicily. There should be a swoop made on the banks, experts set to work on the books, falsified as often as not, of businesses big and small; the register of landed property brought up to date; a check should be made on all those of dubious character, young and old, who spend so much of their time and breath on politics; and on the company kept by the more restless members of the great family group which is the government; and on their families' neighbours, and their families' enemies, and on the luxury villas, custom-built cars, the wives and mistresses of certain civil servants; and their tenor of life compared to their salaries. Then the proper conclusions should be drawn. That's the only way men like Don Mariano can feel the ground begin to give way under their feet ... In any other country in the world a tax-evasion like this one, of which I have the proof, would be severely punished; here Don Mariano just laughs, knowing how little it will take to confuse the issue ... '

'I see the income-tax people don't worry you much.'

'I never worry,' said Don Mariano.

'How's that?'

'I'm not a well-read man: but there's one or two things I do know, and they're enough for me: the first is that we have a mouth under our noses – for eating more than talking ... '

'I have a mouth too,' said the captain, 'but I can assure you that with it I eat only what you Sicilians call "Government bread".'

'I know, but you're a man.'

'And what about the sergeant?' asked the captain ironically, pointing to Sergeant D'Antona.

'I don't know,' said Don Mariano, scrutinizing him with what, for the sergeant, was unwelcome attention. 'I,' went on Don Mariano, 'have a certain experience of the world; and what we call humanity – all hot air, that word – I divide into five categories: men, half-men, pigmies, arse-crawlers – if you'll excuse the expression – and quackers. Men are very few indeed; half-men few, and I'd be content if humanity finished with them ... But no, it sinks even lower, to the pigmies who're like children trying to be grown-ups, monkeys going through the motions of their elders ... Then down even lower we go, to the arse-crawlers who're legion ... And, finally, to the quackers; they ought to just exist, like ducks in a pond: their lives have no more point or meaning ... But you, even if you nail me to these documents like Christ to His Cross, you're a man.'

'So are you,' said the captain, not without emotion. Then, with a twinge of discomfort at having exchanged a 'Present Arms' with a head of the mafia, he tried to justify this by remembering that he had once shaken hands with Minister Mancuso and the Honourable Member Livigni as representatives of the people, surrounded by fanfares and flags amid the din of a National Holiday. Unlike them, Don Mariano, at least, was a man. Beyond the pale of morality and law, incapable of pity, an unredeemed mass of human energy and of loneliness, of instinctive, tragic will. As a blind man pictures in his mind, dark and formless, the world outside, so Don Mariano pictured the world of sentiment, legality and normal human relations. What other notion could he have of the world, if, around him, the word 'right' had always been suffocated by violence, and the wind of the world had merely changed the word into a stagnant and putrid reality?

'Why am I a man, not a half-man or even a quacker?' he asked with harsh exaggeration.

'Because,' said Don Mariano, 'in your position it's easy to trample on a man's face; but you treat it with respect ... Many years ago I had to take a mortal insult from men sitting where you and the sergeant are sitting now. An officer like you slapped me; and, down in the guard-rooms, a sergeant-major pressed his cigar-butt on the soles of my feet, and laughed ... I ask you: can a man sleep after such insults?'

'So I don't insult you?'

'No, you're a man,' repeated Don Mariano.

'And d'you consider it manly to kill or have killed another man?'

'I've never done anything of the sort. But if, just to pass the time of day, discussing life, you were to ask whether it was right to take someone's life, I'd say: it depends whether he's a man.'

'Was Dibella a man?'

'He was a quacker,' said Don Mariano with scorn. It was a slip. Words are not like dogs which can be whistled back to heel.

'Have you any particular reason for so classifying him?'

'None. I scarcely knew him.'

'Even so, your judgment is perfectly correct. You must have had some grounds ... Perhaps you knew he was a spy, an informer of the carabinieri ... '

'I didn't bother.'

'But you knew?'

'The whole town knew.'

'So much for our secret sources,' said the captain ironically, turning to glance at the sergeant. 'And if Dibella did sometimes do his friends a good turn by passing us on selected information ... What would you say?'

'No idea.'

'But on one occasion at least, some ten days ago, Dibella did let slip some genuine information: in this office and sitting where you're sitting now ... How did you get to know about it?'

'I didn't: and if I had, I wouldn't have been interested.'

'Maybe Dibella came and confessed his mistake to you from remorse ... ?'

'He was the sort to feel fear, not remorse. And there was no reason for him to come to me.'

'Are you the kind to feel remorse?'

'Neither remorse nor fear: never.'

'Some of your friends say you're very religious.'

'I go to church, I send money to orphanages ... '

'Do you think that's enough?'

'Of course it is; the Church is great because each can be in it according to his own lights.'

'Have you ever read the Gospels?'

'I hear them read out every Sunday.'

'What do you think of them?'

'Beautiful words: the Church is all beautiful.'

'For you, I see, beauty has nothing to do with truth.'

'Truth is at the bottom of a well: look into it and you see the sun or the moon; but if you throw yourself in, there's no more sun or moon: just truth.'

The sergeant was getting bored. He felt like a game-dog compelled to follow the trail of a hunter over arid stony ground without the faintest scent of game. A long, twisting trail. Murder had hardly been mentioned when the field suddenly broadened: the Church, humanity, death. Club conversation, God Almighty, and with a crook ...

'You have helped many a man to find truth at the bottom of a well,' said the captain.

Don Mariano stared at him with eyes cold as nickel coins. He made no reply.

'And Dibella had already found truth,' the captain went on, 'when he wrote your name and Pizzuco's.'

'Truth? Madness, you mean!'

'He was *not* mad ... I sent for him immediately after Colasberna's death: I'd already had anonymous information which enabled me to connect the murder with certain interests ... I knew that Colasberna had had proposals and threats and even been shot at, just as a warning. I asked Dibella if he could give me any information as to the identity of the person who had made those proposals and threats. Caught on the hop, but not enough to give me the right answer there and then, he gave me two names: one of the two just to confuse me, so I later found out ... I wanted to protect him; but I couldn't arrest both the men mentioned by him. I had to be sure of arresting the right one. Since they belonged to rival *cosche*, one of the two was in the clear; either La Rosa or Pizzuco ... Meanwhile, the disappearance of Nicolosi was reported. And I was surprised at certain coincidences ... Nicolosi, before disappearing, had left a name too. We pulled in a man called Diego Marchica, whom you must know, and he confessed ... '

'Diego?' burst out Don Mariano incredulously.

'Diego,' confirmed the captain; then he told the sergeant to read out his confession.

Don Mariano followed the reading with heavy breathing that sounded like asthma; actually it was anger.

'Diego, as you see, led us to Pizzuco without much trouble; and Pizzuco to you ... '

'No, not even God will lead you to me,' said Don Mariano with assurance.

'You have a high opinion of Pizzuco,' observed the captain.

'I've a high opinion of nobody, but I know 'em all.'

'I don't wish to disillusion you about Pizzuco, especially after Diego let you down so badly.'

'He's a cuckold,' said Don Mariano, his face twisted with a spasm of uncontrollable nausea. It was an unexpected sign of yielding.

'Don't you think you're being rather unfair? Diego never even mentioned you.'

'What have I to do with it?'

'If you've nothing to do with it, why are you so angry?'

'I'm not angry: I'm just sorry about Pizzuco, who's a decent person ... I'm always upset by disgrace.'

'You can guarantee that what Marchica says about Pizzuco is quite untrue?'

'I can guarantee nothing, not even a one-cent IOU.'

'But you don't think Pizzuco's guilty?'

'No, I don't.'

'And suppose Pizzuco himself had confessed, and named you as accomplice?'

'I'd say he'd gone out of his mind.'

'So it wasn't you who instructed Pizzuco to settle Colasberna, by fair means or foul?'

'No.'

'Have you any investments or interests in building companies?'

'I? Heavens no.'

'Didn't you recommend the Smiroldi company for a big contract, which was obtained by somewhat unorthodox methods, to say the least, thanks to your recommendation?'

'No ... Yes, but I make thousands of recommendations.'

'Of what kind?'

'All kinds: about contracts, jobs in banks, school examinations, government grants ... '

'And to whom do you address these recommendations of yours?'

'To friends who get things done.'

'Who in particular?'

'Whoever is friendliest and can do the most.'

'But don't you yourself get anything out of it, any profit, any token of thanks?'

'Just goodwill.'

'Sometimes, though ... '

'Sometimes I'm given a *cassata* for Christmas.'

'Or a cheque: Martini, the accountant of the Smiroldi

firm, remembers a substantial cheque made out to you and signed by Smiroldi himself; the cheque passed through his hands ... Maybe it was a token of thanks for landing an important contract, or had you done something else for the firm?'

'I don't remember: it could well have been a repaid loan.'

'Well, if you don't remember, we'll subpoena Smiroldi.'

'Fine: then I needn't try and remember. I'm old and my memory sometimes sticks.'

'May I just call on your memory about a more recent matter?'

'Let's see what it is.'

'The contract for the Monterosso–Falcone road. You managed to raise the money for an utterly useless road, on a quite impossible plan. That it was you who raised the money is shown by an article of a local correspondent who gave you the credit for it. Apart from this, doesn't the Fazello company also owe the award of a contract to your influence? That was what Signor Fazello told me, and he had no reason to lie.'

'He hadn't.'

'Has he, under any form whatsoever, shown you any gratitude?'

'Yes, he has! He came here and blabbed the whole story: he's paid me back, all right, with interest!'

* * *

An hour before the session was to begin they had collected their invitation cards from the Via della

Missione entrance. They had strolled in the arcade, had a coffee at Berardo's and paused to look at the illustrated weeklies hanging up on the bookstalls. Rome lay in enchantment under a gentle flow of sun and, sauntering along, they were hardly aware of the rush of traffic and the long-drawn-out screech of the trolley-buses. Voices, newsboys' voices shouting the name of their home-town coupled with the word 'crimes', sounded distant and unreal. They had been away from home for two days and had already spoken to two eminent criminal lawyers, a minister, five or six deputies and three or four men wanted by the police who were enjoying the golden idleness of Rome in the taverns and cafés of Testaccio. They felt at ease, and the invitation of their Member of Parliament to visit Montecitorio for a session in which the Government was to reply to questions about public order in Sicily seemed an ideal way to end a hectic day. The evening papers said that the temporary arrest of Marchica, Pizzuco and Arena had been converted into real arrest, since the Public Prosecutor had issued warrants. From what journalists had been able to glean, Marchica had confessed to one murder and attributed another to Pizzuco; Pizzuco had admitted his involuntary complicity in two murders committed by Marchica; two, not, as Marchica had confessed, one; and Arena had admitted nothing, nor had Marchica and Pizzuco accused him of any complicity. Even so, the Public Prosecutor had issued warrants against Marchica for premeditated murder, against Pizzuco for premeditated murder and instigation to murder and against Arena for instigation to murder. An ugly situation but, seen from Rome at an hour which bestowed on the city the gay, airy freedom of a soap-bubble, luminous, iridescent with colours of shop-windows and women's dresses, those arrest-warrants seemed to float upwards, light as kites, to whirl like a merry-go-round over the top of the Antonine column.

It was almost time. The two went down the subway and, amid the multicoloured throng more vivid under the crude neon of display windows, their subfusc overcoats, their faces, swarthy as the patron saint of S., their mourning bands, their language of nudges and exclamatory looks with which they noted and acclaimed the passing of a pretty woman, their hurried gait, attracted momentary interest. Most people took them for plainclothes men following a pickpocket. Really they were a glimpse of the problem of the South.

At the House, the ushers looked at them with misgiving, passed their invitation cards to and fro, asked for their identity cards and made them take off their overcoats. Eventually they were escorted to a box. It was just like a theatre, but the proscenium was quite different. They were looking over the rim of what seemed a huge funnel, at the bottom of which was a mass of dark suits in ant-like movement. There was the same light which in their parts heralded a storm, when clouds driven by winds from the Sahara roll up in a slow surge, filtering light through sand and water: a strange light which makes surfaces look like satin.

It took a little time before the abstract concepts of left, centre and right applied to the concrete topography of the House and to the more familiar party faces. When Togliatti's face emerged from behind a newspaper, they realized they were looking at the left; then, with the slow precision of a compass, they swung their gaze towards the centre, paused for a moment on the face of Nenni, on that of Fanfani, and came to rest on the member to whom they owed the spectacle. He seemed to be looking at them too and they waved but, lost in his own thoughts, he did not notice. What impressed them most was the constant coming and going of messengers from bench to bench, like shuttles imparting to the hall the mechanical movement of a loom. A hum of low persistent talk rose which seemed to come from an empty vault rather than from the groups of persons sitting on the amphitheatre benches, haggard and absorbed.

Every now and then a bell rang. Then a voice began to float on that sandy light, spreading like a patch of oil over the gradually increasing murmur of the hall. They were unable to locate the source of this voice until their eyes travelled down from the President of the Assembly, who was ringing the bell, to what, when present, must have been the Government bench, where they saw, sitting near the man speaking, Minister Pella.

'We want the Minister of the Interior!' shouted the benches on the left.

The President rang the bell. He said that the Minister of the Interior was prevented from coming, that the Undersecretary was there, which amounted to the same thing, that they should let him speak and that he was sure nobody would be lacking in respect for the House. He might have saved his breath.

'The Minister! the Minister!' the left continued shouting.

'Let 'im speak for Christ's sake,' said one of the two Sicilian spectators in his companion's ear.

They let him speak.

The Undersecretary said that as regards public order in Sicily the Government saw no particular reason for concern.

A howl of protest rose from the left. This was just subsiding when a voice from the right shouted: 'Twenty years ago in Sicily one could sleep with one's door open!'

The left and a part of the centre rose to their feet, yelling. The two leant over the rail to see the fascist beneath them who, in a voice like a bull's, was bellowing: 'Yes, twenty years ago there was order in Sicily; but it's been destroyed by you!' He pointed an accusing finger from Fanfani to Togliatti.

The two saw his shaven head and accusing finger and muttered in chorus: 'The order of horns on your head!'

A long, frenzied ringing of the bell: then the Undersecretary continued. About the happenings at S., to which the Honourable Members had referred in their question, the Government, he said, had no comment to make, since there was a judicial inquiry in course. The Government, however, considered these happenings as manifestations of normal criminality and rejected the interpretation put on them by the said Honourable Members. Furthermore, the Government indignantly rejected the base insinuation, spread by left-wing newspapers, that certain Members of Parliament – and even of the Government – had any connection whatsoever with elements of the so-called mafia, which, in the opinion of the Government, only existed in the imaginations of socialists and communists.

From the left-wing benches, now packed with deputies, rose a storm of protest. A tall, grey, hairless member left his bench and advanced to the Government's until stopped by three ushers. The insults he was shouting at the Undersecretary were such that the two spectators thought: 'This'll end with knives!' The bell rang frenziedly. Darting from the right like a cicada, the shaven-headed member reached the middle of the hall; other ushers rushed to restrain him as he hurled his insults towards the left. The word 'cretin' whizzed around him, grazing his massive head as Red Indians' arrows did Buffalo Bill's.

'They need a battalion of carabinieri here,' thought the two, admitting for the first time in their lives that carabinieri might have some use.

They looked down towards their friend, the Honourable Member. He was quite unperturbed. Noticing their look, he waved with a smile.

*   *   *

It was a languorous evening in Parma, touched by a melting light embracing memory, distance, indefinable tenderness. Steeped in a dimension already reflected in memory, Captain Bellodi was pacing the streets of his native city; but uppermost in his mind was the thought of far-off Sicily, with its burden of injustice and death.

He had been ordered to Bologna to attend a trial as recorder of evidence and, when the trial ended, had not felt like returning to Sicily at once; the prospect of a leave in Parma with his family was particularly sweet to one in his state of nervous strain. He had applied for sick-leave and been given a month.

Now, almost half-way through his leave, he had just

learnt, from a bundle of local newspapers sent by the enterprising Sergeant D'Antona, that his whole painstaking reconstruction of the S. case had collapsed like a card-castle under a puff of irresistible alibis, of one alibi in particular, Diego Marchica's. Persons above all suspicion, highly respected for position and education, had borne witness to the sheer impossibility of Diego shooting Colasberna and being recognized by Nicolosi, as on the day and at the time the crime was committed Diego had been no fewer than seventy-six kilometres away: this was the exact distance, in fact, from S. to P., where Diego, in Doctor Baccarella's garden and under the very eyes of the doctor himself, who was in the habit of getting up early to supervise work in his garden, had been engaged in the harmless and peaceful task of hosing. This testimony could be confirmed not only by the doctor, but by peasants and passers-by, sure as they all were of Diego's identity.

The confession he had made to Captain Bellodi, Diego had explained, was due to a sort of spite; the captain had made him think that he had been incriminated by Pizzuco and, maddened by rage, he had tried to get even; just to put Pizzuco on the spot he had incriminated himself. Pizzuco on his part, confronted with Diego's treachery, had spouted a regular firework display of lies just to tie a millstone round Diego's neck for having incriminated him. The gun? Well, Pizzuco was certainly guilty of illicit possession of firearms; but it was this very worry about the weapon being illegal that had made him tell his brother-in-law to get rid of it.

As for Don Mariano, who had been much photographed and interviewed by the press, it goes without

saying that the patient web of clues woven by the captain
and the Public Prosecutor had melted into thin air. An
aura of innocence illuminated that ponderous head
which, even in photographs, wore an expression of wise
cunning. To a journalist who had asked him about
Captain Bellodi, Don Mariano had replied: 'He's a
man.' When the journalist asked whether by this Don
Mariano meant that like all men he was fallible, or
whether on the other hand there was an adjective missing, Don Mariano had said: 'Adjective be damned! A
man doesn't need adjectives and, if I say the captain's a
man, he's a man and that's all there is to it!' – a reply
considered by the journalist as sybilline, surely dictated
by anger and probably by rancour. Don Mariano,
however, had wished to express an objective appreciation,
like a victorious general praising a defeated adversary.
And so a note of ambiguity, of pleasure mingled with
irritation, was added to the turmoil of Captain Bellodi's
feelings.

Other items in the paper, marked in red by Sergeant
D'Antona, announced that, of course, the investigations
on the three murders had all been reopened, and that the
mobile police squad were well on the way to solving the
Nicolosi case and had arrested his widow and her lover,
a certain Passarello, a man under the 'darkest' suspicion;
it was inexplicable, the paper added, how this trail had
been overlooked by Captain Bellodi. Another red-
marked item, on the page devoted to news from the
province, stated that the commander of the carabiniere
station of S., Sergeant-Major Class 1 Arturo Ferlisi,
had, at his own request, been transferred to Ancona.
In a viaticum of good wishes and congratulations the

correspondent of the newspaper paid tribute to his equilibrium and ability.

Brooding over this news and seething with impotent rage, the captain was stalking aimlessly around the streets of Parma with the air of a man afraid of being late for an appointment. He did not even hear his friend Brescianelli call him by name from the opposite pavement and was surprised and annoyed when the other caught up and stopped him, standing, smiling affectionately and claiming at least a hand-shake in the name of their happy but, alas, distant schooldays. Bellodi gravely apologized for not hearing and told him that he wasn't feeling very well, forgetting that Brescianelli was a doctor. The other in fact took a step back to get a better look at him and noticed that he was thinner, as his overcoat hung too loosely from his shoulders; then he came nearer, took a look at his eyes which, he said, had a touch of burnt sienna in them, sign of liver-trouble, asked about his symptoms, and named medicines. Bellodi listened with an absent smile.

'D'you hear me,' asked Brescianelli, 'or am I a nuisance?'

'No, no,' protested Bellodi, 'I'm delighted to see you again. By the way, where are you going? ... I'll come with you,' and, without waiting for an answer, took his friend by the arm; with this gesture, one he had almost forgotten, he really did begin to feel the need of company, of talk, of distraction from his anger.

But Brescianelli now began asking him about Sicily; what was it like, how was life down there; and what about its crime?

Bellodi said that Sicily was incredible.

'Yes, indeed; incredible ... I have Sicilian friends too; quite extraordinary people ... And now they have home rule, their own government. The government of the *lupara*, I call it ... Incredible, that's just the word.'

'Italy's incredible, too. You have to go to Sicily to realize just how incredible Italy is.'

'Maybe the whole of Italy is becoming a sort of Sicily. When I read about the scandals of that regional government of theirs, an idea occurred to me. Scientists say that the palm tree line, that is the climate suitable to growth of the palm, is moving north, five hundred metres, I think it was, every year ... The palm tree line ... I call it the coffee line, the strong black coffee line ... It's rising like mercury in a thermometer, this palm tree line, this strong coffee line, this scandal line, rising up throughout Italy and already passed Rome ... ' He broke off suddenly and said to a smiling young woman approaching them: 'You're incredible too: incredibly lovely ... '

'What d'you mean: "too"? Who's the other?'

'Sicily ... Another woman. Mysterious, implacable, vengeful ... and lovely ... like you. Captain Bellodi, whom I have the pleasure of introducing, was telling me about Sicily' – he turned to Bellodi – 'and this is Livia, Livia Giannelli, whom you may remember as a girl: now she's a woman and won't have anything to do with me.'

'Have you come from Sicily?' asked Livia.

'Yes,' said Brescianelli, 'he's down there as a "filthy policeman", as they say,' imitating the cavernous voice and Catanese accent of Angelo Musco.

'I adore Sicily,' said Livia, moving between them and taking their arms.

'This is Parma,' thought Bellodi in sudden happiness,

117

'and this is a girl from Parma. You're home, and to hell with Sicily.'

But Livia wanted to hear the incredible facts about incredible Sicily: 'I've been to Taormina once; and to Syracuse for the Greek plays, but they tell me that really to know Sicily one must go into the interior ... Where are you stationed?'

Bellodi gave the name of the town; neither Livia nor Brescianelli had ever heard of it.

'What's it like?' asked the girl.

'An old town with plaster-walled houses, steep streets and flights of steps, and, at the top of every street and flight of steps, an ugly church.'

'And the men; are the men very jealous?'

'After their own fashion.'

'And the mafia, what's this mafia the papers are always going on about?'

'Yes, what *is* the mafia?' urged Brescianelli.

'It's very complicated to explain,' said Bellodi, 'it's just incredible.'

Biting sleet was beginning to fall, and a white sky foretold heavy snow. Livia suggested they go home with her: some of her women friends were coming and they could listen to some splendid old jazz records, records unearthed by a miracle; there'd also be some good Scotch whisky and Carlos Primero brandy. 'And food?' asked Brescianelli. Livia promised that there would be food too.

They found Livia's sister and two other girls stretched out on the hearth rug in front of a blazing fire, glasses beside them, and the haunting rhythm of 'Funeral at the Vieux Colombier, New Orleans', on a record-player.

They adored Sicily too. The knives which, according to them, were flashed in jealousy, gave them delicious tremors. Sicilian women they pitied, but also envied a little. The red of blood became the red of the painter Guttuso. Picasso's cock on the cover of Brancati's Bell' Antonio', they said, was a charming emblem for Sicily. The thought of the mafia gave them more tremors: and they asked for explanations, stories of the terrible deeds the captain must have seen.

Bellodi told the story of a medical officer in a Sicilian prison who took it into his head, quite rightly, to remove from the mafia convicts the privilege of residing permanently in the prison hospital. The prison was full of genuine sick cases, even some tubercular ones, living in cells and common dormitories, while these mafia chiefs, bursting with health, occupied the sick-bay in order to enjoy better treatment. The doctor gave instructions for them to be sent back to their ordinary quarters and for the sick to be admitted to hospital. The doctor's instructions were disregarded by both warders and governor. The doctor wrote to the Ministry. The next thing that happened was that one night he was summoned to the prison where, he was told, a prisoner had urgent need of him. He went. At one point in the prison he suddenly found himself alone among the convicts; and he was then beaten up with skill and precision by the mafia chiefs. The warders noticed nothing. The doctor reported the attack to the Public Prosecutor and the Ministry, on which some, not all, of the ringleaders were transferred to another prison. Next, the Ministry relieved the doctor of his post on the grounds that his zeal had given rise to incidents. Being a member of a left-wing party, he applied to it for support, but was told that it was better to let things slide. Unable to obtain redress in any other way he then applied to a mafia leader, who did at least give him the satisfaction of having one of his assailants beaten up in the prison to which he had been transferred. The culprit, he was assured, had been given a thorough working-over.

This episode the girls found quite delightful. Brescianelli was horrified.

Sandwiches were made. They ate, drank whisky and brandy and listened to jazz. Then they talked about Sicily again, then about love, then about sex. Bellodi felt like a convalescent: highly sensitive, susceptible, famished. 'To hell with Sicily! To hell with it all!'

He went home at about midnight, crossing the whole city on foot. Parma lay bewitched under snow, silent, deserted ... 'In Sicily it doesn't often snow,' he thought, 'and perhaps a civilization's character is conditioned by snow or sun, according to which is more prevalent.' He felt a little fuzzy in the head. But before reaching home he knew, with utter lucidity, that he loved Sicily and was going back.

'Even if it's the end of me,' he said aloud.

TAILPIECE BY THE AUTHOR

'Excuse the length of this letter,' wrote a Frenchman or Frenchwoman of that great eighteenth century of theirs, 'but I have had no time to make it shorter.' I cannot make this excuse with regard to the golden rule that even a short story should be shortened. I took a whole year, from one summer to the next, to shorten this one, not working at it constantly of course, but side by side with quite other activities and preoccupations. What I hoped to achieve by pruning was not so much proportion, stripped essence and rhythm, as self-defence against the possible reactions of any who might consider themselves more or less directly attacked in it. In Italy, as is well-known, some things must not be made light of, so think what happens when one takes them seriously. In books and films the United States of America can have imbecile generals, corrupt judges and crooked police. So can England, France (at least up till the present), Sweden and so on. Italy has never had, has not and never will have them. That's how it is and, as Giusti said of those ambassadors whom Barnabo Visconti forced to swallow signet, parchment and seal, a fuss ought to be made about it. I don't feel heroic enough to face charges of libel and slander, not deliberately at any rate. So, when I realized that my imagination had not given due consideration to the limits imposed by the laws of the State and, more than by the laws, by the susceptibilities of those whose duty it is to enforce them,

I began to prune and prune. In the first and second drafts the thread of the story has remained substantially unchanged: some characters have disappeared, others become anonymous, a sequence or two omitted. Maybe, even, the story has gained. One thing is certain, however: I was unable to write it with that complete freedom to which every writer is entitled (and I call myself a writer only because I happen to put pen to paper).

Needless to say, there is no character or event in this book which bears anything but a fortuitous resemblance to any real person or actual occurrence.

EQUAL DANGER

translated from the Italian by
ADRIENNE FOULKE

One must do as the animals do, who erase every foot-print in front of their lair.

—Montaigne

O Montaigne! You who pride yourself on your candor and truthfulness, be sincere and truthful, if a philosopher can be so, and tell me whether there exists on earth a country where it is a crime to keep one's given word and to be clement and generous, where the good man is despised and the wicked man honored.

—Rousseau

O Rousseau!

—Anonymous

District Attorney Varga was conducting the prosecution in the Reis trial, which had been going on for almost a month and would have dragged on for at least two more, when, one mild May night, after ten and not later than twelve, according to various testimony and to the autopsy, they killed him. The testimony, in point of fact, did not strictly coincide with the results of the autopsy: the medical examiner placed the time of death near midnight, whereas friends with whom the District Attorney, a man of rigid habits, was accustomed to spend every evening, and with whom he had indeed spent that evening, stated that at ten o'clock, give or take a few minutes, he had left them. Since it would not have taken him more than ten minutes to reach his house on foot, there remained the blank of at least one hour, and the need to find out where and how the District Attorney had spent that hour. Perhaps his habits were less fixed than they appeared and there were unprogramed hours in his day, hours of solitary and absent-minded perambulation; perhaps he had habits unknown even to his family and friends. Malicious conjectures were privately expressed and also whispered by the police, on the one hand, by friends on the other;

1

but to prevent their publicly exploding, the conjectures were promptly defused by a top-level decision reached at a meeting among the highest authorities in the district which branded any suspicion about that pregnant hour as an attack on the memory of a life that henceforth would be reflected in the mirror of all the virtues. The District Attorney had been found at the foot of a low wall from which hung masses of jasmine; he had a flower clasped between his fingers. This moved the bishop to say that in the fatal moment there had been fulfilled the small yet significant destiny of that freshly plucked flower, symbol of an unsullied life, of a goodness still scattering its fragrance in the halls of justice and no less in the bosom of the family and in every place the District Attorney had been accustomed to frequent, the bishop's residence included. This conceit received various elaborations. Police reports suggested that his pausing to pluck the jasmine had offered the criminal a precise target (a single shot, straight to the heart, fired from a distance of six or eight feet). Eulogies delivered at the funeral averred that the act of plucking the little flower bespoke a delicacy of feeling and a penchant for poetry which, for that matter, had never been belied by Varga, either in the exercise of his calling or in his private conduct. At one point in his oration, the pedantic Mr. Siras quoted, with a groan, *"avisad los jazmines con su blancura pequeña"*—"warn the jasmine with its tiny whiteness"— in his grief forgetting that, given the incontestable auricular faculties of jasmine, the blossoms had got the news instantly from a gun blast which the experts estimated had been quite heavy, as well as from the lawyer's last breath, whereas several hours passed before

2

the police were alerted, by which time at least a third of the city's inhabitants had contemplated the corpse.

The Reis trial was suspended. And since District Attorney Varga had conducted the prosecution with implacable acumen, the police believed one should look to the trial for the motive that had armed the hand of the unknown assassin. Nowhere in the nation's history of crime, or at least nowhere in the experience of the investigators, were there precedents of the kind; never had prosecutors or judges been threatened or struck down for a position taken during a trial or for a verdict delivered. However, considering that the Reis case was based entirely on circumstantial evidence and offered impenetrable obscurities of feelings and facts, the suspicion that someone had wished to silence Varga's inexorable prosecution, or wished merely to muddy the already sufficiently muddied waters of the affair, was deemed promising by the police. But relatives and friends of the defendant (the friends numbering very few at the moment) proved to be above or beneath suspicion. Accordingly, the police proceeded to his enemies, attributing to them a twisted and diabolic design not only to make the misdeeds of the accused appear unchallengeable but also to implicate other persons whom the pretrial examining judges had believed should be left on the sidelines. But even in this area the detectives' chase ended in failure.

Investigations having led to a dead end—i.e., to that hour or more the District Attorney had spent who knows where and how, a dim zone at the boundaries of which the zeal of the police was forcibly curbed—the authorities acted. Whether to restore to public opinion a faith in the efficiency of the police that, as it happens, public opinion had never nourished, or to make the public accept the unsolvability of the mystery, the Minister for National Security decided to assign Inspector Rogas to the case: the shrewdest investigator at the disposal of the police, according to the newspapers; the luckiest, in the judgment of his colleagues. The Minister did not fail to communicate to Rogas, by way of a viaticum delivered by the High Commissioner of Police, the desire of both the President of the Supreme Court and himself that any shadow which might blemish the limpid reputation of the deceased Varga should be evaluated by Rogas in light of the discredit that would unjustly fall upon the entire judiciary; therefore, with the utmost caution, any such shadow was to be exorcised upon its first appearance. Should it loom up irresistibly, it was to be erased. But Rogas had principles, in a country where almost no one did. Therefore, immediately but alone and with discretion, he pushed on into the forbidden zone, and he would have emerged—like a dog who comes out from the vapors of a swamp, the coot between his jaws—bearing who knows what snippet of Varga's reputation, had he not been stopped short by the news that Judge Sanza had been found dead on the beach at Ales (a pistol shot to the heart).

Ales was about sixty miles from the city where Rogas was checking into the assassination of Varga, but he could not go there without the permission of his chief. He requested it by telephone; he received it by letter. He arrived in Ales three days later, when the local police had already arrested a dozen people who had nothing whatever to do with the case but from among whom the police

4

were all agog to draw the guilty one virtually by lot. Rogas made a brief study of the motives attributed to those under arrest; the motives were such that only if fueled by madness could they have brought anyone to plan and carry out a murder. Since none of the twelve men appeared mad, whereas Inspector Magris, who commanded the local constabulary, *was* a bit mad, Rogas had them released. After which, having settled himself into the best hotel in town, on the magnificent beach where during his solitary walk Judge Sanza had met death, Rogas gave himself over to an indolence that verged on the ostentatious and bordered on the scandalous. He swam, he went out with the fishermen in their boats, he dined on the catch at its freshest, he slept hours on end. Inspector Magris hovered around him frantically, humiliated to have to be subordinate to someone who was equal to him in rank and superior to him in prestige; although full of bitterness, at the same time Magris savored the failure his colleague was heading toward, the brusque recall to the capital, the derision of the press.

However, Rogas's head was working. Two major public officials murdered within the space of one week, in two cities not very far from each other, in the same manner, with bullets of the same caliber fired perhaps from the same weapon (he never relied on reports from police laboratories to contain hard facts). He considered there was enough at hand to work on the hypothesis of a revenge that an unjustly condemned man might have vowed to carry out against his prosecutor, against his judges. Except that District Attorney Varga and Judge Sanza had never, at any point in their careers, been as-

5

sociated in the same trial; this fact Rogas had readily confirmed upon learning of the second crime. Yet the hypothesis held up. Rogas found reasons for not abandoning it: (1) The murderer could have been found guilty first in a court where Varga was conducting the prosecution, and later in a court where Sanza shared the bench with fellow-judges. Or it could have been the reverse—Sanza functioning in the lower, Varga in the appellate court. (2) The murderer could have made a mistake in the case of one of his two victims because of erroneous information, a lapse of memory, a case of homonyms (phonogram: IS THERE, HAS THERE EVER BEEN ANOTHER DISTRICT ATTORNEY VARGA, ANOTHER JUDGE SANZA?), for, as everybody knows, entire families have dedicated themselves, generation after generation, to certain public offices. (3) The murderer could have deliberately sought to confuse things, to make his game indecipherable, his identity impenetrable, by killing one of the two gratuitously, either the lawyer or the Judge (phonogram: WHO FROM AMONG THOSE SENTENCED IN TRIALS IN WHICH VARGA AND SANZA TOOK PART HAS LEFT PRISON IN THE LAST SIX MONTHS?). However, out of a superstitious attachment to the number three, which he considered characteristic of the neuroses of others as well as of his own, Rogas was convinced that there would be a third victim, and that it would be the good one; that is, the one that would turn up the clue necessary for him to solve the problem. As it presented itself at the moment, the problem was insoluble. And so Rogas was waiting. The third victim glowed in his mind, trespassing into the realms of yearning and fantasy, like an abstract sign that was on the verge of becoming name, body, funeral, inheritance, pension, and, above all, the element with which to advance the investigation on some basis firmer than thin air.

He did not have to wait long. Four days later, in Chiro, Judge Azar was felled: a sullen, reclusive man, who had spent the years from youth to death in terror of being infected by illnesses and emotions. Never had he shaken hands with a colleague or with a lawyer; when he could not avoid shaking hands because some newly arrived superior offered his own, Azar would suffer until he managed to slink behind a curtain or to some place where he, not seeing, believed himself unseen; taking out a tiny flask of alcohol, he would pour a generous amount (the only thing in which he was generous) over his bony hands, which were roped with veins and spotted like lichen-covered stones. Yet in his funeral eulogy, the highest-ranking magistrate in Chiro must perforce invent the wealth of human kindness that Azar concealed beneath a rough and callused hide. The other wealth, the real wealth, was discovered by the son of a sister, the Judge's only heir. Having rushed to Chiro upon receiving news of his uncle's tragic end, he would have remained who knows how long a guest in the local jail had Rogas not arrived to set him free. The young man, somewhat dissolute, had no alibi for the evening Azar had been murdered, and although by now it was clear to everyone that somebody, whether seeking revenge or simply mad, was running around murdering judges, the police did not renounce the almost ritual habit of swiftly, even joyously, sacrificing the reputation of persons who were the last to see a murdered man alive or who stood to gain by his death.

Having won the nephew's confidence, Rogas, as if to help him, and actually being helpful, kept after the young man to make an inventory of the estate. It turned out to be worth a sum at least twenty times larger than the amount the State had paid the Judge in salary over twenty-two years, assuming that in twenty-two years the Judge had spent not one penny for food, lodging, clothing, and disinfectants. Nor, insofar as the nephew could recall, had the Judge begun his career owning anything; on the contrary, the young man had been forever hearing from his mother the exemplary tale of the privations and the hunger against which her brother, now a judge of high rank and incorruptible prestige, had struggled in his younger years. Accordingly, Rogas began to inquire into that fortune, convinced that even if the investigation would not prove useful in uncovering the reason for which Azar had been murdered, it would surely provide some clue to what kind of judge he had been.

But Rogas, acting on the hypothesis of Azar's corruptibility, had no sooner begun to bestir himself, to speak with this or that person, to solicit confidences, than there arrived from the capital an authoritative exhortation not to forage for gossip; Rogas should keep on the trail, if trail there was, of that crazy lunatic who for no reason whatever was going about murdering judges. The crazy-lunatic thesis had by now come into favor at the very top levels: the Minister for Security, the Minister for Justice, the President of the Supreme Court, the High Commissioner of Police. Even the President of the Republic, Rogas's boss informed him confidentially, was asking every morning whether the homicidal madman had been caught. So far, and Rogas was astonished at this, the

8

affair had not been tossed into the political arena, not even by those papers that were always ready to attribute every senseless or monstrous crime to one of the many revolutionary groups that swarmed throughout the country.

Luckily, before Rogas could register disagreement with his superior's directives, the information he had requested immediately on learning of Azar's death did arrive: for about two years, Azar and Varga had served in the Criminal Court in Algo. Rogas abruptly disappeared from Chiro, just as he had disappeared from Ales. Newsmen lost track of him until a local correspondent reported his presence in Algo. Thereupon, the most disparate conjectures were bandied about, and they grew positively wild when, right in Algo, Judge Rasto was killed. Had Rogas known that the assassin would fell his fourth victim in Algo? And if he knew, why on earth had he not managed to prevent the crime? Had he made a lucky guess? Had he prepared a trap for the assassin? If so, the trap had not worked, and to bait it with a judge was a bit too much. *The Fuse*, a newspaper whose editors had impartial faith in violent social rebirth and in the equally violent adverse powers of the evil eye, insinuated that Rogas possessed innate malefic gifts. This insinuation, passing from the paper's few readers to the many who did not read it, became a certitude, so that at the mention of the name "Rogas" at least two-thirds of the adult population of the country knocked on wood and stroked good-luck charms for the better part of a week. At the end of which time, fearing that the attribution of fatal powers might be extended to the entire police corps and to the very Ministry he headed, the Minister for

9

Security hastily summoned newsmen to explain the intentions of the police and of Rogas and, above all, to clarify the reason for the Inspector's presence in Algo only shortly before Judge Rasto was killed. Rogas, he explained, had gone to Algo on the strength of a clue he had managed to uncover, the only clue that somehow connected two of the three murders committed to that point: ten years ago, Varga and Azar had served for about two years in the Criminal Court in Algo. Now, the fact that the unknown assassin had struck again, in Algo, was to be explained by the papers' having published news of Rogas's presence in the city, and, accordingly, was to be understood as a challenge hurled at the police, a challenge the police accepted; on the basis of the clue discovered by Rogas, they were hard at work tracking down the homicidal madman.

The Minister's statements made Rogas so nervous that he telephoned his chief begging to be relieved of the assignment if the Minister was really determined to put a spoke in the wheels. His chief comforted him and ordered him to go on with his investigation. But, as Rogas feared, the assassin's reply to the Minister came promptly: in a city far, far from Algo, Judge Calamo fell —a man who, as far as could be immediately learned, had had no connection with any of the other four victims. Which meant one of several possible things: the murderer had killed Judge Rasto according to plan, unaware of Rogas's presence; or he had known of Rogas's presence and had wanted to challenge him; or he now realized he had made a false step, a mistake, and was trying to lure the Inspector away from Algo and from the clue he had discovered there, drawing him into a labyrinth of counterfeit clues.

But Rogas did not stir from Algo. He had assembled the records of all the trials in which Varga as prosecutor and Azar as judge had taken part, and after a summary examination he divided and regrouped them according to simple criteria. A first group, nineteen trials that had ended with a verdict of not guilty, he eliminated immediately. The second group, thirty-five trials in which the defendants had been found guilty either because they had confessed or because they had been apprehended by the police in the act of committing the crimes or because the evidence and proofs were incontestable, he also eliminated after carefully examining four cases that, in the police reports or in the statements of witnesses, seemed to him to strike some false note. He returned the fifty-four eliminated trial records to the court archives, and retained a group of twenty-two in which the accused had been found guilty on the basis of assumptions and circumstantial evidence but had always, throughout police interrogations, pretrial examinations, and trial proceedings, protested their innocence.

Rogas made a list of those in the twenty-two trials who had been sentenced. It was complete in every detail that might serve to track them down. He distributed the list to judicial and police offices that were in a position to know the fate of those persons, whether they were still in prison or had left. In this way, he learned that fourteen of the men were still in prison; eight had regained their freedom, either because they had served their sentences or had had them reduced for good conduct or by amnesties, or because they had been found innocent upon appeal. Rogas concentrated for more than a week on these eight men and the documents relating to their trials. It was a kind of escape, a kind of game for him. He extracted from the documents the elements that could have been used to prove the innocence of the defendants. It gave him a sense of freedom, it amused him to skirt or suppress reactions of his own that, conditioned by habit and professional experience, continually suggested guilt.

In all eight cases, according to Rogas, the elements that could have persuaded the judges to find the defendants innocent prevailed over those they had used to justify a verdict of guilty, a conviction. And supremely unjust, it seemed to him, was the element of "previous acts of misconduct," as in the phrase "demonstrated tendency toward delinquency," which in five out of the eight cases was accepted as an incontrovertible, definitive argument. If someone had stolen some plums from a neighbor's orchard when he was twelve, it was assumed that at thirty he could very well kill with intent to rob. And if he had stolen those plums from a canonical orchard, it was entirely credible that ten years later he would be capable of murdering his mother. And so on and so on, with "previous acts of misconduct" being constantly referred to—and this in a country which boasted a whole body of literature dealing with the unforeseeable moods, contradictions, gratuitous actions, and radical changes to which human beings are prone. But while Rogas considered that attaching importance to "previous acts of misconduct" was an offense and an impediment to justice, he lingered longest over three

12

cases in which the protagonists had committed no such "previous acts," and it was with these three cases that his on-the-spot investigation began.

The three persons lived in the district of Algo. Their cases, upon appeal by defense or prosecution, had moved up from one level to another of the judicial hierarchy until, after a period of years (rather long years if measured within the cell of a prison, brief as a puff of air in the sidereal course steered by the administration of justice in the country), the cases had finally reached the Supreme Court. Here doubt, not about the facts on the basis of which these men had been found guilty but about the application of the law that had condemned them, had become manifest to the judges; the defendants had been remanded for new trials. The results: one had had his sentence confirmed; one had had his increased by two years; one had been cleared. Rogas began with the last man, because it seemed to him that, both for reasons of the man's character as it emerged from· the proceedings and for the very fact of his being finally absolved, he was the one to be ruled out immediately.

The man had neither a fixed residence nor an occupation. Not that he had been ruined by the trial and the four years he had spent in prison; on the contrary, his troubles had come from a vocation to laziness that he flaunted, considering it a design of Providence. Since, as everyone knows, laziness is the father of every vice, to the police and to the judges in the court of first instance it had seemed in order to charge him with homicide with intent to rob. There were no "previous acts of misconduct," but there was laziness.

Rogas found him in the square, seated in the sun at the

foot of a monument to a General Carco who, a hundred years earlier, had freed the region from one tyranny only to impose another on it. The man had pulled his beret down over his eyes. He sat motionless, in a position of total abandonment. Perhaps he was asleep. Rogas stopped in front of him, to cast a shadow over him. As if in play, he lifted the man's beret. A disgusted, questioning glance fixed him. So the man was not asleep. Then a shadow of suspicion passed through his eyes. Rogas saw himself being brought into focus, recognized for what he was. Without shifting position, apparently relaxed, the man was now tense, watchful.

"How are things going?" the Inspector asked. The tone sought to be, and was, cordial; nonetheless it was a question, the beginning of an inquisition.

"They're not," the man said.

"What's wrong?"

"Everything."

"And before?"

"Before what?"

"Before, I mean, things went all right?"

"Never."

"So then?"

"So then here I am."

"All the time?"

"Not all the time. Sometimes I sit in the square by the market, sometimes at the café."

"A little trip somewhere?"

"I'd like that. But the last one I took was to Rus. Seven miles, on foot. Three years ago."

"What's your hunch about these judges being murdered?" Rogas spoke to him familiarly because the fel-

14

low was the type that expected old-buddy treatment from the authorities even if they were being ruthless.

"I'm sorry about them," the man said, like someone who knows he is giving an unsatisfactory answer and meanwhile is feverishly preparing more satisfactory responses to the questions to come. He was moving from tension into fear.

"District Attorney Varga—" Rogas began.

"He seemed convinced that I'd killed that shopkeeper. He talked well, he was convincing. He wanted them to give me thirty years. He was sorry, he said, that there was no death penalty anymore."

"And Judge Azar?"

"He gave me twenty-seven. Not all by himself, though. There were two other judges."

"I know. And they're still alive. And you?"

"What could *I* do? I rolled with the punches. I was lucky the court assigned me a young lawyer who wanted to make a name for himself. He appealed, carried my case right up to the Supreme Court. And now here I am."

"And those four years in jail?"

"Over and done with."

"Over and done with, all right. But you did four years unjustly, didn't you?"

"I've done fifty-two years of life unjustly. Actually, the four I spent in jail don't bother me much. Prison is safe."

"Safe how?"

"For eating, sleeping. Everything's regulated for you."

"And freedom?"

"Freedom is here," the man said, pressing a finger against the middle of his forehead.

"But you said you'd been lucky to find a lawyer who got you out of jail."

"It's a manner of speaking. Sure, it wasn't bad luck. They said I'd killed a man to take his money. The lawyer proved I was innocent; that's good luck. But as for the rest . . ." With his hand, he made a gesture of dismissal, of indifference.

Rogas rested a hand on his shoulder, by way of saying goodbye. He walked away. Turning when he reached the edge of the square, he saw that the man had again tipped his beret over his eyes and had resumed his relaxed position. Sun. Rest, idleness. The dignity of rest, the civilization of idleness. Luis Cernuda, *Variaciones sobre tema mexicana*. Fine book. "Freedom is here." Well, no; in the end, they don't leave you even that.

For the second man, on the other hand, things were going very well, at least as the world judges such matters. He owned a machine shop, he worked night and day. He was making money, and this money he invested in a flourishing trade in new and secondhand cars. But maybe things were going better for the first man, Rogas reflected when he saw the second man come out, sweaty and covered with grease, from under an automobile he was repairing.

He did not realize that Rogas was from the police. He said he was busy; a car belonging to some American tourists had to be repaired immediately. He couldn't imagine what urgency there could be about the interview Rogas was asking for.

"Police. Inspector Rogas."

The grease and sweat became a mask on the man's

suddenly ashen face. "All right," he said. "Let's go in there." They went into a little glass-walled room. There were two chairs; he motioned for Rogas to take one; he fell into his like a puppet whose strings have been cut, disarticulated, lifeless. Then, groping, he felt for his cigarettes on the table, lighted one, staring at the Inspector with eyes that seemed to be looking out from behind a wall, from within a cave. His hands shook.

"I'm here just for a little checkup. No doubt it will be useless, but in our work to move ahead you must first clear the ground of superfluous things, useless things; otherwise you end up finding them in the way when you least expect them. . . . For example, when I came in here I realized immediately that it would be difficult for you to leave your shop for a day or even just for a few hours without your workmen and customers not only noticing your absence, and remembering it, but also asking for explanations and excuses. 'The boss is not here?' 'He's sick.' . . . 'He's gone to a wedding.' . . . 'He's been called down to the tax bureau.' . . . 'And when will he be back?' . . . In other words, your being away can't help but be noticed."

"It can't help but be noticed," the mechanic said, a bit reassured.

"But you've understood why I've come to see you?" Rogas asked.

"I think so."

"So tell me. In the last weeks, have you been away from here for periods of, say, hours or days that would reasonably allow you to have got as far as places like Ales, Chiro—"

"No, absolutely not."

17

"—and in connection," Rogas continued, "with the murders of District Attorney Varga and Judges Sanza, Azar, Rasto?"

"As I said, no, absolutely not."

"But you remember District Attorney Varga? Judge Azar?"

"I dream about them at night," and he brushed his hand over his face like someone who is emerging from a dream and wants to wipe any recollection of it away.

"You think of yourself as their victim?"

"Not exactly their victim. A victim."

"What effect does it have on you to know that they've been murdered?"

"None. It was the system. I got caught in the system. It could have done me in. Instead I got out alive."

"But you were innocent!"

"Do you really believe that?"

"I'm here because I believe it."

"Yes, I was innocent. . . . But what does it mean to be innocent when you get caught in the wheels of the system? It doesn't mean a thing, I can tell you. Not even to me, at a certain point. Like crossing a street, and a car runs you down. You're innocent, and you're run down by a car. What sense is there in such a thing?"

"But not everybody is innocent," Rogas said. "I mean, not all the people who get caught in the wheels of the system."

"The way the system works, they could all be innocent."

"But then you could also say, as far as innocence goes, that we could all get caught in the wheels of the system."

"Perhaps. But I'm not a Party man, so I put it differently."

Rogas thought, He knows how to develop an idea, how to reach a conclusion quickly. And he added cynically, Prison did him good. Aloud, he said, "I understand." He resumed his professional tone of voice. "And so, in these last days, you have not left your work even for a day; you have not gone out of town—"

"Sunday the shop is closed, naturally. But I'm here, taking care of the books, putting everything in order. And if someone comes in with a small repair job, I don't say no."

"Sunday . . ." Rogas said. None of the crimes he was investigating had occurred on a Sunday. "And evenings during the work week? How do you spend your evenings?"

"I close up after ten and go to the restaurant."

"Which one?"

"The Hunter."

"Every evening?"

"Every evening. I live alone."

"Why?"

"You read the transcript of my trial?"

"Yes, I read it. I see." He stood up. "I must warn you that I will have to check on your evenings at the Hunter."

"I'm sorry about that because people will start talking about me again, my case, new suspicions the police have about me. But what can I do? It's the system."

"I'll try to do it discreetly, tactfully."

"Thank you."

Rogas left the Hunter at three in the afternoon. He had had an excellent lunch, half a wild rabbit in sweet-and-sour sauce, a bottle of red wine, full-bodied, with a just discernible trace of jasmine in it, and he had verified the mechanic's alibi beyond any shadow of doubt. He felt satisfied, confident, both because he belonged to the ever more numerous ranks of those who celebrate and rejoice in wild game, home-grown fruit, homemade bread, and a simple table wine as relics from the golden age, and because it seemed to him that in the person he was now going to seek out were crystallized the ideal elements of the capacity to commit a kind of ideal crime. The process of crystallization, not dissimilar to that of love (Stendhal, *De l'amour*), had taken place in Rogas as he read and reread the trial records, talked with all the people who had had something to do with the case, and collected the most minute information about the protagonist.

The facts, as related to him by his colleague Contrera, who had been in charge of the inspectorate in Algo, were these (but they were not facts only; they spilled over into impressions, judgments): on the evening of October 25, 1958, a Mrs. Cres appears at the inspectorate. She asks to speak with the Inspector. The officer on duty and, subsequently, the Inspector note that she is upset, agitated, frightened. The woman is carrying a parcel, cylindrical in shape. She undoes it; out comes a small enameled pot; the woman takes off the lid and pushes the pot under the Inspector's nose. The Inspector looks at it: a granular, chocolate-colored pulp.

"Black rice," the woman says.

"What?" the Inspector asks.

"Rice with chocolate," the woman explains. "Have you never eaten it?"

"Never."

"I like it so much."

"It probably is good," the Inspector says, and he begins to feel a slight apprehension.

"Yes, but not this," the woman says.

"Why not?" the Inspector asks, feigning interest as if he were playing a child's game. "Is there something wrong with this rice?"

"It's poisoned," the woman says, terrified and solemn.

"Oh, poisoned," the Inspector says to keep up the game, convinced that he is dealing with a madwoman. "And who has poisoned it?"

"I don't know," the woman says, "but the cat's dead."

"Oh, the cat . . . And who had any reason to kill the cat?"

"No one, I think. But I was the one who gave the black rice to the cat."

"So it was you. Why?"

"Because I didn't know it was poisoned."

"Tell me everything in order," the Inspector says. He thinks, Either a story is going to come out that will have to be transcribed for the record or it's a case of calling the ambulance. But from the woman's last response, his conviction that she is crazy is beginning to waver. In fact, the woman relates her story coherently.

Her husband is a pharmacist, and she helps him in the pharmacy. Rather, they spell each other, for now doctors rarely write out prescriptions in the old way—so much of this and so much of that—and with the nonprescription medicines she works with greater dispatch than her husband because she has a better memory. When she comes down to the pharmacy, her husband goes upstairs to their living quarters or goes out to his club for a game of billiards. Most often he goes upstairs, because he loves to cook, and to tell the truth, some things he cooks to perfection. Black rice, for example—how he can cook that. . . . And she is a glutton for it. Now, that very day the pharmacist had prepared black rice. When he had returned to the pharmacy, he had said nothing to her; it had been a surprise for her to find the black rice in the kitchen, in the form of a conch shell, black and shining on the flowered serving dish. It was fragrant with cinnamon, perhaps a little too much cinnamon. Ordinarily she cannot resist tasting it and then serving herself a portion. But that day she had had an inspiration, surely heaven-sent. The cat had followed her upstairs from the pharmacy, where he habitually stayed; he was meowing, his whiskers trembled at the perfume of the cinnamon, and she—like that, impulsively—had taken a spoonful of black rice and given it to him right there, on the floor.

"Why?" the Inspector asked. "Why on the floor?" His wife would never have done that; she grew angry when the children dropped a tiny bite of meat for the cat who was under the table. (Thanks to his wife, Rogas reflected, his colleague Contrera had asked the only sensible question in the entire investigation.)

"But I told you—like that, impulsively, a kind of inspiration."

"I don't believe in impulses that conflict with habits, and much less in divine inspiration," the Inspector said.

"Wasn't there something that aroused your suspicions and made you act like that?"

"Maybe the overstrong smell of cinnamon."

"Well-l-l," the Inspector said, loading his doubt with two or three "l"s. "Anyhow, let's go on. What about the cat?"

"The cat ate the spoonful of black rice with gusto, licked the floor clean, and looked up, meowing and waiting for a second helping. Then suddenly he shrank; he seemed to withdraw into himself, puffing like a little organ. . . . But the bit about the organ occurs to me just now. At the time, he made me think of the sleeve of an empty fur coat that goes through the motions of turning inside out all by itself. . . . Then he leaped up like a spring and fell down on his side, stretched full length and stiff on the floor."

"And you?"

"I was frightened to death. But I kept myself from crying out."

"Why?"

"I don't know about why then. Now, having collected my wits, I can say that perhaps it was a flash of suspicion."

"The suspicion that only your husband could have put some poison in the whatchamacallit?"

"In the black rice," the woman corrected him, and she did not reply to the question. She was very calm now. A beautiful woman, between thirty and forty, the Inspector had noted; a vibrant, restless body.

"But why did you think of poison?"

"What else could I think of?"

23

"Cats can perfectly well die the way people often die. On the street, chewing a mouthful of food, lighting a cigarette—"

"The smoking cat," the woman said, with half a smile. "Excuse me, in my mind's eye, I just saw the sign of a Paris café."

"It's a dog—Le Chien Qui Fume," the Inspector said, irritated. "In any event, a cat can die suddenly, too. He finishes eating the black rice, and he dies. How is it you haven't thought your cat might have happened to die suddenly?"

"I don't know; perhaps because for some time I've not been sure my husband loves me."

"Loves you? But between not being sure your husband loves you and being certain, all of a sudden, that your husband meant to kill you with the black rice, there is, I'd say, a big difference."

"I've never said anything about being certain. I'm talking about impressions, presentiments, fears. Certainty must come from analyses. I've brought you the black rice, and the cat, too; I put it in a bag in the trunk of the car. And there is no point in going on about my impressions before one knows the results of the tests. To you I say simply this: I believe someone wanted to make an attempt on my life, but who I don't know. If the cat is really dead from poison, if there is poison in the black rice . . ."

The cat was dead from poison; in the rice there was enough to kill a dozen people. The pharmacist did not deny having prepared the dessert; he excluded the possibility that anyone other than his wife could have added poison to the sweet. A check showed that the quantity of

24

poison found in the dessert was precisely the amount that, according to the register, was missing from the pharmacy supply; and on the glass jar there were only the fingerprints of the pharmacist. The envelope in which the poison had been put was found in the pocket of his dressing gown (he put on his dressing gown when he was acting as cook), and in his wallet was found (a serious clue) a very brief letter that seemed to have been written by his wife (the experts found the handwriting well imitated but denied its authenticity): "I can live no longer. You have nothing to do with it. It is not your fault, so feel no remorse. Live in peace."

Missing was a motive, apart from the woman's vague impressions as to the diminishing of his love for her (never did she allow another expression to pass her lips, and with intransigent modesty rejected every allusion to sexual relations). However, when something is lacking, God provides, and an anonymous letter arrived opportunely to supply a precious clue: ten days, two weeks before, the pharmacist had stopped by the house of a local whore; he had told her some things in confidence. The lady, having been summoned to police headquarters, did not require much working over to confess the secret that the pharmacist had confided in her: he had a "cold" wife. The Inspector did not find it plausible that a husband would try to do away with his wife because she was "cold"; the motive was not serious—after all, all women are "cold." But he took note of the whore's confession and passed it along, without embellishing it by so much as a word, to the pretrial judge, whose dreams, at the side of a "cold" woman, were populated with "hot" women. Accordingly, the effects of the coldness that Mrs.

Cres exhibited with regard to her consort became the basis on which District Attorney Varga and Judge Azar and company built up a sentence of five years for attempted homicide, which sentence was confirmed by the appellate court then presided over by Judge Riches, who subsequently moved up to preside over the Supreme Court.

In the course of his trial, defended by a lawyer by no means convinced of his innocence, pharmacist Cres maintained an attitude that seemed disdainful. He said that in the light of common sense nothing prevented his accusers, or his judges, from thinking that the whole affair might be the machination of his wife. The appeal to good sense irritated the District Attorney and the presiding judges. The District Attorney asked him if his wife was attached to the cat. The pharmacist conceded her affection. "Very much attached?" District Attorney Varga insinuated. Cres replied that he was unable to establish the degree of affection, and added ironically, "She seemed to be attached to me, too." An appeal to good sense, irony—things an accused man must never permit himself. Varga delivered a tirade against the defendant's cynicism, and concluded with the declaration: "And therefore, even admitting that the lady might have been capable of conceiving and carrying out such a diabolic design (yet why, since not even her husband has managed to point to a motive), is it thinkable that she would have gone to such lengths as to sacrifice the innocent creature to which, by the admission of the person who would wish to saddle *her* with the charge that pinches him, she was so greatly attached?" Whispers of indignation, of incredulity, serpentined through the courtroom; the lady president of the Society for the Protection of Animals, present at every session both in her official capacity and as a friend of Mrs. Cres, cried out "Impossible!" and the defense lawyer turned to the pharmacist with a gesture that meant their case was irremediably lost.

After the appeal, Mrs. Cres disappeared. Without warning, without even saying goodbye to the women friends who had been so close to her for the duration of the wretched case. For all they knew at the police station, she could even have been dead. But at that point Inspector Contrera had a theory of his own. During the trial, he had already had some suspicions; nothing factual, one must understand, only the suspicion that in that concatenation of clues there was something contrived, and that of the two, in their loveless life together, the boredom—the desperate, limpid boredom—was more on her side than on her husband's. When, later, Contrera learned that she had disappeared, suspicions fed his theory: the woman had plotted that crime, leaving it up to the police and the judges to execute it, as it were, by filling in the blanks, and she had done so in order to be quit of her husband for as long as it would take her to disappear. Since a woman, according to Contrera, never disappears alone, there must be some man whom the lady had managed, before and after, to keep in the most secret, most impenetrable shadow. Whereupon Contrera made an attempt to turn up something on the woman's score, but without results.

Having served five years, the pharmacist returned home. He did not expect, naturally, to find his wife sitting by the hearth, nor did he bother to learn where she might have gone. He liquidated the pharmacy, sold everything he possessed except for the building, in which he still lived. The house was very dear to him, despite sad memories of the black rice, the cat, the years he had spent there with his wife—years that now, in every remembered image, must appear to him in the cold and sinister light of betrayal. He left the house rarely, rarely sought the company of the two or three friends with whom he had once played billiards and who, invariably of an evening, used to stop by the pharmacy for a summary of the day's happenings.

Rogas, before leaving the restaurant, had made sure that Cres was at home. For three days, with an unobtrusiveness that was facilitated by there being a café opposite, a medieval castle in ruins on one side, and the residence of a brigadier on the other, Cres's house had been assiduously kept under surveillance. He was there. As late as the evening before, toward nightfall, they had seen him walk out onto the balcony in a dressing gown. (Maybe he was preparing black rice, Rogas thought.) Lights burning until past midnight. After which, until now, no sign that he was at home. But he was.

When Rogas arrived, the stakeout gave an almost imperceptible nod to confirm that Cres was there. Rogas searched for a doorbell. There was none. He lifted the lion-head knocker, let it fall. From the empty reverberations in the entrance hall, from the wave of more intense silence that overwhelmed them, Rogas had a presentiment that Cres had gone away. But he continued to pound, louder and louder, with the knocker. Then he turned toward his watchdog, called him over with a wave of his hand. The man came on the run, clutching the glass of ginger beer with which he had been regaling himself. He said, with a mixture of rage and amazement, "He's got to be there!" and fell to pounding in a frenetic crescendo.

"That's enough," Rogas said, for the situation was beginning to look ridiculous to the habitués of the café.

"It was to be expected," Rogas said, and he was not talking about Cres but about the men who for three days had been keeping Cres under surveillance and who had orders to stop him if he tried to get away. It was not the first time; it would not be the last.

"He's got to be inside. Maybe he's asleep, maybe he wants to make us think he's not there," the policeman said.

"It could be," Rogas said, out of pure kindness to the distracted man, who was gasping and breathless, like a runner nearing the post.

"What'll we do?" the policeman asked.

"You go back to the café," Rogas said. "I'll come tonight with a search warrant and a locksmith." He went off, careful not to look in the direction of the spectators.

Cres had gone. Clearly, he had become aware of the surveillance and, at some moment when the man on duty had turned away, he had tranquilly walked out of his house. In two days, he had had time to study the habits of his surveillants; on the third day, he was in a position to carry out his flight. It did not call for much, after all; it was almost a tradition with the police to allow persons under surveillance at any distance to escape. On the surface, the phenomenon suggested an inveterate and

29

widespread negligence; in reality, it had a more dangerous root—the inability of police agents and of their superiors to conceive of the existence of an individual who was to be kept under surveillance and not to be arrested. The prescribed structure of the police had been, until only a few years before, purely repressive; that psychology, that habit, endured.

But while saying to himself that it was to be expected, Rogas felt a searing disappointment at not having found Cres, both because his fellow had walked off with perfect composure from a house that could have been well staked out even by a blind man and because the flight, if flight it was, would complicate matters. Perhaps it was not a flight. One could not exclude the possibility that Cres had been aware of nothing, that he had simply gone off without any plan, without any precautions, under the very nose of the plainclothesman who, in the oppressive hallucination of the midday heat, between the snare of drowsiness and the solace of a cold drink, had forgotten why he'd been hanging around the café for hours and had come to see in the man he was supposed to be watching merely someone leaving his house to go about his own business or to get some fresh air on the town ramparts. And there was a still more serious consideration: not all the people who took to their heels when favored by the attention of the police could be accounted guilty. On the contrary. In Rogas's experience, there were more flights of innocent than of guilty people. The guilty would often sit tight until the attention of the police took the tangible form of a warrant for arrest, sometimes impatiently even going so far as to confess, thereby crossing over the police domain to the more secure, more reliable terrain of the judicial realm where even confessions required proof and proof was almost always lacking. It was the innocent who took flight. Not all, of course. And an innocent person, someone like Cres, would have good cause to flee. Innocent, perhaps —in any event, convicted on the basis of weak evidence, he had been caught up in the police and judicial system. Five years later, he had come out of it without even the satisfaction that an appellate court, although it would not recognize his innocence, at least had taken cognizance of how inadequate were the proofs of his guilt.

Whether Cres had been unfairly convicted Rogas was not sure. Had he been in the place of his colleague Contrera, who had investigated the case and delivered Cres over to the judges—washing his hands of him, like Pilate—Rogas would have been sure of Cres's guilt or innocence, and with discreet but tenacious insinuation he would have judiciously seeded the reasons for his certainty into his reports. For Rogas, having the man before him, talking with him, getting to know him, counted more than clues—more than facts. "A fact is an empty sack." One had to put the man, the person, the character inside the sack for it to hold up. What kind of man was this Cres, sentenced to five years for attempted homicide, with the aggravating circumstances of premeditation and base motives? What kind of man had he become after his conviction, during the five years in prison, during the other five in which, having returned to freedom, he had lived in his own house almost as if it were a prison? Rogas could only imagine, fantasize. And the most tenable point he had reached, while imagining and fantasizing, was this: Cres was a man who had a kind of vocation for prison; he had made his life into one long prison sentence. One of the most fateful professions a man can choose. And Cres had chosen it at eighteen, barely out of school. He had chosen freely, not because of tradition or family pressure, for his father had been a lawyer and would have liked him to take up the study of law.

Then there was the life he had led, his habits, his pastimes. And a "cold" woman beside him. He had made a prison for himself and, it appeared, was comfortable in it. Therefore, the discovery of a prison in which he could be held unjustly, by force, by violence, through the machinations and decisions of others, had kindled in him a lucid and implacable hatred, a cold and deadly madness. After all, the greatest affirmation of freedom in life is made by the man who creates a prison for himself. (Rogas was contradicting himself.) Montaigne, Kant. Why laugh at poor Cres, at his name being placed side by side with such names as these? Why ridicule Cres if Beethoven, from heaven, from the castle of illustrious spirits, decrees that a perfect performance of his A-Minor Quartet should reach the ears of some English schoolgirls, yet they hear only the murmur of a sea shell, the fanfare of a regiment? The author of this anecdote of Beethovian fantasy, E. M. Forster, called these phenomena "the central sources" of melody, of victory, of thought. (Rogas preferred the term *"res nullius."*) Austerlitz on a picnic. Beethoven in a sea shell. The *Critique of Pure Reason* on a billiard table. The Montaigne *Essays* in pharmacy jars. But the real prison, the one to which others hold the keys, the one to which others constrain you, is the precise negation of the prison to which each man, perhaps, aspires and which some, unconsciously or not, realize in their own lives.

In any event, Cres had gone off. Because once again he felt unjustly persecuted? Or simply because he wanted to continue his insane revenge and escape punishment? This, for Rogas, was the question. A question of conscience, however, not of technicalities. Technically, when Cres became a "wanted man," incriminating himself by his flight (for officially flight signifies guilt, despite Rogas's dissenting opinion), the investigative problem could be considered resolved: tomorrow or within a year, Cres would be captured or killed ("killed in an exchange of gunfire with the police"); or he would continue to flee and to elude his hunters, and at a certain point he might even die a natural death; yet even if hundreds of people, following his example, were to devote themselves to the sport of killing judges, all the murdered judges would be laid at his door, just as all rivers flow (or used to flow) into the sea.

From the police station, Rogas telephoned the district attorney in Algo, requesting a warrant to search the Cres house, the search to be carried out at night and in the absence of the owner. The district attorney, not informed of the course of the investigation, wished to know the whole story, but Rogas had only to mention the verdict rendered against Cres, attempted homicide, for his curiosity to fade to a "So we're dealing with a jailbird" and for him to promise the warrant. After which, having got directions to the General Carco Culture Club, where he knew he would be able at that hour to find one of Cres's oldest and most trusted friends, Rogas set out

33

for the club, allowing worries and frustrations to be dispelled in the contemplation of the doorways, balconies, and courtyards that followed one after another on the narrow, tortuous streets of that old quarter of the town. Upon entering the club, located in a charming little triangular square, one did not see what it might have to do with culture. For that matter, its being named after General Carco, to whom the world is indebted for the burning of the entire Palatine Library, would have been enough to put one on one's guard. Inside the club were two billiard tables and four card tables, a side table on which lay a hunting magazine and a newspaper, numerous chairs, and two consoles with mirrors that reflected the absorbed, almost funereal, groups of card and billiard players. The silence was broken only by the dry click of the balls on the flat, faded-green surfaces of the billiard tables, and by the more prolonged and, it would seem, more joyous sound of the balls that rolled into pockets. For a moment and almost imperceptibly, the entrance of Rogas distracted the players' attention. Rogas made a small bow, to which no one responded, and then he asked, "Dr. Maxia?" Without raising his eyes from his cards, one of the players said, "I am Dr. Maxia. What do you want?" "I want to talk to you," Rogas said. Brusquely, so as to allow him no illusion about being able to put off the conversation until after the end of the game. The tone of voice had its effect. "I will be with you at once," Maxia said. Delicately, he laid down the fan of cards, relinquished his place to a man who had been standing behind him, an attentive spectator of his game. He walked over to Rogas. "At your disposal," he said.

"Thank you. I am—"

"Let us go outside, if you don't mind," the Doctor interrupted. And no sooner outside: "You are Inspector Rogas. I've seen a photograph of you in a newspaper."

"Yes, I'm Rogas."

"And you're investigating this chain of crimes that —"

"Yes," Rogas admitted.

"But I don't see how I can be of any help to you." The smile ceremonious, the forehead creased with uneasiness.

"Please. Indeed, I must ask your pardon for having taken you away from your game. But it's a matter of a little verification, a check I must make. It concerns your friend Cres. Nothing directly related to the investigation I am working on, of course. It is simply a check to eliminate the coincidences, those apparent connections that turn up in the course of an investigation and that one must eliminate in order to move ahead."

"I understand," Maxia said, who did not understand.

"I have been told that you are the only person Cres frequents."

"That is not quite the case. He, to use your expression, does not frequent me. It is I who look him up, who try to draw him out of his shell, make him pick up old habits again, bring him in contact with other people. But it's a waste of time. Now and then I'm tempted to give up, particularly because it seems to me that I am annoying him with my attentions."

"Interesting," Rogas said.

"What?" Maxia asked, in a flush of suspicion.

"What you say."

"But, excuse me, what exactly do you want to know?"

35

"Nothing exactly. I just want you to talk to me about Cres, about his personality, how he lives."

"I'd rather you ask me questions. Talking like that, freely, I'm afraid I may say something that someone who doesn't know him can misconstrue, something that, if picked up by you, can even turn out to harm him."

"Don't be afraid of that. Nothing you tell me will appear in any memorandum, any report. Our talk is confidential. I want to get an idea of the man, of the personality."

"A strange personality," Maxia said.

"Look, I'll ask you a specific question. In your opinion, was he innocent?"

"I want to be frank. For a while, I believed he really had tried to put his wife out of the way. He's always been a closed sort, taciturn, morose; you can believe anything, good or bad, of a man like that. Just try to understand what goes on in the head of a man like that. So, an indictment comes along, based on circumstantial evidence but in theory credible; the indictment is followed by a verdict of guilty; the verdict is upheld on appeal. . . . A person believes that. I believed it."

"Guilty."

"Yes, guilty . . . Then his wife begins to behave in a kind of way . . . as if she were satisfied, gratified, happy —a happiness she'd like to hide but which bursts out in every gesture, every word. . . ."

"Nothing more?"

"Nothing more. And then, as you know, she disappeared."

"She could be dead. Killed, I mean."

"Why? By whom? Where? . . . Her husband was in jail.

36

And no one else could have any reason to take revenge on a wife who, unjustly or justly, had had her husband thrown into prison for five years."

"It could have been a hired killer."

"I rule that out. Without passing any judgment on whether or not Cres would be capable of hiring a killer. I rule it out for the simple fact that the very day before she disappeared, his wife had completed transactions to convert everything she owned into cash."

"Right," Rogas said approvingly. "Now tell me, did Cres know while he was in prison that his wife had disappeared?"

"I believe so."

"You don't know?"

"No, I don't know. Never once, from the day he got out of jail, has he said one word about his wife."

"Not even about the machinations he was the victim of, not about the unfair verdict?"

"Not even that. Never."

"What does Cres talk about? When he's with you, I mean. There surely must be some topic that turns up frequently in your conversation. . . . An interest, a preference . . . Books, politics, sports, women, crime news . . ."

"Let's see. . . . But, if I'm not mistaken, a moment ago you said 'unfair verdict.' Did you say that to pretend you're on my side, or are you really convinced that Cres was convicted unfairly?"

"Not entirely. Seventy percent, let's say. . . . So what does he talk about when he is with you?"

"He doesn't talk about women. You know, that wouldn't be talking about a rope in a hanged man's

37

house; that would be the hanged man himself talking about a rope. . . . He doesn't know anything about sports, doesn't care about politics, doesn't read many books. . . . I'd say he likes to talk about human-interest stories —the most obscure, complicated kind, full of double meanings. . . . But with detachment, with a light touch— with relish, the way a person would talk who enjoys an absurd spectacle, a hoax. . . . Come to think of it, like someone who's been the victim of a hoax and now is amused to see other people fall into the same trap."

"Amused?"

"Maybe he's pretending to be amused. . . . The Reis trial, for example. He's followed the news reports on it in three or four papers, talked about it often."

"Ah, the Reis case!"

"Don't misunderstand me, please. Cres doesn't side with the defendant. He isn't convinced the man's innocent, nor does he find any justification for the crime he's accused of."

"And when they killed District Attorney Varga?"

"Nothing."

"But he did talk about it?"

"Yes, but only from what you might call a technical angle. Since the District Attorney was dead, would there be a new trial or would the law allow for a substitute—"

"And Cres hoped for a substitute, not for a new trial."

"How do you know that?"

"I'm guessing."

Maxia's expression became diffident, perplexed. He was beginning to wonder whether he had said too much, whether he should watch his tongue. Rogas sensed that the moment had come to change the subject. "Cres isn't here," he said.

"He's not where? At home? In town?"

"He's not at home or in town. Disappeared."

"What do you mean, disappeared? How can you be sure he's not at home?"

"I went to his house, I knocked again and again. Not a sound."

"He's pretending not to be home. With me, too, sometimes. But I ignore it, I don't get offended. He doesn't like to be with people, sometimes not even with me. . . . Once, I read the diary of a sixteenth-century Florentine painter—pretty squalid stuff, a neurotic's story. But I was reminded of it precisely in connection with Cres. Because the painter used to hear his friends knock and call out to him, and he would pretend not to be at home; then he would write in his diary, 'So-and-So and So-and-So knocked; I don't know what they wanted,' and he would think about it for two whole days. . . ."

"Pontormo," Rogas said.

"That's right, Pontormo. . . . How did you know?"

"I'm guessing," Rogas said, ironically this time.

"Pontormo," Maxia repeated, disconcerted. "Well, when I'm standing outside Cres's door, sure that he's there and doesn't want to open, I take the edge off the irritation that grips me for a second by thinking of Pontormo, and how Cres is letting me stand there for the pleasure of wasting two days daydreaming about what I might have wanted—when he knows perfectly well I don't want a thing—and feeling remorseful for having treated me badly."

"Pontormo comes through in his diary as a hypochondriac. What would you say to that?"

"I'd agree."

"Cres, too, then."

"Since I'm a doctor, with regard to Cres I'd be more cautious."

"Right. But this time, my dear Doctor, I believe that Cres really isn't at home, that he's gone away. . . . Now, tell me this: are you sure he was at home all those times you found yourself waiting in front of his door?"

"What do you mean, sure? I've no proof. Nor can I say always. It's possible that sometimes he actually wasn't there."

"But you have always suspected that he was."

"The first times, no. Then, after checking with the neighbors, who said they hadn't seen him go out, I came to that conclusion. And for that matter, it fits the type of person he is, as far as I know him."

"Has it happened recently that you've been left standing more often than usual in front of a closed door?"

"I don't remember. . . . It's happened to me often enough, yes, but I can't say whether it's been more often than last year or three years ago."

"I want to tell you, in all candor, that we are looking for Cres to question him in connection with this massacre of judges. In the last few days, we've had him under surveillance, and up until yesterday evening, according to the police, he's been at home. Now, I have the clear impression that he's no longer there, that he's managed to elude the stakeout and make a getaway. I've asked the district attorney for a search warrant. Tonight, if Cres is not there, as I assume, or if he pretends not to be there,

40

as you believe, we will force the door and search the house. In the circumstances, I hope you, as a friend of Cres and in his interest, will be willing to accompany me."

"I'll come. But first I'd like us to go together now and try to get him to answer the door."

"That's fine with me," Rogas said.

Cres was not there. Rogas observed with what order and neatness the house, too large for a man living alone, was kept. But something sinister hovered in the air, as in prisons or convents. A more concretely sinister detail, it seemed to Rogas, was a portrait of Mrs. Cres (languid glance, lips half-parted as if she were about to pronounce a word of love) that looked out from a heavy silver frame: it was placed opposite the double bed in which, evidently, Cres had continued to sleep, since on top of the bed table there were ranged, in orderly fashion, water thermos and glass, bicarbonate of soda, cough lozenges, ashtray, and the third and last volume of *The Brothers Karamazov*. Under the book was one of those memorandum cards that come packaged with expensive cigarettes; the Inspector surmised that Cres had used it as a bookmark; if it was not inside the book, one could assume that he had come to the end: "Well, now we will finish talking and go to his funeral dinner. Don't be put out at our eating pancakes—it's a very old custom and there's something nice in that!" . . . Perhaps he had finished the book while waiting for it to be time for him to slip away, having set everything in order in anticipation of the police's breaking in during his absence. A precise, meticulous man, he had left nothing that could serve to

41

identify or trace him—not a photograph, not a hotel bill, not a railroad ticket stub, no receipt whatever. The identity of the man who until a few hours ago had inhabited the house was fading away into the few things that remained by the bed: the bicarbonate, the cough lozenges, the *Karamazov*. . . . Bicarbonate and lozenges were almost finished, and so he had left them behind; one could deduce that he consumed them in quantity, since he ate complicated things (in the kitchen were some of the more rare and highly spiced culinary ingredients) and smoked Turkish cigarettes. As for the *Karamazov*, one could account for that choice by virtue of the fact that in the meager collection on the bookshelves, the Russians up to Gorki were in the majority.

The empty portrait frames in the house sparked a sudden seizure of awareness in Maxia. He remembered very well one of the vanished photographs. It was of Cres standing and leaning slightly, in an attitude of affectionate concern, toward his seated mother; the old lady, holding an open fan in one hand, was all intent that the camera's eye should capture that gesture of abiding flirtatiousness. Why had Cres removed it? Obviously because he did not want a likeness of himself to fall into the hands of the police; this was confirmed by the fact that photographs of his mother, his father, his wife, and many strangers who must have been relatives or friends were found by the dozen in a large box, but not one of him, not even of his first Communion. Maxia's loyalty to his friend began to wane, the more so as that sleepless night began to weigh on him. For Rogas, however, the disappearance of the photographs presented itself as a problem within a problem: either Cres had removed them out of some kind of superstition, dictated by a neurotic fear about leaving his own likeness to fall into the hands of people who were not friendly toward him (for even in the nervous disorders of a reasonably cultivated man, the most primitive and unlikely superstitions may surface), or he had done so to prevent the police's using them to track him down by distributing them throughout the country and having them published in the papers. But in this case, the ploy was of little moment: within a few hours, Rogas would have—both from the office that issues passports and from the records of the prison where Cres had sojourned—the photographs necessary for the hunt that would be unleashed. Not to mention that also in newspaper and picture-agency files there must be some photographs from the time of the trial. Unless . . . And there flashed into his mind the recollection of what disorder and neglect reigned over things that were supposed to be preserved and cared for; how relatively easy it was to remove from historical archives a decree of Charles VI or a note of General Carco, and from court archives the bound copy of trial proceedings. Rogas had a presentiment that he would not find a photograph of Cres anywhere.

He did not, in fact, find any. Nor could he make use of the two published in newspapers ten years before: in one Inspector Contrera appeared in focus, and in the other the defense lawyer; in both, Cres was like a shape behind smoked glass. There was a famous police artist who had once succeeded in having a thief arrested by sketching his face from a description supplied by the robber's victim; in two days of work, with Dr. Maxia constantly offering descriptions and suggesting corrections, the artist eventually produced a portrait the distribution of which would have risked causing harassment to a celebrated film star.

What was circulated was the verbal description of a man five feet eight inches tall, thin, dark-skinned, slightly bald, with some white hair, perfect teeth, and slightly aquiline nose; by preference, the man wore gray; he had a great deal of money. This last was the factor that made him virtually invulnerable, provided that in his travels and stopovers he kept to first-class accommodations, which the police were reluctant to search.

Cres had become, in a word, invisible.

Rogas also suspected exactly how Cres had managed to get himself documents for a new identity. In prison, he had known one of the most able counterfeiters in the country, perhaps the best known to the police of four or five nations. The counterfeiter was a reliable man, scrupulous and loyal in regard to his clients. Fellow-prisoners, questioned in this respect, recalled that he was very close to Cres during their years in jail. Rogas went to visit him, for he, too, was now at liberty, but the man said that in prison he had played chess with Cres and talked about books, that he remembered him warmly, but that outside of prison he had not seen him again and, indeed, was eager to have news of him. Was he well? Had they reviewed his trial? If the Inspector had occasion to see him, would the Inspector be kind enough to give Cres his greetings? Rogas had not expected a different attitude.

At this point, Rogas's investigation had reached a fairly reliable presumptive solution. Now it was necessary to find Cres, and the first thing to be done was to

44

check hotel registers in the cities where the crimes had been committed for the days when they had occurred, verifying whether from one city to the next, on the dates of the crimes, the same name might not turn up; that name would be the one Cres had taken for his false papers. Not that Rogas really hoped to get any positive results, but it was a job that had to be done. Furthermore, so many criminal cases he had worked on had taught him that no matter how perfect the plan, how carefully worked out the details, subtleties, and nuances, the most stupid, the most clumsily patched-up mistake always and unforeseeably slipped in to ruin its author.

But while the Inspector, having returned to the capital, was preparing a complete report on his work, District Attorney Perro was felled in the capital. This time there were witnesses: a night watchman, a prostitute, and a man who, because of the heat, was out on his balcony. None of the three had actually seen the crime committed, but immediately after hearing the shot, all three had seen two people running away. From the speed and agility of the culprits' flight, the witnesses could say positively that they were young; from their hair and style of dress (since, for a second, they had paused uncertainly under a street lamp), the witnesses could say further that they were young men of a certain type. "First the rebels revolutionized the style of wearing their hair . . . not molesting the mustache or beard, which they allowed to keep on growing as long as it would . . . letting it hang down in great length and disorder in the back. . . . [They] decided to wear the purple stripe on their togas. . . . And the sleeves of their tunics were cut tight above the wrists. . . . Their cloaks, trousers, and boots were also different:

45

and these, too, were called the Hun style, which they imitated." (Procopius of Caesarea, *Secret History*.)

The news cheered the entire, or almost the entire, nation. Uplifted were the morale and morals of Parliament, Administration, press, clergy, fathers of families, and academics. Also of the working class and of the International Revolutionary Party, which represented it. Not one paper spared the police veiled sarcasm or open derision. The question that reporters and commentators, members of the government and of the opposition, asked each other and asked in diverse ways was: How was it possible that, in a country agitated by insurrectional cadres that preached violence as both means and end, the police had opted for the thesis of the solitary criminal, the mad revenger?

The High Commissioner of Police and the Minister for National Security were asking themselves the same thing. Their questions descended on Rogas like an avalanche. In vain, the Inspector tried to make his chief understand how nothing that had occurred lessened the validity of the thesis pursued to that point, that the unanimous testimony of three well-deserving citizens must be considered within the limits of what actually had been seen; i.e., two young men running away from the scene of the crime. His chief took umbrage at this: he enjoined Rogas to get that Cres out of his head; poor man, perhaps he had run away because he was being unjustly persecuted; Rogas should set to work instead with his colleague in the Political Section, if he wished to redeem himself and redeem the police force from evident error.

Rogas did not get Cres out of his head; now, thanks to a night watchman, a prostitute, and a gentleman suffering from the heat, Cres could proceed with the execution of his plan, enjoying practically boundless freedom and immunity. Rogas's professional interest had ebbed; however, there remained his human concern and punctilio. He would meet Cres, one day or another—maybe not to arrest him, but if he had to do so, he would. Meanwhile, off to work under the orders of his colleague in the Political Section—punishment; in effect, demotion.

The offices of the Political Section looked like a newly established branch of a Benedictine library: at each table, an official immersed in reading a book, a leaflet, a magazine; everywhere piles of books, leaflets, and magazines with threatening or incomprehensible titles. "We're in the process of scanning all the publications the revolutionary cadres have put out over the last six months. We concentrate on articles or passages that attack the administration of justice in our country," his section-head colleague explained to him. "So far, we've found three or four that are more or less violent, but our favorite is this one." He picked up a magazine printed on heavy, pale-yellow paper, opened it, showed Rogas a page marked in the margin in red and densely underlined in blue. "Read that; it's one of those things deliberately designed to inflame weak minds, to unhinge people who have already lost their grip on reality."

Rogas read it absently. He was thinking about a grip on reality—his colleague's, Cres's. "Actually," he said, handing the magazine back, "it is a pretty strong article. Prosecutable, I'd say, for contempt; maybe also for inciting to crime."

"Already attended to, my dear colleague, already attended to." Condescending emphasis on the word "colleague," as if to convey that in fact they were no such thing. "But the problem is, who wrote it? Yes, of course, on the incrimination angle we've got the editor of the magazine. But the article is anonymous. Did he write it, did he not write it? . . . Because, you see, I've got an idea that the shots—these murders of judges, I mean—come from the cadre that publishes this magazine. Do you know how I got the idea? Because lately this group—we keep it under surveillance, of course—has sort of fallen apart. There are maybe ten people left for us to keep an eye on. Most of the cadre has disappeared, and we can't find them."

"You don't suppose it's the time of year that has scattered them?" Rogas was struck by the fact that the police were so mesmerized by the word "cadre" that they pronounced it as if it were within quotes. "They've gone off to the shore, to the mountains; they're traveling abroad. . . ."

"We've thought of that. Maybe they are at the shore or in the mountains. But in hiding."

"No, no. They're at their fathers' country houses or on their fathers' yachts. I'll bet the ones who've stayed behind under surveillance are the poorest ones."

"That may be." Letting the objection drop: "The editor of the magazine has disappeared, too. . . . Now, I would like you to fish him up for me—not to arrest or detain him, of course."

"It won't be easy."

"Easier for you than for us, I assume. You are almost a man of letters." This in a tone of voice that tried to be ingratiating but that betrayed facetious scorn, for Rogas had this bad reputation among his superiors and colleagues on account of the books he kept on his office desk and the clarity, coherence, and succinctness of his written reports. These were so unlike the ones that had been circulating in police offices for at least a century that they often sparked the shout "How this character can write!" or again "What's this fellow trying to say?" It was known, furthermore, that he frequented journalists and authors. And he was said to go to art galleries and to the theatre.

"I am not 'almost a man of letters,'" Rogas said brusquely.

"I'm sorry. I meant to say, you are well acquainted with those people."

"Not even that. I know three or four newsmen; very few literary men, actually. And I've been a friend of the writer Cusan from grammar-school days."

"In any event, you are in a better position to handle this job than we are. . . . You will, first, find out where the magazine editor is hiding and inform me immediately, so that I can set up a strict surveillance; second, when the stakeout is functioning, you will pay the fellow a visit, talk to him, pump him for all the information you can get about the magazine and the cadre—scare him a little so that he does something to scare his friends, too. Needless to say, we'll tap the phone of the house where he's hiding. . . . O.K.?"

"O.K.," Rogas said wearily.

The editor of the magazine *Permanent Revolution* was the guest, as Rogas promptly learned, of the writer

Nocio. Rogas notified his colleague in the Political Section, who immediately arranged for house surveillance and a wiretap. Two hours later, he was knocking at the door of a small villa on the outskirts of the city, where Nocio habitually went each summer to write that summer's book.

A maid in apron and starched lace cap opened the door, examined him with distrust, and, before Rogas had uttered a word, said, "Mr. Nocio isn't in."

"I am a police inspector."

"I will see if he's in," the maid said, flushing either over the lie she had just proffered or from the emotion, never before experienced in that household, at finding herself confronted by a police inspector.

Nocio was in. The maid ushered Rogas into a large, dark study; at the far end, before a desk on which the light of a gooseneck lamp fell—and it was bright daylight outdoors—sat Nocio. When the Inspector was two steps away, he raised his eyes from the manuscript he appeared to be correcting; he rose, leaning on the arms of his chair as if with an effort, came around the desk, offered his hand.

"I am Inspector Rogas."

"Delighted. I am at your service." Spreading his hands wide, as much as to say that there was very little he, in his inveterate state of innocence, could do for the police who, everyone knows, are always looking for the guilty.

"I am disturbing you," Rogas said, "because it appears that Dr. Galano, the editor of the magazine *Permanent Revolution,* is your guest."

"Not mine. My wife's."

"Ah," said Rogas.

50

"Don't think what you're thinking," Nocio said, laughing. "My wife has passed the canonical age. The fact of the matter is, she acts as his housekeeper; she is housekeeper to a priest of the revolution. Furthermore, strictly between ourselves, Galano—"

"His personal tastes are known."

"Of course, you people know everything. . . . And so you knew"—ironically—"that Galano is my guest: a piece of information that is not entirely correct. He is the guest of my wife. Just between us, I can't stand him. He's a hysterical little provincial intellectual. What am I saying, intellectual! He's one of those cretins who create the illusion of intelligent discourse. It takes very little today to acquire that magical skill. 'Words, words, words . . .' You read his magazine?"

"Some articles. In line of duty."

Nocio fell into a chair, prey to almost silent but uncontainable, visceral laughter. " 'In line of duty!' Do you know, you've just made one of the most marvelous remarks I've heard in years? 'In line of duty.' Too utterly marvelous! . . . But please, do sit down." He gestured toward the chair opposite.

"Have you seen," Nocio continued, composing himself after his abrupt outburst of mirth, "the department in the magazine that deals with books? It's a column called 'The Index.' This cretin—Galano, I mean—has discovered the Index Librorum Prohibitorum. Four hundred and some years after the fact, when the Catholic Church itself is revoking it! . . . My books, all of them, systematically get put on his 'Index.' Think of it: *my* books! The most revolutionary books that have been written in these parts in the last thirty years."

51

Simple-minded, Rogas thought. He's come straight to the sore point. "That's right," he agreed aloud. But only by way of consolation.

"The fact is," Nocio went on, "they're all Catholics. Old-style, fanatical, funereal Catholics, and they don't know it. What a pity the Church is in such a hurry to bring itself up to date. If it were to retreat behind its old lines of defense, if it were to go back to being closed and cruel the way it used to be in the days of Philip II, the Inquisition, the Counter Reformation, these people would be joining up in droves. Prohibit, investigate, punish—that's what they want."

"But if that were to happen, the Church would bear down hard on us again, the way it did during the Counter Reformation. And you certainly don't want that," Rogas observed.

"No, I don't want it. And anyhow it can't happen. But I've got this crazy wish that it would; it's a dream of mine. Everything would be clearer, tidier: they on one side, me on the other. Instead, the way things are, I'm forced to be on their side, on the side of Galano, who puts me on his 'Index.' The revolution, you understand? This word, and it's only a word, involves me, blackmails me, binds me to Galano and his ilk." Almost a shout: "I hate him!"

A pause. Then Nocio stood up, went to the desk, picked up some sheets of paper; he came back and sat down in front of Rogas. "Do you know what I was doing when you came in? I was rereading and correcting a poem I ripped off—like that, in a rage—last evening. Poetry! I haven't written poetry since I was in high school. . . . Read it." He thrust the papers into Rogas's

hand with a nervous gesture, as if he had made a decision
he was ashamed of. Rogas read.

> Arrogant, you repeat from memory
> what you do not know,
> idea-spray, scum of old and new ideas
> (more old than new)
> that your mouths
> drool and dribble
> the way only yesterday
> in Mama's arms
> —Mama, Mama—
> they slobbered ice cream.
> And flowing from
> your beards of protomartyrs—
> that faddist fakery,
> fiction of a maturity
> that makes you
> equal to your fathers
> and therefore fit for incest.
> Mama . . .
> The whole problem right here,
> the woman who lies in your father's bed,
> and you announce her reign;
> and behind your beards you have faces
> like the San Luigi of a neo-neo-capitalism—
> all the flaws of the Gonzagas in his thin face,
> all the flaws of the middle class in your own;
> he grown up among dwarfs and buffoons,
> among hunchbacks and eunuchs;
> distilled by the pox,
> a saint because never did he look his mother,
> who was a woman,

in the face;
but yours you look in the face and think
she is a whore if she lies in the bed of your father
because you are holier than he
even if you do not know it,
and you have grown up—you, too—
among buffoons, dwarfs, and eunuchs,
between the gold and the lues;
the beard, then, to make sinister
the delicate faces of pimps
inverts
perverts;
and Robespierre, who had no beard,
laughs at you, at your revolution;
his skull laughs,
his dust,
his last particle of dust that is worth more
than your whole life—
that is, than the fact that you are alive while he is dead;
and Marx, too, who had a beard, laughs,
laughs with every bristle of his beard,
laughs at the empty husks he has left you,
the necklaces of jingling bells
of dry sperm, dead sperm
that you bedeck yourselves with like show mules;
you shake them in idleness, in discontent, in disgust
(the living seed of Marx is in those who suffer,
who think,
who have no flags).
Robespierre and Marx are laughing,
but perhaps they also weep
over the man, no longer human, who is fleshed in you,
over mind that does not think,
over heart that does not love,

over the perpetual fiasco of sex and mind
with which you announce the reign of the mothers.
"That is not what I meant at all;
that is not it, at all—"
Not that, not that,
not even we wanted that,
we buffoons
vitiated
corrupted;
we fathers,
not even we,
since we prostituted life but understood love,
prostituted mind but understood thought,
reason
sex
man and woman
male and female
grief
death.
Talleyrand said that the sweetness of life
was known only to those who, like him,
had lived before the Revolution,
but after you (not your revolution,
for you will not make one) there will no longer be
relic reflection echo
of the sweetness of life,
nor of you will there remain any record
unless it be
in the files of the federal narcotics bureau.
The human man has had his moon,
the human goddess
quiet light of love;
you have your
gray pumice pox-infected desert

deserving of your no longer human bones,
dead nature with the dead lights of judgment;
but you know nothing
of the Ariostoan fable of Orlando
restored to his senses by Astolfo
on a lunar voyage
of the mind sealed in a flask
like yours (but yours is
irrecuperable). The flask, still life,
the flask of Eros,
as Stendhal said in Italian in the text,
Stendhal whom you do not know,
Stendhal who speaks
the language of passion to which you are all dead.

"Interesting," Rogas said. "Will you publish it?"

"You must be joking." The delicate, thoughtful lines of his face changed and coarsened. A merchant, Rogas thought, who feels he's making a bid that will ruin him. "You must be joking. They're already pointing their fingers at me as a reactionary. If I bring out a thing like this, I'm done for. It would be my gravestone, my epitaph."

"But you had the impulse to write it; you've written it."

"I blew up, I blew up. It's of no importance. Crazy. You'll tell me there are some truths, some insights in it. But they don't count, not in comparison to the great, unique fact of the revolution. Which will come, which will come as surely as day follows night. . . . Oh, no, Galano won't make the revolution; people like him won't. . . . But it will come. And Galano and the rest who talk about it without understanding it and without really expecting it—they're all in there, in the front line. . . .

Maybe they'll be the first to be devoured, but meanwhile there they are, and there they will be until the moment it explodes." Changing his tone of voice: "You've read Pascal?"

"I've read him."

"You remember his idea about the wager? At first glance, it seems scandalous—"

"Monstrous, I'd say."

"It isn't. . . . If I believe in God, in eternal life, in the immortality of the soul—even if these things don't exist —what price must I pay? Nothing. But if I don't believe, and if these things do exist, the price to be paid is ever-lasting death. . . . Today the possibility of making the wager has shifted from metaphysics to history. Now the 'beyond' is the revolution. I would risk losing everything were I to bet against the revolution. But if I bet on it, I lose nothing if it doesn't take place; I win everything if it does. . . . And this is not, as you say, a monstrous proposition. Its utilitarian formulation mustn't make us forget that we are still caught up in the problem of what Augustine and Pascal called free choice, what I call liberty. . . . You don't have this problem? You don't bet? You don't like to bet?"

"I detest every kind of betting. I don't want to risk winning. And I've a soft spot for losing, for losers. I can tell you, too, that I'm discovering in myself a kind of affection for the revolution—precisely because it is already defeated."

"I would say, and I haven't the slightest wish to offend you, that that is a professional point of view. Because you are a part of the structure of the bourgeois state, in order to defend it you've come to the point of believing it has a practically inexhaustible survival potential. But don't you see what's happening in our country? Sooner or later, we must pay for our mistakes."

"When there is something to pay with," Rogas said morosely.

"Right, when there's something to pay with." He scrutinized Rogas with absent-minded attention. Then, jokingly: "Isn't talking about revolution a punishable offense?"

"Professionally, this time, I assure you that the more one talks about it, the better."

"O Galano!" he apostrophized comically. And suddenly he remembered why Rogas was there. "But you came to talk to Galano! Forgive me, I'll have him called at once." He went to the desk, took up a little silver bell, and rang it loudly. At the sound, the maid came. "Tell Mr. Galano—and, naturally, my wife, too—that a police inspector is here who wants to talk to him." The maid had no sooner disappeared than Nocio hastily gathered up the pages he had had Rogas read, put them in a drawer of the desk, locked the drawer, and pocketed the key.

"You'll destroy the poem?" Rogas asked.

"Why?" Surprised, irritated.

"You can't leave anything lying around that may make you lose your bet. . . . But I wonder—what if you could win the bet with the poem?"

"For the love of heaven!" Nocio said. Perhaps referring to the momentary folly of those verses, perhaps warning Rogas not to speak of them further, for Galano had entered the room in a kind of soundless balletic flight. He halted his dance before Nocio; feigning anxiety, consternation, he asked, "A police inspector? For me?"

Nocio indicated Rogas, who had risen to his feet.

"Are you going to arrest me?" Galano asked, languidly peering up at Rogas. He turned to Nocio. "Do you think he's come to arrest me?"

"I don't know," Nocio said brusquely.

"But you'd like that," Galano said, shaking his finger like someone who's caught another out and is scolding him.

"What is it he would like?" Mrs. Nocio asked from the door, in an I'll-fix-you tone of voice. Rogas bowed slightly. He thought, Tallemant des Réaux would say that few women are less lovely than she.

"For them to arrest me," Galano said.

"Oh," the woman murmured, looking with horror at her husband.

Fearing a small explosion of domestic resentments, Rogas said, "I must disappoint you. I haven't come to arrest you."

"You disappoint me indeed," Galano said. "And you disappoint him." Pointing to Nocio.

"I have come," Rogas said, "to inform you that, as editor of the magazine *Permanent Revolution* and, presumably, author of an unsigned article on the administration of justice, you have been accused of contempt and of inciting an act against the security of the state."

"The same old story," Galano said.

"Yes, the same old story. But this time in a different climate, you understand."

"No, I don't understand. Rather, I refuse to understand. Because if they want to make me the scapegoat for

59

that carrousel of murdered judges, it means that the administration of justice goes beyond our denunciations of it, so I will have material to write even more violent pieces about it."

"Then you did write the article?"

"I don't deny it and I don't admit it. You have informed me of the charges; we'll see each other in court. But I assure you, I am not someone who goes around killing judges."

"I am sure of that."

"Personally, or is it the police who are sure of it?"

"Personally."

"Why?" With a touch of disappointment.

"Perhaps out of pride in my work."

"Of course, I remember. You were on another scent. . . . But the police, instead, have some suspicions about me."

"I haven't said that. The police—this I can tell you— have some suspicions about your article; that is, about the effects an article like yours can produce on a reader who is *non compos mentis*, or on a group of readers, on an extreme group of your aficionados."

"Oh, no, my articles don't produce such effects, worse luck. If they did, he"—he pointed at Nocio—"would long since have been installed in the pantheon of Christ's Church, at rest among the nation's heroic dead."

Nocio's chin shook, like that of a child about to cry. But perhaps it was anger. "You are a swine," he said. And he tried to sweeten the insult by smiling as if it were a joke.

"Why, please? Because I maintain that you are a middle-class writer who has far more to answer for than the

60

Minister for Security or the President of the Supreme Court or the most abominable American financier?"

"I? A middle-class writer?" Turning to Rogas: "Did you hear? Now I am a middle-class writer! You tell him whether the police consider me a middle-class writer."

"Vilfredo, don't be ridiculous," his wife intervened. "Do you really need a certificate from the police: 'Vilfredo Nocio is not a middle-class writer.' Signed Tamborra?" (Tamborra was the High Commissioner of Police, known for his perfervid aversion to intellectuals.)

"Shut your mouth," Nocio said.

"There's instant proof of how reactionary you are: 'Shut your mouth.' Because I'm a woman, because I'm your wife—"

"You don't even have a mouth; you've got a beak, a parrot's beak, a magpie's beak," Nocio said ferociously.

"Oh, no, there's no help for it," Galano said. "You are a middle-class writer; you yourself are middle-class, you live like a middle-class man; you eat, sleep, and amuse yourself like a middle-class man—"

"I am *not* middle-class!" Nocio shouted. He was on the verge of breaking down.

"Excuse me," Rogas said to Galano, and his question was also a sympathetic attempt to ease Nocio's anguish. "You say, 'You live like a middle-class man; you eat, sleep, and amuse yourself like a middle-class man.' Precisely what do you mean?"

"You don't understand?"

"No, I don't understand."

"Why, all this . . ." Galano said. He raised his arms to encompass and circumscribe all that was implicit in the study, the house, the encircling garden, and the life that Nocio led in those surroundings.

"Meanwhile you are staying here. And your own house is not all that different," Nocio said.

"But I am staying here with a difference, that's the point," Galano shrilled triumphantly.

"You eat the way I do; blue-collar people working for a wage serve you the way they serve me; you sleep in a canopied bed like mine. . . . In fact, in your own house you sleep in a bed they sold you, fobbed off on you as the Marquise de Pompadour's. . . ."

Galano bristled. "They did not fob it off on me. It's authentic. But that desk of yours, it doesn't come from D'Annunzio's villa at Arachon; it was manufactured a couple of years ago in Évian." He turned to Rogas. "Very significant, don't you think? He bought a desk because they made him believe D'Annunzio used to sit at it reading Petrarch."

"All right, my desk is a copy, your bed is genuine. The point is, you bought it and you sleep in it. . . . In a word, you live like me, spend your money like me, have the same friends and acquaintances I have. You do nothing but come and go between Saint-Moritz and Taormina and Monte Carlo. You gamble and you pay for your love affairs, which I don't do, which I have never done. But I am middle-class and you are not."

"To be or not to be middle-class depends on this," Galano said, and with his index finger he tapped the center of his forehead.

"Very convenient," Rogas said. He arose to leave.

"You wouldn't understand," Galano said scornfully.

The Chief of the Political Section was disappointed and tired. "No sooner had you left Galano," he related to Rogas, "than he got on the phone. He called, in this order, the director-general of the West Bank; the president of Schiele Pharmaceuticals; the editor of the government paper *Order and Freedom;* the editor of the opposition's weekly, the *Evening Red;* that famous tailor, Gradivo; the actress Marion Delavigue; the Count of Santo Spirito; and the ex-Queen of Moldavia. . . . *Merry Widow* stuff, isn't it? He informed all these people, with screams of laughter, that he had had a visit from a police inspector and it seemed the police suspected him of being the perpetrator of this systematic picking off of judges. Everyone was greatly amused. Now, do you believe people like that can be part of a revolutionary plot —what's more, that they can approve of actions like killing judges?"

"What about you?" He thought, In another minute, he'll be saddling me with responsibility for the idiotic idea of going after Galano.

"Not in my wildest dreams . . . All the same, from Galano's telephone calls we've come up with one useful little detail. At one point, when he was talking with the actress, he said that, if anything, the police should be looking into the people in Zeta. Zeta's the neo-anarchist group that's headed up by that ex-priest; he's a theorist in Christian evangelical anarchism. The group's financed by Narco, who is practically sole owner of the big SD store chain. SD—you know—it stands for Square Deal. I must say, it strikes me as a little much that evangelical neo-anarchists would be devoting themselves to an open season on judges. But I will have to read the Bible, also all the publications these Zeta people put out."

"As far as the Bible is concerned, I can tell you unqualifiedly that you will find a great many injunctions against judging others and against judges. There is nothing evangelical, of course, about resorting to violence—slugging it out, as we policemen say. However, one doesn't know how priests and ex-priests read the Bible, when they read it. And then there's 'I came not to send peace, but the sword.' "

"Who says that?"

"Christ said it."

"Right, there is some talk about a sword. Still, I would never have thought that Christ—"

"It could be a metaphor. The sword, I mean."

"But a .38-caliber gun isn't. And *that*'s what we're dealing with. . . . That's why I don't trust the clue Galano's been kind enough to hand us."

"Nor do I."

"But we've got it, and we can't not look into it. . . . I think you're the person who should look into it. . . . Galano, while he was still talking to the actress, said, 'This evening, everybody's going to be at Narco's. If only the police knew . . .' "

"In my opinion, Galano suspected that the telephone was tapped and wanted to play a joke on us."

"You think so? . . . Well, joke or no joke, this evening you'll go to the Narco home. The house, naturally, will be surrounded—but discreetly—by plainclothesmen who will arrive a few at a time."

"Why don't you come along?"

"I can't. I've been called to see the Minister."

64

"Well, then, tell me what I must do, what I must say."

"Say that you want to have a talk with the ex-priest—I don't remember what the devil his name is—or that you're looking for such-and-such a person who you've been told is at the Narco home—invent any old name. . . . This notion, to be looking for someone who doesn't exist, strikes me as extremely good. . . . Anyhow, I trust your judgment, your discretion."

As Rogas, accompanied by a brigadier, was entering the baroque palace built by a cardinal and now occupied by Narco, the President of the Tribunal in Tera was shot dead. At that moment, however, the Inspector was not thinking of the crimes, or of Cres, who in all likelihood was their author; he was worried that he himself was slipping into a ridiculous position, and that his colleague in the Political Section would turn a cold shoulder to him once he hit rock bottom—rock bottom of the ridiculous, as well as of the erroneous.

He stated his name and rank to the doorman. Pressing a button, the man shouted that name, that rank into an invisible microphone. An authoritative voice was heard: "Have him come up. Servants' entrance." With a gesture of indolent scorn, the doorman pointed out the servants' stairway to Rogas.

The door was open, and the major-domo was standing there as if to bar their passage. "What is it you want?"

"To speak with Mr. Narco."

"I don't know if he can receive you now."

"Go ask him."

The man came back with an expression in which arrogance was diluted with amusement. Rogas felt a certain foreboding: the faces of servants always foretell the mood of the masters. A long hallway, a deliciously furnished sitting room, a salon with many paintings. Watteau, Fragonard, Boucher. May they at least be fakes, Rogas hoped. Still another door, and they were in a great drawing room crowded with people. Instantly, Rogas knew that his colleague in the Political Section had lied to him: he had not been summoned by the Minister if that same Minister was now walking toward him together with a man who must be Narco.

With a grave face and in a menacing tone of voice, the Minister asked, "What do you want?"

Rogas elected not to recognize him. "To speak with Mr. Narco," he said quietly.

"I am he," the other man said. The Minister made him a sign that signified: You be quiet. It's up to me to put these boors in their place. He turned to Rogas: "Who are you?"

"I am Inspector Rogas. And you?"

"He's asking me who I am," the Minister said to Narco, smiling with irony and spite.

"Yes, he's asking you who you are," Narco shot back. Doubly pleased: both at the Minister's wounded vanity and at the painful situation in which the Inspector would shortly find himself.

"You really do not recognize me?"

"*I* do," the brigadier said, as exultant as the boy who answers the question his classmate has been unable to answer. Rogas was a good actor; he looked at the brigadier with surprise and vexation. Almost in a whisper, the brigadier said to him, "It's our Minister."

That "our" placated the Minister. He looked at Rogas

66

with the expression of a man who is disposed to be merciful but is waiting to be asked. Rogas said, "I beg your pardon, Excellency, but I did not expect—"

"You did not expect what? To find me here, at the home of my friend Narco?"

"I meant to say, I didn't expect to intrude on an evening among friends."

"You have intruded. So?"

"We came to ask Mr. Narco just one bit of information: whether he knows a man by the name of Zervo."

"Why should I know him?" Narco asked.

"Because they have told us that he belongs to the Neo-Anarchic Christian Movement, or that he frequents the group without belonging."

"I've never heard that name," Narco said. "But let's see if some of our friends know him. . . . Come along." All four moved toward the circle of people, seated or standing, who had drawn closer together to whisper and snicker the moment Rogas and the brigadier had entered. Moving into the circle, Rogas noticed Galano elegantly curled up in a big armchair. And that was no surprise.

"My dear Inspector," Galano greeted him cheerfully. Turning to the Minister, "I must say to you, my dearest Evaristo, you are one big liar. You've always denied that the police tap our telephones, but they do tap them, and how! The presence of the Inspector here is absolute proof of it."

Evaristo turned pale. He asked Rogas, "Is this true?"

Rogas said, "I've heard nothing about it."

"How delicious!" Galano said. "This one asks whether it is true, the other one says it isn't. . . ." He stood up to confront the Minister. "Do you think I'm an imbecile? Don't hesitate, tell me: 'You are an imbecile, and I expect you to believe what I say and what the Inspector says.'"

"I give you my word, I know nothing about any wiretaps. . . . I can't exclude the possibility that sometimes they are made, but always on a court order and in the case of people under serious suspicion. . . . But political wiretaps, no. I rule that out absolutely."

"Well, then, I am a person under serious suspicion, because certainly my phone is tapped. . . . Not mine, to be exact: the phone of Vilfredo Nocio."

A salvo of outraged surprise arose from the bystanders.

"However that may be," Galano continued, "I want to give you some advice. Instead of playing out the farce with your Inspector, call him to the Ministry and have him tell you how and why he came here this evening."

"Be at my office tomorrow at ten," the Minister said to Rogas.

"Naturally," Galano said, "I won't know what you'll say to each other tomorrow. But I do know what I know. And I'm sorry, but in the next number of the *Permanent Revolution* you'll see—"

"Let it go," Narco said.

"Oh, no, I can't let him get away with this."

"Meantime, let's have a drink," Narco said. And he shouted to the waiter, "Bring the Inspector a drink."

Rogas remembered the phrase "but meanwhile bring the father something to drink" in a famous, tedious Italian novel, and thought how well the episode of that earlier trying visit matched the present moment. But he said to himself, "You're becoming paranoid; you're not Fra Cristoforo."

"Scotch, Armagnac, champagne?" Narco asked.

"No, thank you."

"Have a drink," the Minister said. "You're not on duty. The assignment you came here on is over and done with."

The next day at ten, in the Minister's anteroom, Rogas found the Chief of the Political Section. He, too, had been summoned, and on barely a half hour's notice; he was, therefore, breathless, upset, terrified, and Rogas's calm heightened his terror, in his certainty that such calm on Rogas's part came from the latter's decision to unload on him all responsibility for the unfortunate expedition to the Narco home. It would have been fair for him, in the Minister's presence, to assume the responsibility, but instead he was frantically wondering how he might attribute to Rogas defects in the execution of the plan, if not the idea for it.

But the Minister's mood, jovial and just short of hail-fellow-well-met, dissolved the terrors of the Chief of the Political Section proportionately as, on the other hand, it troubled Rogas.

After a cordial, vigorous handshake, the Minister sought to underscore the friendly nature of the meeting by moving from his cold and gleaming desk, crowded with telephones and push buttons, over to a corner of the big room which, thanks to armchairs, a small table, and a tiny bar, seemed family-like and intimate. To get the conversation started and, even more, to remove a thorn that was hurting him, he asked Rogas, smiling, "Tell me, did you really not recognize me yesterday evening?"

"I recognized you immediately, Your Excellency, but I wanted to play for time, to find out just what the situation—"

"Good," the Minister said. And turning to the Chief of the Political Section: "No point in telling you that last night's business was a mistake on your part, but—"

"Your Excellency, I—"

"—but, as I was saying, I never cry or lose my temper over spilt milk. Also, mistakes sometimes produce results that, even if they're not what one wanted, turn out to be useful beyond one's hopes. Last evening's blunder in the Narco drawing room produced, as its first effect, a victory for Galano, who had contrived to play a trick on the police and to get proof of wiretaps. . . . It embarrassed me, too, of course. . . . But then, after I'd left, it occurred to me, as I was thinking about the conduct of the police and the coincidence of my being at Narco's that very evening—I hadn't been there for two weeks—that the whole thing could be construed quite differently. That is, that neither I nor the police are fools, and, on our side, there must be a trap into which Galano, thinking he'd trapped us, had fallen. Devilishly sensitive, these people, full of fantasies. . . . By dint of turning themselves inside out to guess what our scheme was—we, unfortunately, weren't able even to think one up—within the space of two hours they had slipped from sarcastic self-confidence into abject terror. Galano, during the night, moved from Nocio's house to Schiele's: he was afraid of being arrested. And there were a lot of other transfers—from one host to another, from the person's own house to the house of a friend."

"Crazy," Rogas said.

"Crazy," the Minister said. "But, my dear Inspector, I am playing precisely on these crazy reactions of theirs. I stand in the middle; I offer protection one moment, a threat the next. The more they believe in the threat, the higher the price I put on protection. Because groups like those of Galano and Narco—and especially Narco's, those Catholic revolutionaries—are a convenience for me. They're almost as great a convenience for me as the Square Deal chain, which, as you know, is Narco's thing. To put it crudely, I deal (and that's the word that fits the case) in today's egg and tomorrow's chicken by being with them. The egg of power and the chicken of revolution. . . . You know what the political situation is—the, so to speak, structured political situation. One can sum it up in two words: it has suddenly dawned on my party, which has been misgoverning for thirty years, that it would misgovern better in collaboration with the International Revolutionary Party; and especially if that chair"—he gestured toward his own, behind the desk—"were to be occupied by the I.R.P.'s Secretary-General, Mr. Amar. Now, the vision of Mr. Amar sitting in that chair and ordering out the troops to fire on striking workers, or on farmers asking for water or students asking not to study—like my late predecessor, but even going him one better—this vision, I must confess, beguiles me, too. But today being today, it's a dream. Mr. Amar is no fool. He knows very well that it's better for me to sit in that chair than for him, better for me to sit

71

there in the sense that so long as I am there everybody is better off, Mr. Amar included."

"Under the leadership of Your Excellency, this Ministry—" the Chief of the Political Section began unctuously.

"It's trumpery, I know. I also know that you'd prefer to take orders from Mr. Amar, but you'll just have to be patient—"

"Your Excellency!" protested the Chief of the Political Section.

"Come, come—I know and I don't mind at all. As I told you, I'd hand over my post to Mr. Amar willingly. But, you see, this country hasn't reached the point yet of despising Mr. Amar's party as much as it despises mine. And in our system, contempt is what puts the seal of approval on power. Mr. Amar's people are doing their level best to deserve it, and with time they will. And once they've got it, they will know what to do to legitimize it. Because, while the system allows us to come to power via contempt, it is iniquity, the practice of iniquity, that legitimizes it. We—those of us in my party who succeed each other in ministerial posts—we are blandly iniquitous. Constitutionally and contingently iniquitous because we do not know how, we are unable, to be more iniquitous. On the contrary, we grow increasingly less so. But you people thirst after iniquity. Not only you, the police, I mean."

The Chief of the Political Section was looking at the Minister with the eyes of a hare caught in the beam of a headlamp. The Minister was looking sardonically at him. Rogas, too, who was thinking about the Minister. No cretin, he—even if he had the impression that the man was reciting things he had heard others say.

"To cheer you up," the Minister said to the Chief of the Political Section, "and also to make you realize what credits you are accumulating—you'll be able to turn them to good account someday—let me tell you that what you are doing, what I am having you do, corresponds fully to the wishes of Mr. Amar."

"What am I doing, Your Excellency?"

"You don't know?" the Minister said, with ironic amazement. "Well, just keep it up, all of you keep it up. . . . Bedeviling the cadres, as much as you can. Searches, distraints, arrests—always, naturally, with the authorization of the courts. . . . Another judge was murdered last evening, so they'll give you everything you want."

"Your Excellency," Rogas said," it seems to me we have gone off the right track to follow a wrong one. In connection with the murders of the judges, I mean."

The Minister looked at Rogas with sympathy and suspicion. He said, "Perhaps. But, right track or wrong, stay on it, stay on it."

Leaving the Ministry, "What do you make of that?" the Chief of the Political Section asked Rogas.

"I have no opinions. If I did, I'd change jobs. I've only got principles. What about you?"

"I've got neither opinions nor principles. But this talk of the Minister's—"

"I saw. You were upset by it."

"No, it didn't upset me. It takes something else to do that."

"What, then?"

"Nothing . . . I was just thinking. Why is he telling me —us—these things?"

"Right, us."

"There has to be some reason, some purpose."

"I am sure you will discover it," Rogas said, veiling sarcasm with flattery.

"Of course." Swallowing the flattery.

"Meanwhile what do we do?"

"What do we do?" the other man echoed.

"With your permission, I'd like to call on the President of the Supreme Court. Sooner or later, it will be his turn."

"What?"

"To be murdered. Whether it's my man who does it, or your cadres."

"You believe they'd dare go as far as the President of the Supreme Court?"

"Why not?"

"My god!" It was almost a groan.

"I'd say one should warn him."

"Of course. But with care, with tact."

"Do you want to go?" It was the right way to make the Chief of the Political Section feel reconfirmed in his authority and fearful of the responsibility.

"No, no, you go. I have too much else to do." That is, nothing.

"All right, I'll go this afternoon."

The President of the Supreme Court lived on the top floor of a small mansion buried in a green park just outside the city walls. It had once been the summer residence of the Dukes of San Concordio. The Society for the Protection of Forests and Woodlands had made a fuss over the park's being turned into a residential area, but now in that area there resided two or three members of the Society's board of governors, as well as a pair of Ministers, a dozen Deputies (of diverse political allegiances), as well as the Attorney General and the President of the Supreme Court.

One entered this residential enclave through well-guarded gates. Rogas got in by showing the porter his identification card and with the endorsement of a police agent stationed beside the glass-and-concrete booth in which the porter was caged. The small avenue that led to the building where President Riches lived was pointed out to him. It unfolded in an S shape between tall trees, so that it debouched abruptly into an open space at one side of which the three-storied mansion rose in ungraceful, indeed ungainly geometry. In the open space stood five big cars which Rogas instantly recognized from the size, color, and the license plates bearing State Service initials (for he knew nothing about makes and models) as official government cars. The five chauffeurs were standing together in a group. One of them was in uniform: an Air Corps sergeant. Drawing nearer, Rogas singled out and recognized among the five the chauffeur of the High Commissioner of Police. He was in mufti, but he gave Rogas a military salute.

Inside another cage, this one all glass, in the middle of the entrance hall, sat yet another porter. Again Rogas showed his identification card, said that he had come to speak with President Riches. Could His Excellency receive him? The porter shut the window of the cage and spoke into the intercom. He reopened the window and advised that the President could receive no one at that moment; in any case, calls had to be announced in advance, confirmed in advance. "May I hope," Rogas said, with a touch of irony, "that the President will receive me tomorrow at this time?" "You may hope," the porter said sourly. He noted down on a slip of paper: "President Riches, Police Inspector, tomorrow, 5 P.M." "Thank you," Rogas said; and involuntarily, out of habitual curiosity, he added a question: "These gentlemen"—he gestured toward the automobiles outside—"are with the President?"

The porter looked at him with waspish suspicion. He countered with a second question: "Why do you want to know?" and closed the window to the cage again. He expected no reply, nor did he want one. His "why" had been purely punitive: there could be no "because" for the curiosity of a little police inspector about persons so much more powerful, with whose power the porter felt he was osmotically invested. To himself, Rogas said, "Why indeed?" Not about his own curiosity but about that meeting.

Once more he passed by the little group of chauffeurs, and once more he received the salute of the Commissioner's driver. Why indeed? The High Commissioner of Police . . . A high-ranking officer in the Air Corps . . . And the other three cars? That the High Commissioner of Police should have reason to confer with the President of the Supreme Court—nothing surprising about that. On the contrary, normal, standard, routine. Normal, however, in an office; a little less than normal at home. But an Air Corps officer? Unless he were a judge advocate. But why the two of them, High Commissioner of Police and judge advocate? And the other three?

He went out through the iron gate. The street, rather narrow, was one-way. He walked a hundred feet or so, as far as the bus terminal.

From that terminal, the bus left only every hour: the area was inhabited by people who had no need of it. It had not yet arrived. Rogas pulled out his paper, opened it to the literary supplement. There was a piece about the translation of a Moravia novel, a Solzhenitsyn short story, essays by Lévi-Strauss, Sartre, Lukács. Translation, translation, nothing but translation. He tried to read, but with every automobile that passed he raised his eyes from the paper. He had decided, without deciding, to wait for the five official cars to pass by to see who was inside; it could well be that inside would be the wives of those powerful men, because official cars were used more by them than by their husbands. It was likely, in fact, that it would turn out to be the wives. A meeting of high-ranking wives would be more logical, more obvious, than a meeting of their husbands. But no, President Riches was a bachelor and a misogynist; it was to be excluded, then, that he would be receiving ladies.

The bus arrived hours later; that is, with the delay that customarily confronted travelers in that country, even if they were taking planes. Luckily, this time, for a person would have drawn attention to himself if he remained at the terminal, letting the bus leave without him. Thus Rogas saw the five automobiles pass by, at about five-minute intervals one from the other. Five times five, twenty-five: twenty-five minutes that were within the

77

bus's delay. But why not together, one right after the other? Precaution? Concern? Against what? Over what?

In addition to his superior, Rogas recognized inside one of the automobiles the Commanding General of the National Gendarmerie, and he thought he recognized the Minister for Foreign Affairs crouched down into a corner of another car as if to make it appear empty. The other two he did not recognize, but in the automobile driven by the Air Corps sergeant there must have been a general from the same branch of the armed forces, even if he were dressed in civilian clothes. Stupidity typical of a general, Rogas thought: he takes the precaution of dressing in civies, and has himself driven by a chauffeur in military uniform.

When the bus arrived, Rogas stumbled aboard, very weary. While he had been absorbed in his thoughts, he hadn't noticed any fatigue. Now he felt it, even in his head. But he had developed the ability, when an idea became almost an obsession, to put it firmly out of his mind. The literary supplement to the newspaper helped him banish all other thoughts for the entire evening.

The next day, he was summoned urgently by the High Commissioner of Police, whose expression was dark and threatening. Without responding to the salute, letting Rogas remain standing, he said abruptly, "Yesterday you went to the home of the President of the Supreme Court. Why?"

Rogas explained why. The Commissioner's lowering expression was diluted with mockery. "With your infallible nose"—charging the infallible with being fallible—"you are still pursuing your Cres."

"Not exactly," Rogas said. "I am pursuing the possibility, which from one moment to the next could become fact, that an attempt will be made on the life of President Riches—on the part of my Cres or your cadres."

"The President is well guarded," the Commissioner replied.

"I know. But I should like, if you are not against it, to have a talk with him."

"Because you aren't willing to put that Cres out of your mind; there's the truth of the matter. Anyhow, go see the President; he's expecting you this afternoon. He telephoned me last evening. He told me you'd come in the afternoon but that he hadn't been able to see you. Also, that the porter had mentioned to him certain questions of yours. He was quite put out, you know."

"Only one question," Rogas said. And he thought, Now we're in for it.

"All right, only one. But indiscreet."

"Seeing your car, I thought you might have gone to the President for the same reason that I—"

"There were other official cars. Did you think we were all with President Riches for the same reason?"

"The other cars didn't interest me."

"No?" the Commissioner said, with sardonic disbelief.

"No. I asked about all of them because I didn't want to pinpoint my curiosity for the porter's benefit."

"However that may be, we were not all at Riches's. The Italian Ambassador, who lives in the same building, had invited us to a small afternoon reception. You know how the Italians are. They live in the expectation of being, so to speak, snubbed; they're quick to take offense. . . ."

"I understand," Rogas said.

"So go see the President. And please, be discreet." He made a gesture of dismissal and turned his attention to the papers lying before him.

Naturally, Rogas checked immediately. He went to a phone booth, closed the door, looked up and dialed the number of the Italian Ambassador (and he actually did reside in the same building as the President). He was about to hang up when an irritated voice answered. "Excuse me," Rogas said, "but General Fabert thinks he forgot a small portfolio at the Ambassador's home yesterday." "Who? When?" "General Fabert, yesterday afternoon." "Where?" "With you, at the Ambassador's home." "Look here, the Ambassador has been on vacation for two weeks; his apartment is closed. I happen to be here at the moment by chance. Your General What's-His-Name probably left his portfolio at the Embassy." "I think so, too. Thank you." He hung up, content.

Lunchtime had come, and Rogas set out for Thursday's restaurant; he had one for every day of the week—seven, then, that thought of him as a good client but not so faithful, so settled in, that they could give him poor service. Like every self-respecting investigator—that is, every investigator who entertains the same respect for himself that he wishes to arouse in his readers—Rogas lived alone; nor were there women in his life. (It seems —it seemed vaguely to him, too—that he might once have had a wife.)

He sat down at his customary table in the corner, chose food and wine with care. But he ate listlessly, absent-mindedly. Within the initial problem of a series of crimes that he, because of his duty, because of his profession, felt called upon to solve, whose author he must try to bring to court if not to justice, another problem had arisen, supremely criminal in kind—a crime contemplated in respect to fundamental principles of State, but one that would have to be solved outside the confines of his duty, in conflict with his duty. Practically, it was a matter of defending the State against those who represented it, who held it captive. The imprisoned State must be liberated. But he, too, was in prison: he could only try to open a crack in the wall.

He thought of his friend Cusan and of going to spend the evening with him, after his conversation with President Riches.

As he left the restaurant, the idea suddenly occurred to him that the Commissioner, immediately after dismissing him, had certainly picked up the phone to arrange to have him shadowed. Elementary—he should have thought of it before. And he felt he was being watched by someone; those eyes interfered with his walking, they mired him. He refrained from stopping in front of shopwindows, even when he was attracted by them, because stopping in front of shopwindows is typical of the person who fears or knows he is being shadowed. He went home, strenuously resisting the temptation to look behind him. He spent an hour shaving and reading desultorily. As he came out of the elevator and started to leave the building, he saw, beyond the glass door, on the pavement opposite, the man who had shadowed him. According to the rules, another man would follow him now; he would discover the new tail on the bus. And, in fact, he did discover him: at the terminal a furtive glance, as he was stepping down from the bus, was enough.

The man followed him as far as the outer gate to the park. He walked on ahead, naturally; without seeing him, Rogas could count his footsteps, draw the map of his movements. He would walk a hundred and fifty feet and he would turn back, but without entering the gate; he would go in search of a telephone, put in a call for his relief; then he would wait in front of the gate, making himself as inconspicuous as he could. Dog eat dog, Rogas thought. But there are dogs and dogs.

In the glass-walled cage in the middle of the entrance hall, the porter, because of the light, looked like a shark who was rushing against the walls of its tank. He recognized Rogas. He raised three fingers toward him: third floor.

On the third floor, one of four doors opened as Rogas stepped out of the elevator. A servant in a striped jacket, assuredly a police agent (or an ex-agent, given the age he looked to be), wordlessly ushered him into a spacious, well-ordered room. At the far end, in a corner armchair, behind a pale-blue cloud of smoke, sat the President. He said, "Come in," and when Rogas was near him, pointed to a chair: "Sit down."

Rogas saluted, sat down. The President peered at him over his glasses, acerb and caustic. Twice he drew on his cigar, puffing the smoke toward a ray of light that diffused it like a veil. Then slowly, contemptuously, he, invulnerable and immortal before the vulnerable, mortal little philistine, said, "So you believe they will kill me."

"I believe they will try."

"The cadres or that fellow who, according to you, was

82

the victim of a mistake? Of a judicial error, as it is usually termed." As he pronounced the words "judicial error," he made the syllables grate, like a blade against a whetstone, throwing off sparks of disdain.

"That fellow. Cres."

"Cres, that's it. . . . He had tried to do away with his wife. A rather ingenious plan, I'd say, but one of those that easily manage— What sentence did he get?"

"Five years in the court of first instance, confirmed by you on appeal."

"Not by me," the President said, placing his open hands before his chest and moving them out toward Rogas as if to repulse a disagreeable impact.

"Excuse me, I meant by the court over which you were presiding."

"That's right: by the court over which I was presiding." With condescending satisfaction, like a teacher who has at last got an acceptable reply from a dull student. "And so?"

"It was an error. A judicial error, as it is usually termed."

"Which is to say?"

"He was innocent."

"Really!"

"I believe so."

"He was innocent or you believe he was innocent?"

"I believe he was innocent. I can't be sure of it."

"Ah, you can't be sure of it!" Smiling, sardonic, from the summit of his certainties.

"I only think, not absolutely and indeed with a margin of doubt, that he was unjustly found guilty."

" 'Not absolutely, a margin of doubt' . . . That's amus-

83

ing." And passing from the sardonic to the tragic, as if assailed by a sudden pain in the middle of the chest: "Have you ever thought about the problem of passing judgment on a man?" For a moment, he threw himself back in his chair, as if he were in the throes of death because of that problem.

"Constantly," Rogas said.

"Have you solved it?"

"No."

"Exactly, you have not solved it. . . . I have, obviously. . . . But not once and for all, not definitively . . . Here and now, speaking with you, and mindful of the next case whose outcome I shall have to preside over, I can even say I have not solved it. But, mind you, I am speaking of the next case. Not about the case that has just ended for me or about a case from ten or twenty or thirty years ago. For all the cases in the past, I solved the problem, always; and I solved it by the very fact of judging them, in the act of judging them. . . . You are a practicing Catholic?"

"No."

"But Catholic?"

Rogas made a gesture that signified: like everyone else. And in fact he did believe that all men everywhere were a little bit Catholic.

"Of course, like everyone else," the President interpreted correctly. Assuming the posture of a priest at catechism: "Let us take, well, the Mass, the mystery of transubstantiation, the bread and the wine that become the body, blood, soul, and divinity of Christ. The priest may even be unworthy in his personal life, in his thoughts. But the fact that he has been ordained means that at each celebration of the Mass the mystery is com-

84

pleted. Never, I say never, can it happen that the transubstantiation not take place. And so it is with a judge when he celebrates the law: justice cannot *not* be revealed, not transubstantiated, not completed. A judge may torment himself, wear himself out, tell himself, 'You are unworthy; you are full of meanness, burdened by passions, confused in your ideas, liable to every weakness and every error'—but in the moment when he celebrates the law, he is so no longer. And much less so afterward. Can you imagine a priest who, after celebrating Mass, says to himself, 'Who knows if the transubstantiation took place this time, too?' There's no doubt; it did take place. Most assuredly. I would even say inevitably. Think of that priest who was seized by doubt and who, at the moment of the consecration, discovered blood on his vestments. I can say this: no judgment has ever bloodied my hands, has ever stained my robes. . . ."

Without meaning to, Rogas made a sound much like a groan. The President looked at him with disgust. And as in a fireworks display, when everything seems to be over, in the stunned silence and darkness one more luminous, elaborate, and thunderous rocket explodes, Riches said, "Naturally, I am not a Catholic. Naturally, I am not even a Christian."

"Naturally," Rogas echoed. And indeed he was not surprised.

The President was disappointed and irritated, like someone who has just performed a magic turn only to have a child jump up and say he has understood the trick. With a note of hysteria, he proclaimed, "Judicial error does not exist."

85

"But the different levels of courts, the possibility of petitions, of appeals—" Rogas objected.

"—postulate, you mean to say, the possibility of error. But this is not so. They postulate merely an opinion—let us call it a lay opinion—about justice, about the administration of justice. An outside opinion. Now, when a religion begins to take lay opinion into account, it is already dead even if it doesn't know it. And so it is with justice, with the administration of justice. I use the term 'administration' to please you, clearly, and without granting it the slightest statutory or bureaucratic meaning." More subdued and persuasive now, and even melancholy: "Everything began with Jean Calas. . . . More or less, I mean. . . . Since we must establish definite points—a name, a date—when we try to apprehend the great defeats and the great victories of mankind. . . ."

"It began with—?"

"Jean Calas . . . 'The murder of Calas, committed in Toulouse with the sword of justice, on March 9, 1762, is one of the most remarkable events that deserve the attention of our age and of posterity. Soon forgotten is the numberless multitude of those who die in wars, not only because those dead belong to an inevitable fatality but also because they were in condition to visit death upon their enemies and not to fall without having defended themselves. There where the danger and the advantage are equal, pained astonishment ceases and even pity is weakened; but if the innocent father of a family falls into the clutches of error, or of passion, or of fanaticism; if the accused has no defense other than his own virtue; if the arbiters of his life run no other risk, ordering his throat to be cut, than that of being wrong; if they can kill with impunity through a sentence, then the public voice is raised, everyone fears for himself. . . .' Have you ever read it?"

"*An Essay on Tolerance, Upon the Occasion of the Death of Jean Calas,*" Rogas recited.

"Ah, you have read it," the President remarked. Banteringly, but with an undertone of menace: "Our police permit themselves unimaginable luxuries."

"I permit myself some reading," Rogas amended.

"And the police permit themselves to have you on the force. But let's let that go. . . . Jean Calas, then . . . The *Essay,* and everything else Voltaire wrote about the death of Calas, I know almost by heart. It was the starting point of error—the error of believing there could exist such a thing as judicial error. . . . Naturally, this error does not spring out of nothing, nor does it remain like that, isolated or at least isolatable; there is soil, there is a context for it to grow in. . . . I've spent a great deal of my life, an infinity of those hours one calls free—free from the burdens of office, and for me there are never any free hours in that sense of the word—in confuting Voltaire about the case of Jean Calas. That is, in refuting the idea of justice, of the administration of justice, which, so Voltaire assumes, was belied in that case." He pointed to a thick stack of notebooks on the table. "There it is. My refutation, my essay."

"Will you publish it?" The same question he had, a few days before, put to Vilfredo Nocio.

Unlike Nocio, the President was not horrified. "Certainly I will publish it. As soon as conditions prevail that will favor its success. And I do not speak, quite obviously, of material, practical success. I am speaking of an ideal

87

success. . . . I'd say the time is not far off. . . . Because, you see, the advent of the masses is the condition that allows us to turn back and to start out again on the right foot. Follow my reasoning. . . ." He edged forward in his chair, leaned toward Rogas with a winning smile, his eyes bright with a feverish anxiety. The way it happens in asylums, Rogas thought, where you always run into the man who stops you to confide in you about his Utopia, his Civitas Dei, his phalanstery. "Now follow my line of reasoning. . . . The weak point in Voltaire's tract, the point where I take off to set things right again, occurs on the very first page, when he proposes the difference between death in war and death at the hands, let us say, of justice. This difference does not exist; justice sits in a perennial state of danger, in a perennial state of war. It was so also in Voltaire's day, but it was not perceived, and in any event, Voltaire was too gross to realize it. But now it is perceived. What earlier could be gleaned by a subtle mind the masses have made macroscopic; they have brought human existence to a total and absolute state of war. I'll risk a paradox that can also be a prophecy: the only possible form of justice, of the administration of justice, could be, and will be, the form that in a military war is called decimation. One man answers for humanity. And humanity answers for the one man. No other way of administering justice will be possible. I'll go further: there never has been any other. But the moment is coming to give this fact theoretical expression, to codify it. To prosecute a guilty man, guilty men, is impossible—practically, technically impossible. It's no longer a question of looking for the needle in the haystack, but of looking in the haystack for one single

88

straw. Among other idiocies in circulation, someone said once that it is impossible to remember the face of a Chinese because all Chinese look alike. Then it was noticed that at least three faces of Chinese are unforgettable, and they do not look alike. But millions of men, hundreds of millions of men do look alike—I don't say physically. Or, rather, not only physically. There are no more individuals; there are no more individual responsibilities. Your profession, my dear friend, has become absurd. It presupposes the existence of the individual, and the individual does not exist. It presupposes the existence of God, the God who blinds some men and enlightens others, the God who hides—and has remained hidden so long that we may presume Him dead. It presupposes peace, and there is war. . . . This is the point: war. . . . War exists, and dishonor and crime must be restored to the corpus of the multitude the way in military wars it is restored to regiments, divisions, armies. Punished by lot. Tried by fate."

"Number can never be indefinite," Rogas said.

"How's that? What did you say?"

Rogas did not answer. He was trying to remember how it went: "*Argumentum ornithologicum.* I close my eyes and see a flock of birds. The vision lasts a second or perhaps less. I don't know how many birds I saw. Were they a definite or indefinite number? This problem involves the question of the existence of God. If God exists, the number is definite, because how many birds I saw is known to God. If God does not exist, the number is indefinite, because nobody was able to take count. In this case, I saw fewer than ten birds (let's say) and more than one; but I did not see nine, eight, seven, six, five, four, three, or

89

two. I saw a number somewhere between ten and one, but not nine, eight, seven, six, five, etc. That number, as a whole number, is inconceivable; *ergo*, God exists." When the brief page had reconstituted itself in his memory as it is reproduced here, he turned from it to give his attention once more to what the President was saying, but with the sense that that flock of birds, which for a second or maybe less had flown before Borges's closed eyes, might be much more real, not to say definite, than the man who was talking to him and than everything else around him.

The President, continuing that part of his dissertation which Rogas did not regret having missed, was saying, "For that matter, the problem of justice, for Voltaire and those who descend from him, seems to converge on those crimes he calls local—*délits locaux.* But today the masses, running roughshod over legal codes like a thirsty herd—thirsting for crime, I mean—have trampled local crimes underfoot. The judge need no longer ask himself, 'Would I dare punish in Ragusa what I punish in Loreto?' What is punished in Ragusa *is* punished in Loreto. But it would be more accurate to speak of what is *not* punished. . . . Few things are punished, at this point."

"It doesn't seem so to me," Rogas said. "And as for local crimes, Loreto is in Italy; Ragusa now calls itself Dubrovnik, and is in Yugoslavia. One can't say that what is punished in Italy is necessarily punished in Yugoslavia."

"Maybe not, maybe not." With an air of absent-minded skepticism.

"You don't think so?"

"If you really want to know, no. Because you are making the mistake of considering local those crimes which are instead universal and eternal—in other words, everywhere and always punished. Those crimes against the legitimacy of authority that only authority, by reversing itself and taking the perpetrators' part, can cancel out as crimes and transform into acts of witness for the entrance of God into the world, presupposing that this reverse authority is unalterably ready to receive Him. . . . The only entrance the world allows God. . . . Not the God who hides Himself, of course. Now, it is precisely these crimes, the way in which these crimes have always been judged and punished—the method, the procedure —that offers secure elements to my treatise. In trials of this type, the guilt has been, and is, prosecuted with the most total disregard for the accused individual's pleas of innocence. Whether an accused man may or may not have committed the crime has never had any importance for judges. . . ."

"But the fact that in such trials one tries by every means to obtain the defendant's confession to a crime he has not committed—"

"You are saying exactly the opposite of what you mean. . . . You remember that famous pamphlet attacking the trial in Milan, in 1630, in which persons were accused of spreading the plague with unctions? The author, an Italian Catholic, says the trial lays bare an injustice that could readily have been seen by the very people who perpetrated it—by the judges, that is. Well, of course they saw it! They would not have been judges if they hadn't seen it. But even less would they have been judges had their seeing it led them to absolve rather than

91

to convict. No matter that the organized, institutional-
ized unleashing of a plague was not morally conceivable,
ergo not possible then—whereas today, as we know, it is.
And no matter that a motive was lacking with which to
charge the defendants, that there was not a glimmer of
proof, and that even circumstantial clues did not tally.
There was the plague; this is the point. The fellow who
denied it—actually a character created by the author of
the pamphlet—in point of fact represented the one lay
attitude then possible. Ridiculous, naturally. But Voltaire, a hundred years later, is no less so. And likewise,
two hundred years after Voltaire, Bertrand Russell and
Sartre."

"But confession—"

"If you give a religious rather than a technical sense to
the word, confession of a misdeed on the part of someone who has not committed it establishes what I call the
circuit of legitimacy. That religion is true, that power is
legitimate, which brings man into a state of guilt; guilty
in body, in mind. And from the state of guilt it is easy to
abstract the elements for the conviction of crime, easier
than from objective proofs, which, for that matter, do not
exist. On the contrary, if anything, it is objective proofs
that can give rise to what you call judicial error."

"Exactly, in the case in question it was the objective
proofs that gave rise to error. Cres was found guilty—"

"It doesn't interest me," the President said.

"I understand," Rogas said. "I understand very well.
But you see, Your Excellency, it is my job to look for the
single straw in the haystack, as you so well put it. And
that straw is armed, it shoots, it has already murdered
some seven high officials—to this point without making

92

a false step, without ever being diverted. Now, I am willing also to admit that I may be wrong, that the attacks may come from some other quarter. There remains nonetheless the problem of assuring you adequate protection, enough to frustrate the plan of Cres or of the cadres. . . . Do you consider yourself sufficiently protected, sufficiently safe?"

A shadow of fear passed over the face of the President.

"What do you think?" he asked, with an arrogance tempered by anxiety, an anxiety masked by arrogance.

"I think that you will be as protected and as safe as possible so long as you feel unprotected, unsafe."

"Ah," the President said, impressed.

Like a sleepwalker, Rogas found himself once again in the elevator; in the entrance hall, as the gates swung quickly open, he had the sensation for a moment of finding himself before a mirror. Except that in the mirror was another man.

"Excuse me," the other man said, entering the elevator as Rogas left it.

"Not at all," Rogas said. Suddenly alert, tensed, senses and memory exploding within him in the most delicate tentacles. His same build, five feet eight inches tall: therefore, the sensation of the mirror on finding himself suddenly face to face in the artificial light of the entrance hall. Very dark-skinned, in contrast to the white hair. Slightly bald. Slightly aquiline nose? Maybe not. Not exactly thin: robust, healthy. He had put on a little weight, his hair seemed whiter; he had perhaps had plastic surgery done on his nose. But what identity had he assumed? How had he managed to get entrée into the building where, among other powerful personages, President Riches lived?

Rogas controlled his own impulses—with no excessive effort, it must be said to his credit or discredit, as you prefer. The sudden temptation to reënter the elevator, to return to the President's apartment, came as a flash that was immediately quenched in the recollection—rather cynical, given the circumstances—of what Innocent says as he aims the revolver at the Schopenhauer professor (G. K. Chesterton, *Man Alive*): "It's not a thing I'd do for everyone. But you and I seem to have got so intimate to-night, somehow." The remark aimed now at the President, of course, with whom the revolver of Cres was perhaps at that moment about to settle accounts. The phrase, visually repeating itself in an elegant italic, made a kind of selvage edge to his ruminations, and it was fading into rhythm, into music ("It's-not-a-thing-I'd-do-for-everyone," to the theme of a shower song; and then, "But-you-and-I-seem-to-have-got-so-intimate," in a broad Puccinian phrase, baritone air, and timbre), when he realized that he had already been on the bus for some time, that the street lights in the city had come on, haloed by the sirocco, that shops were closing, that he was therefore no longer in time to give his tail the slip by dragging him along behind, as he had planned, into a big store (Square Deal) where the many doors, elevators, escalators, and, above all, the crowd allowed one to confuse the most skillful operative of the police or of the Center of Special Information. Because, according to Rogas, the two who had first followed him were from the police, but the man who was following him now, and who in the almost empty bus had planted himself so that he could not be caught off guard by his quarry's suddenly departing, was certainly from the C.S.I.; it was evident from the good cut of his clothes, his short hair, his well-fed appearance. Unlike Americans of the same calling, whom they considered models and tried to emulate, C.S.I. agents indulged more than they should in good food (expense-account funds) and less in the gymnastics and sports prescribed by their order on the same frequency as prayers by Benedictines.

The agent opened the evening paper he was holding, and Rogas glanced at the headlines: another judge had been killed.

He suddenly remembered a detail: Cres was carrying a small traveling case. And from that detail there flowed a deduction: the man had not gone into the mansion to kill the President but because he lived there. He was coming back from a trip, that was it—from the city where, a few hours earlier, he had succeeded in doing away with one more judge. He could kill the President whenever he wanted to, but the cover of living in that building was so perfect that, in order not to compromise it, surely he was postponing, and would continue to postpone, the decision to act. But perhaps more than the security and invisibility he had managed to create for himself, what counted with Cres in keeping the President alive were considerations of order, of planning; for these reasons he was holding the President in reserve, as if on a game preserve or in a hen coop, for the final banquet.

His sudden discovery of Cres, who had found the most comfortable and privileged asylum under the same roof as the President of the Supreme Court, disquieted Rogas. Professional eagerness, impatience to verify, to make sure, were combined with the fear that, in that fleeting encounter, Cres might have recognized him: in his uncertainty whether the Inspector might have discovered his refuge or, in the casual and rapid meeting, might have been brushed by a suspicion or even by only an impression, he would disappear again, renouncing his plan to put the President to death or deferring it to a better time. But there would never *be* a better time to kill the President. Only, if Cres had recognized the Inspector and believed he had been recognized in turn, he could never imagine that that police inspector, who, the papers said, was tenaciously but vainly tracking him down, had actually passed over to his side. Nevertheless, like an aficionado who sits before his television and enjoys (or suffers through) a football game, anticipating, imploring, calling for the decisive play, the impetuous descent on the opposing team's field, the winning pass, Rogas was turning over in his mind what, in Cres's place, he would do, what Cres should do. Meanwhile he wanted to be sure that he had not made a mistake, that the man really was Cres. Go back and ask information from the porters and the agents? Look up the manager of the building? But if Cres really lived there, there was the risk of his coming to know about Rogas's inquiry and then of his taking fright and running away.

At the Clio Square stop, Rogas indolently stepped down from the bus. He bought a paper. The news report on the judge's murder, in boldface, was brief. Turning the pages of the paper, he walked along under the arcade. The C.S.I. agent seemed to have disappeared, but Rogas knew that he was standing in the least illuminated area of the square.

He went into a café, ordered a cup of cold milk and one of hot coffee. He sugared each, drank them in quick succession. The two opposed and almost simultaneous sensations, cold, hot, canceled each other out, and for a few moments his body acquired a kind of imperviousness to the terrible pall of the sirocco which was descending on the city. Then a good idea came to him. The café was nearly deserted, and the telephone was well placed to prevent any curious person from coming close without being noticed. Rogas dialed the number (secret) of President Riches. As he foresaw, the butler answered. He said, "I am Inspector Rogas. I'm calling to ask you some routine information. . . . Yes, you. . . . I would never dream of disturbing His Excellency. . . . Yes. . . . So, I should like to have the names of the people living in the building: their names and, if possible, some information about their activities, their professions. . . . The Ambassador of Italy, then; the president of National Radio-Television; the Duke of Lieva; Mr. Ribeiro, Carlos Ribeiro . . . Spanish? . . . Ah, Portuguese. And what does Mr. Ribeiro do? Is he with the Portuguese Embassy? . . . No, if you don't mind, let's pause a moment over Mr. Ribeiro. What's he like? Physically, I mean. . . . Ah, a fine-looking man . . . very good . . . Let's go on. . . ." This simply so as not to arouse the suspicions of the butler, ex-police agent, about his special interest in Mr. Ribeiro.

So Cres had taken the name of Ribeiro. A Portuguese businessman. Portuguese face. Portuguese passport. And wealthy like a wealthy Portuguese.

The next morning, standing a long time under the shower, Rogas made up his program for the day. But the program could be carried out only if he managed to shake the agents who were tailing him. Because from now on all the people he met would automatically come under surveillance also, and who knew for how long and with what consequences.

He stayed in his office for several hours to write a report on his visit to President Riches. He put into the account all the irony that none of the people who would read it would be able to grasp—the whole hierarchy through whose hands it would pass, the future archives researcher, the historian. A world unsuited for irony, but Rogas was nonetheless amused to employ it. He closed the report thus: "From the moment the undersigned left the home of the President of the Supreme Court, he has had the clear impression of being shadowed by experts —that is, by persons particularly fitted for such an assignment, as if they might have been trained in an official or private police corps. If higher echelons have taken the trouble to make such arrangements for the protection of the undersigned, the undersigned can only express his appreciation but at the same time permit himself to observe that such vigilance, so costly because of the employment of so many men who work in shifts, would be better directed toward the protection of judges. If, however, higher echelons have not ordered the surveillance and are completely unaware of it, the undersigned deems it would be opportune, and indeed absolutely necessary, to take measures whereby equally able police agents devote themselves to tailing the tails."

The time had come for the daily report that the Chief of the Political Section received from the subordinates in his office. But that day there was no report; the Chief of

Section, a colleague informed Rogas, was questioning a girl who was one of the most active members of a cadre on the rampage in the city where the day before a judge had been killed. She had been brought to the capital by plane, together with three companions; the Chief of Section had wished to start with her. Because she is a woman, Rogas thought. And, Will he beat her with a flower?

He peeped into the waiting room; three young people were waiting to be questioned, and a dozen policemen were guarding them. Bearded, jacketless, with contemptuous glances and smiles for the fuzz, the three did not talk and did not even look at each other. Poor things, he thought: not because they were about to meet an idiot, not because they were living through that little scrape (in a few hours, they would be free, toasted by their friends and virtually awarded decorations and patents of nobility for their day spent in captivity). He pitied them, he pitied all young people whenever he found them caged in their scorn, their anger. Not that there was nothing to be angry and scornful about. But there was also something to laugh about.

He went downstairs and out into the square. It was the hour when traffic tangled the city in a fierce snarl. He struck off on foot, since finding a taxi was out of the question. For a quarter of an hour, at a brisk pace, he walked under the sun; finally, he turned in to Frazer Street, tranquil, bordered by a fringe of shade. It was a long, straight avenue, closed to traffic in both directions. Rich people lived here, not recently rich people but those whose money dated back to a time when wealth was at least converted into decorum (*Deco*, in this case).

He entered No. 30: here lived three generations of Pattoses, shipowners, proprietors of the newspaper *The Star*, friends of the High Commissioner of Police ("Report to me tomorrow, for this evening I'm having dinner with the Pattoses"). Rogas, on the other hand, enjoyed the friendship of the porter; he had proved the man's innocence once when the police were firmly intent on charging him with a big robbery at the Pattoses' residence. Cutting the effusions short, Rogas rapidly explained to the porter what he should do: pretend to speak over the intercom with the masters of the house, who were on vacation, as if he were announcing a call; accompany Rogas to the elevator; wait until the gentleman out on the street (not there yet but sure to appear in a second) came to ask about him, about whom he had gone to see; tell the man that he had gone to call on old Mr. Pattos. The tail turned up as the porter was talking into the house phone (he was simply reëvoking the trouble from which Rogas had rescued him). He hung up and arose to accompany Rogas to the elevator. Rogas went up to the second floor and then walked down the stairs. He placed himself so as to hear, without being seen, the dialogue between the C.S.I. agent and the porter.

"That gentleman who went in just now, whom did he go to see?"

"Why do you want to know?" The habitual counterquestion.

"Just curiosity," the agent said, coldly threatening.

"He went to see Mr. Pattos."

"Pattos who?"

"Pattos Pattos," the porter said, with a certain pride.

"The shipowner?"

"The shipowner."

"All right . . . When he comes down, don't tell him someone was here asking questions. Clear?"

"Clear."

He left. And Rogas left, too, walking through the cellar and coming out into Pirenne Street, parallel to but not connected with Frazer Street. To catch up with him, the C.S.I. agent would have had to walk an extra half mile, but at that moment the suspicion did not occur to him that Rogas might have escaped him; he was relishing the importance of the information he had just learned, which would be immediately communicated to his principals; one does not go to see important people except on important matters.

From a café, Rogas placed one call to Cusan, making an appointment to meet him in a restaurant outside of town, and a second call to a taxi stand for a cab to come and pick him up. A half hour later, he was sitting under a pergola, sipping a well-chilled white wine. Cusan's being late was a small advantage: it allowed him to sort out his facts, hypotheses, conjectures. He reordered them lucidly in the cool of the breeze filtering through the vine leaves, in the cool of the wine, but there was an undercurrent of apprehension, of insecurity, perhaps of fear.

He told Cusan everything.

Cusan was a committed writer; therefore, to find himself in any way responsible for those secrets, those dangers, plunged him into consternation. But he was an honest man, a loyal friend. After trying, from every angle and at every weak point, to demolish Rogas's castle of impressions, deductions, hypotheses, he realized that he

101

was trapped inside it together with Rogas, as if they were in a labyrinth and must find the thread in order to get out. One thread lay within reach: the one that would lead them out by their simply forgetting. More than once, in their thoughts, they brushed by this thread; each was on the point of grasping it. The pleasure of the place, the food, the wine; the dear, good paternal and maternal figures repeating the who-says-you-must-do-it? formula that two thousand years of their country's history made prophetic and fatal; the memories of a carefree youth that always crowded their meetings; the longing for things still to be understood, a world still to be seen, books still to be read in the perspective of a maturity and a serenity they felt they were approaching (cancer or embolism permitting)—everything converged to turn their minds toward that thread of salvation, of oblivion. But neither mentioned it to the other, and each was ashamed to be thinking of it yet not to speak of it, although they would have been even more ashamed to speak of it. But also concealed under will and conscience was the cowardly reciprocal anticipation that the other would give in.

Cusan did give in a little when, both having arrived at the most obvious solution, he volunteered for the mission that had to be carried out. In his tone of voice rather than in his words, there were almost imperceptible nuances of resignation and, at the same time, of heroism. And the more he insisted, the more reasons he adduced that made him suitable for the mission, the more perceptible the nuances became.

"I know Amar very well. I'm sure that he thinks well of me, that he trusts me. . . . Also, I can approach him without arousing suspicion. . . . A writer goes to see the Secretary-General of the International Revolutionary Party: nothing merits greater inattention on the part of the police or the C.S.I. What can a writer want from Amar? A literary prize, the good will of the Party paper? And what can Amar want from a writer? A signature on a manifesto of protest, a statement about this or that suppressed freedom, this or that right that's been trampled on? . . . No risk for me. Whereas you . . ."

Rogas said no, he continued to say no. "I'll go see Amar. Tomorrow. And I'll find the safest way. It's my job. A hunter who casts himself in the role of the hare is certainly better able than the hare to stay clear of trouble. . . . Don't worry. Tomorrow, after I've talked with Amar, I'll come see you—always assuming that I manage to get rid of my guardian angel."

"But if, before you go see Amar, you're not absolutely sure no one is following you, telephone me and *I'll* go," Cusan offered again.

"I'll get rid of him. As you see, I did today," and with his hand he made a gesture to include all the innocuous patrons in the restaurant garden who were lingering over the good wine and enjoying the cool breeze.

But he was mistaken. "One can be cleverer than another, not cleverer than all others." (La Bruyère?)

Rogas did not put in an appearance the next day, Saturday, nor on Sunday morning; that is, at the times when he was still able, in the literal sense of the phrase, to put in an appearance.

At midday Sunday, while Cusan was eating his lunch, he had the television in the next room turned on, as usual, to hear something of the day's events without having to watch the gray, monotonous pictures, and thus he learned that Rogas was dead. The voice of the newscaster, with that tremolo of emotion and commotion reserved for earthquakes and air disasters, announced: "This morning at eleven o'clock, in a room in the National Gallery, a group of foreign visitors came upon the corpse of a man apparently in his forties. The police arrived promptly and identified the dead man as Inspector Americo Rogas, one of the corps's best-known and most able investigators, and quickly determined that the cause of death was three revolver shots. The Inspector was gripping his service pistol in his right hand. . . . But immediately after, police agents made another and far more serious discovery: In the adjoining room, also felled by gunshots, probably from the same weapon, lay the body of Amar, Secretary-General of the International Revolutionary Party." The toothachy face of the newscaster dissolved (Cusan was now standing before the TV screen). Next appeared the entrance to the National Gallery, the stairway, the succession of exhibit rooms. Room XII. A dark mass at the feet of a standing portrait. "The body of Mr. Amar was found under a famous portrait by Velázquez." Room XI. "The body of the Inspector of Police, under the painting of the Madonna of the Chain by an unknown fifteenth-century Florentine artist. . . . This is how, on the basis of testimony and of hypotheses suggested by those investigating the crimes, the facts can be reconstructed." A terrified face appeared. "You were on duty this morning at the entrance to the museum. Did you see the two men who have been killed come in?" "I saw them come in. First the gentleman they say was a police inspector arrived. About ten minutes later, the other one, Mr. Amar, arrived." "They were not together, then?" "No, definitely not." "Then what?" "Then a young man came, blond, tall, with a well-kept beard." "What kind of a beard?" "Short, fringed, I'd say." "How was he dressed?" "Black trousers, very tight-fitting. Embroidered shirt. He was carrying a small black pouch in one hand." "How soon after Mr. Amar did this blond young man with the beard arrive?" "Two, three minutes after." "Did anyone else come in?" "No one until about eleven, when the herd of Americans— Excuse me, but we call tourist parties herds, like that, as a joke." "Did you see the young man leave?" "Yes, a few minutes before the tourist group came in." "Was he upset, was he running?" "Not at all, he was very calm." "Tell me, if you were to meet him would you recognize him?" "By now, he would have shaved his beard. How can I recognize him without the beard?" And the man disappeared from the screen, grinning with relief. "Here now is the guard on the second floor of the museum." Worried face, nervous tic between eye and mouth. "And what did you see?" "Nothing. The three men walked by me, one after the other, in the order and at the time my colleague said." "Where were you?" "In the first room." "And you never moved away?" "Never." "You heard nothing?" "Nothing." "Did you see the young man as he left?" "I saw him." Dissolve. "Now let us hear from the police inspector who is in charge of the investigation. He is Dr. Blom, Chief of the Political Section. . . . Inspector, can you tell us why the investigation has been undertaken by the Political Section?" The Inspector's face, lined by bureaucratic tribulations and dyspepsia, broke into a commiserating smile. "Mr. Amar was a political man, and a political man is usually killed for political reasons." "Have you a precise idea about the political reasons for which he was killed?" "I have." "Naturally, at this juncture you cannot talk about them." "Naturally." "Can you tell us, at least, what, according to you, was the sequence of events?" "Well, we must assume that both Mr. Amar and my colleague Rogas, who as far as I can discover did not know each other, liked to visit galleries and museums in their free time. Mr. Amar was, as everyone knows, a cultivated man; also my colleague was considered by the rest of us to be a man of exceptional culture." This with a slight grimace, as if exceptional culture must finally, inevitably, be gunned down. And no more than right. "This morning, by chance, both happened, almost at the same time, to visit the National Gallery. I should say, to revisit, because each of them, their respective friends tell me, enjoyed looking at certain paintings again and again. Mr. Amar, for example, considered that the portrait by Velázquez, near which he was killed, was one of the masterpieces of world art. So they were both here. Rogas arrived first, then Mr. Amar. The gallery, as always in the early morning hours, was deserted. The third arrival was not, evidently, an art lover. He was following Mr. Amar (he entered the gallery a few minutes behind him), if not with a precise plan, then certainly with criminal intent. The gallery deserted, Mr. Amar, contrary to his habits, alone—what better opportunity to carry it out? He did not take into account the possibility that someone else could have entered the museum first. But this was a minor oversight, since, as far as the murderer was concerned, the presence of Rogas was resolved by committing a second crime. . . . According to me, Rogas was in Room XIV, or in Room XV, when he heard the shot fired in Room XII. . . . Very probably, the assassin's revolver was equipped with a silencer; therefore, the guard in the first room did not hear. But the sound did not escape Rogas, he being nearer and having a trained ear. He ran to Room XII, he saw the body of Mr. Amar. Then he drew his own revolver. And here a small question arises. When Rogas caught up with the assassin in the next room, did the assassin, who was still holding his gun in his hand, turn and fire three shots? Or, hearing someone arrive from the rooms up ahead, did he stand back against the wall, beside the door Rogas had to pass through, in order to shoot him down from behind? According to me, the second hypothesis is the correct one, but confirmation will come from the autopsy." The Inspector disappeared, the newscaster reappeared. His previously stricken face was now sculpted in a violent rictus of grief. "Before asking the Vice-Secretary-General of the International Revolutionary Party to speak, we must announce further fearful news: His Excellency Ernest Riches, President of the Supreme Court, has been murdered in his home. The assassin, who was able—how is not known—to gain access to the well-guarded residence, took advantage of the customary Sunday-morning absence of the President's old and faithful servant. . . . We will have further details during the two-o'clock news telecast."

Cusan knew by whom and how President Riches had been killed. He knew that Amar and Rogas had not been at the National Gallery by chance. And from what he knew, from what he believed he knew, he readily imagined that their meeting—what Rogas would have told Amar, what Amar would have set in motion on hearing Rogas's revelations—must be sealed in death. Of course, it was not impossible that the tall blond young man with the fringe of beard and the embroidered shirt was of the extraction which television and newspapers were shortly to hint at and then, with absolute certainty, affirm, and that he was following Amar in order to eliminate him at the most likely opportunity. But for Cusan it was easier to imagine—in fact, he felt it was indisputable—that the man being shadowed was Rogas; shadowed by a C.S.I. agent opportunely bearded and disguised, for there were surely a lot of them set loose among the cadres and in the heroin and LSD cult centers. Rogas must have had more than one agent tailing him, so, having eluded the first (and he would not have gone to the appointment if he had not been absolutely sure of having ditched him), he did not realize he had the second on his heels. At this point, Cusan felt, in the heat of the day and the hour, the cold sweat of fear. What if the same had been true yesterday, too, he thought, at his meeting with Rogas in the restaurant outside of town? Rogas had considered himself safe because he had given the slip to the agent who followed him to the Pattos house, but there could have been another one, and even more than one, in a car, ready to move in any direction. Nor would the trick of entering by the main door and leaving by a smaller door on another street have been such an impenetrable ploy for people like the C.S.I. operatives, who were capable of performing any and all shrewd stratagems and therefore quite up to foreseeing them. Maybe the maneuver with the two doors was enough to elude the police. But not *them*. Already Cusan felt them diabolically omnipresent and omnipowerful, implacable lemurs who brushed by, slunk by, reeking of violence and death, fouling the elements of his own life. That Rogas. What a mess he'd dragged him into. But the rancor that welled up in Cusan immediately subsided to focus on one particular, one detail. Rogas used to do his job well, but he tended to disparage the tools that technology put at the disposal of his profession. Refusing to make use of them himself, he ended up forgetting that others did make use of them. What had finished him—what was about to finish him, Cusan—was perhaps a tiny receiving and transmitting radio, the kind that by now is to be found even in the toy departments of big stores.

Don't panic, he told himself. Poor Rogas. Poor Amar. This poor country of ours. Meanwhile, from behind the window curtain he was scrutinizing the sunny, deserted street as if it were the maw of a canyon: the silent ambush, the crack of the sniper's rifle striking down the explorer who ventured there. And suddenly he drew back from the window, for the sniper could be standing by the window opposite.

He was alone in the house; his wife and children were at the shore. Always alone in the difficult moments of his life. Which difficult moments? He searched for some that resembled the one he was living through now. But this was not a moment; it was the end. And with the thought of the end, of the death that was awaiting him in the canyon, slowly he regained a sense of quiet, perhaps even peace. Like a transparency beyond which actions,

109

persons, things were encamped as if in quarantine. Disinfected. Antiseptic.

He became fearful again because the canyon was in shadow. "Now I'll write it all down," he said to himself.

He wrote for more than two hours. Reread it. Good. Very good. Maybe these are the only pages of mine that will survive: a document. He folded the document. Where do I put it? *Don Quixote*, *War and Peace*, *Remembrance of Things Past*? A book that would be saved, a book that would save the document.

He chose, naturally, *Don Quixote*. Then he wrote a note: "In my library, bookcase E, third shelf, between the pages of *Don Quixote*, a document concerning the death of Amar and Rogas. And mine." He slipped the note in an envelope. But to whom to address it? To his wife, to the Vice-Secretary-General of the Revolutionary Party, to the president of the Writers' Union? He thought also of the Abbot of St. Damian, for they had been friends in school. He finally decided to address it to himself. But he had to go out to post it.

He left the lamp on in his study, and did not light any others to reach the stairway. He walked down in the dark, went out. A few passersby; also, at the corner of the street, right by the letter box, two bodies, clutching each other and writhing. Cusan crossed over to the other pavement; when he was opposite to the couple, he stopped a moment to look at them, like a voyeur but actually scrutinizing them to distinguish in that tangle the real from the sham. He was reassured; sham could not be carried to those lengths. He crossed the street, dropped the letter in the box. Through a shock of hair and beard, one eye, hers or his, glinted with derision, as if to say, "If you want to look, there's no need for the excuse of mailing a letter." Annoyed, Cusan thought, It's the libertines who are preparing the revolution, but it's the puritans who will make it. They, the two grapplers, the whole generation they belong to, would never make a revolution. Their children, maybe; and they would be puritans.

Reflecting on these things, he returned home. He was no longer afraid, but all the same he did not sleep.

The next day, he telephoned a friend, an erstwhile literary critic and theoretician of commitment (but a homemade commitment, like cookies for which the family hands down the recipe, and which seem an altogether different thing if one adds a dash more of salt or ginger or vanilla); the man was now an eminence, not gray but multicolored, nuanced, iridescent, in the cultural affairs of the Revolutionary Party. Cusan asked his friend to set up for him, with all possible urgency, a private appointment with the Vice-Secretary-General. "Go tomorrow to the funeral"—cultural politics—"and I'll be able to have some word for you." "Of course I'm going"—he still felt himself a committed writer—"but don't you forget to speak about this to the Vice-Secretary as soon as you can. It's about something urgent and very confidential."

He stayed in the house all day Monday. Tuesday, the funerals: Rogas's in the Church of San Rocco, filled with police and flags (poor Rogas); Amar's in the great hall of the Party's headquarters. There was a third, in the Palace of Justice: that of President Riches. The nation was in mourning, but the city, with the colors of the flags at half

111

mast on a splendid summer day, seemed on holiday. Every now and then, people were seen suddenly to coagulate: citizens, lovers of law and order, were surrounding some rash person who had come out in beard and long hair to dispute his right to kill policemen, judges, and representatives of the Revolutionary Party, as well as, obviously, his right to exist. There were attempted lynchings; many persons, especially the blond-haired and bearded, ended up in the hospital, but there were no fatalities, thanks to the timely intervention of the forces of law and order against the lovers of law and order.

In the confusion and commotion that swirled around the coffin of Amar, Cusan was able for a moment to get to his friend and to hear from him "Tomorrow afternoon at five, here"—that is, at Party headquarters. After which, having acquitted himself of the obligation to be seen at the funeral, he went back home. He noted in the mailbox the letter he had sent himself. He left it there; his wife would be the one to pick it up, if there were reserved for him, before he met the Vice-Secretary of the Party, the same end as Rogas (poor Rogas). But now when he felt afraid he realized he was perhaps injecting a measure of pretense, of complacency, into his reactions; nonetheless, real desperate tremors crept in, especially when the furniture creaked or the windowpanes tinkled.

Wednesday afternoon, at four, he phoned for a taxi and had himself driven to the headquarters of the Revolutionary Party. He arrived, naturally, way in advance of the time set for the meeting; he walked up and down the street with heroic, provocative slowness, waiting for the shot. It did not come.

At three minutes to five, he went in by the main door, crossed the main hall, climbed the great baroque staircase. He was still ruminating over the baroque when the Vice-Secretary came forward to meet him in the large, austere office that had been Amar's, and in which Amar appeared now only in a youthful portrait painted by one of the most prestigious artists who were militant activists in the Party.

"We still cannot believe it," the Vice-Secretary said, motioning toward the portrait. The classical phrase that mourners and condolers pronounce during visits of mourning. But he did believe it.

"Ah, yes, incredible," Cusan said.

Silence. Then the Vice-Secretary said, "I was waiting for you. . . . No, I don't mean now, not for this appointment our mutual friend set up. . . . I've been waiting for you, let's say, since Sunday evening. . . . Knowing your seriousness and your loyalty, your good will for our Party. . . . Amar admired you very much, you know? . . . I had no doubt, in a word, that sooner or later you would come to explain to us, to clarify for us—"

"But—"

"We knew that you'd met with that Rogas the day before he went to Amar—Saturday."

"Yes, I met with Rogas." Alarmed, he asked himself, Why "*that*" Rogas?

"We—let me be quite clear. We do not know this directly, but from information passed on to us by others. . . . And to these other persons we have said that we trust

113

you completely, trust your seriousness and discretion.
. . . And your intelligence, naturally."

The intelligence of Cusan was, however, at that moment like a flooded motor. "I've come to report on everything that Rogas told me at that meeting."

"Do you mind if I make a tape of what you're going to tell me? For your own protection, so that those other persons may know exactly what part you had in the thing." He smiled. "This way, they'll leave you alone." And again he asked, "Do you mind?"

Cusan minded. And he did not understand. He said, "I don't mind."

The Vice-Secretary pressed a button on his desk. "There," he said.

Cusan began to talk. Insomnia and the anxiety of the last few days made his memory clear; he delivered a recapitulation of what he had written in the memorial hidden in *Don Quixote.*

When he had finished, the Vice-Secretary drummed nervously on his desk, staring at him with an indecipherable expression. Then he assumed an air of funereal solemnity and said, "Mr. Cusan . . ." A long pause. "What would you think, Mr. Cusan, if I told you that Amar was killed by your friend Rogas?"

As if a trap had opened before him. And, falling into it, he said, "Impossible."

The Vice-Secretary opened a drawer in the desk, pulled out some papers, pushed them toward Cusan, who mechanically picked them up.

"Read that," the Vice-Secretary said. But since Cusan, instead of reading, kept staring at him, he explained, "They are photocopies of the ballistic evaluation,

114

autopsy, agents' reports, and of the statement made by the agent who killed Rogas."

"So Rogas actually was killed by an agent. As I suspected."

"Yes, but because Rogas had killed Amar."

"I can't believe that."

"Listen to me, Mr. Cusan. . . ." For Cusan sat as if lost in painful mental confusion. "Listen to me. Saturday morning, Rogas went to the Chamber of Representatives. He managed to approach Amar. He talked to him about a plot he had discovered. I do not know exactly what they said to each other. Amar merely told me that someone from the police had come to make some disclosures about a plot, and that they were to see each other again at the National Gallery. Our firsthand information stops here. Now the Center of Special Information enters the picture. For some time, on the basis of suspicions that unfortunately did not prove unfounded, they had been running a surveillance on Rogas—"

"But precisely because Rogas had got wind of the plot."

"Maybe. But the fact is that Rogas, and not one of the people in the plot, killed Amar."

"But why? . . . I mean, why do you believe Rogas killed Amar?"

"Because in the documents I've given you to read, there is a logic, a truth. . . . Amar was killed by the revolver that Rogas had in his hand when he in turn was killed. Trustworthy experts and some of our own Party people have verified this beyond any doubt. . . . You will think—and we also thought—that Rogas was killed first, and then came the *mise en scène*. . . . But it has been

115

ascertained that there was only one agent from the Center of Special Information at the National Gallery, and he would have had to kill Rogas, take away his revolver, and then kill Amar. And Amar—what would Amar have been doing while the agent was removing the revolver from the dead Rogas's hand? Would he have waited for his turn? . . . He was a man of quick reflexes. You know, he'd fought with the Underground, he swam and played tennis regularly. He would have reacted, right? And in this case, for the agent to carry out the plan, he would have had to kill Rogas, strike Amar hard enough to stun him, take the revolver away from Rogas, shoot Amar. But no trace of a bruise or abrasion has been found on Amar's body. So then what? . . . Then we should have to grant that Rogas was an accomplice of the agent: that he killed Amar, not expecting to be killed in his turn."

"Impossible," Cusan said.

"We think so, too. But not out of regard for the memory of Rogas."

"I knew him well," Cusan said.

"Not well enough, Mr. Cusan. Not well enough."

"But why *would* he have killed Amar?"

"This we don't know. But he killed him."

"But what could Amar have said that would unhinge Rogas—"

"Mr. Cusan—" in a tone of sorrowful reproach.

"I mean to say, to unhinge Rogas, to drive him to do such a thing?"

"Look, your friend certainly did not care for us. . . ."

"No, I suppose not, but he made a fetish of opposition, and inasmuch as the Revolutionary Party is *the* opposition . . . He respected it, in a word. . . . And when he

116

talked with me, when I advised him to talk with Amar—advice that he surely expected from me—he said there was no other way."

"Indeed," the Vice-Secretary said ironically. "There was no other way: talk to Amar out of the mouth of a revolver."

"Incredible. Enough to drive one out of one's mind," Cusan said.

"Read the reports," the Vice-Secretary said.

Cusan read them.

"But why kill Rogas?" he demanded. "Why not hear him, put him on trial?"

"Reasons of State, Mr. Cusan. They still exist, as they did in the time of Richelieu. And in this case they coincided, let us say, with reasons of Party. . . . The agent made the wisest decision he could make: to kill Rogas, too."

"But reasons of Party— You— The lie, the truth—in short—" Cusan was stammering.

"We are realists, Mr. Cusan. We cannot run the risk of a revolution's breaking out." And he added, "Not at this moment."

"I understand," Cusan said. "Not at this moment."

NOTE

Just ten years ago, I contrived to stub my toe, as the saying goes, by appending a note to my book *The Day of the Owl*. I had added that note by way of pointing to the moral of the fable: pretending, since I had written against the Mafia, to be afraid of the law—I afraid, whereas the Mafia were not. But most people took my note literally, and even today some reproach me for it.

Now I hope that this note will be understood as the other should not have been—literally, I mean. So: I wrote this parody (a comic travesty of a serious work that I had thought of writing but then did not write, a paradoxical utilization of a given technique and of current clichés), taking a news item as my point of departure. A man is accused of attempting to murder his wife; the charge is made on the basis of a concatenation of clues that, it seemed to me, might have been made up, prearranged, and supplied by the wife herself. Around this case, I sketched the story of a man who goes about killing judges, and of a police officer who, at a certain point, becomes the man's alter ego. An amusing pastime. But then I went off in a different direction for, at a certain point, the story began to unroll in an entirely imaginary country; a country where ideas no longer circulate, where principles—still proclaimed, still acclaimed—are made a daily mockery, where ideologies are reduced to policies in name only, in a party-politics game in which only power for the sake of power counts. I repeat: an imaginary country. One can think of it as being Italy; one can also think of it as being Sicily, but only in the sense in which my friend Guttuso is speaking when he says, "Even if I paint an apple, Sicily is there." The light . . . the color . . . And the worm that is eating the apple from within? Well, in this parody of mine the worm is entirely of the imagination. The light, the color (after all, is there any?), the incidents, the details—all can be Sicilian, Italian, but the substance (if there is any) must be that of a fable about power anywhere in the world, about power that, in the impenetrable form of a concatenation that we can roughly term *mafioso*, works steadily greater degradation. Lastly, I should add that I kept this fable in a drawer in my desk for more than two years. Why? I don't know, but this could be one explanation: I began to write it with amusement, and as I was finishing it I was no longer amused.

L. S.

AFTERWORD

The detection of crime is a theme of many great novels, but the present century has seen the development of the highly specialized detective or crime story which, in its purest form, is more of a puzzle than a novel. In books of that sort the interest is almost entirely in the intellectual exercise; you must decide what the clues are, for they are sometimes concealed or deceptive and sometimes ostentatious. The detective with whom you are working may be eccentric, an aristocratic loner or a sharp schoolmistress or an Australian aborigine; but the story will only in passing or by inadvertence say anything serious about the society in which these people work, and in which a particular crime occurred. And although the detective will often be contrasted with the policeman, representing the powers of intuition or the free spirit as against routine and plodding intellect, each has society on his side and will bring its enemies to book.

It is true that entertainments of this kind are now less popular than they once were; the delights of problem-solving have given way to the more generalized pleasures of the crime novel, looser in organization but more eventful, less sedentary. And in crime novels we are apt to find representations of a less ordered society, a society that looks more like the one we inhabit. Policemen and politicians may be corrupt, detective work quite unlike chess or pure mathematics. But usually the forces of order, however disheveled, triumph. Only very rarely can we say of such works that they look at questions of social justice with the informed eye of the intelligent artist. We can, however, make that claim for the stories of Leonardo Sciascia. He has reinvented the detective story and made it worthy of himself—that is, of one of the best living writers.

Sciascia is a Sicilian, born in 1921 in Racalmuto, the small town where he still lives part of the year, and which figures (as Regalpetra) in several of his books. He quotes a painter compatriot as saying that he couldn't even paint an apple without Sicily getting into it, and something like that is true also of Sciascia. He is conscious of his descent in a line of important Sicilian writers—Verga, Pirandello, Quasimodo, Lampedusa—who achieved international fame without losing their native tone and color. Sciascia is now famous in Italy and France; acclaim for his work in the English-speaking world has been slow to come, but it is bound to increase. He is no more to be thought of as the novelist of a limited region than Faulkner or Lampedusa.

His Sicily is not the country of the aristocratic Lampedusa; or, rather, it is Sicily seen in a wholly different perspective. Sciascia is of working-class descent. As a boy, his grandfather Leonardo worked in the sulfur mines, and to the writer those mines remain an emblem of Sicilian cruelty and rapacity, a dreadful blend of human and natural malevolence. At the beginning of

The Day of the Owl, the face of the shocked ticket-collector is the color of sulfur. In a later novel, *A Man's Blessing*, an abandoned sulfur mine is of mortal significance. It seems that the ruthless exploitation of this natural resource brought little prosperity; the exploiters, too greedy or embattled to invest in modern methods of extraction, succumbed to more efficient international competitors. The conversation between two high-placed *mafiosi* in *The Day of the Owl* concerns central government subsidies to the sulfur industry; clearly they went not into the mines but into the pockets of businessmen, who then swindled the workers.

In such a country it seems to be in the very nature of things that the innocent should be oppressed, and that the forces of justice and order should be at the disposal of evil and unassailable men. And so Sciascia's Sicily, though he loves it as his native place, becomes a figure for privation and corruption, and the *mafia* a kind of human version of the horrors of the sulfur mine and the *chiarchiaro* of *The Day of the Owl*, that "black-holed sponge soaking up the light flooding the landscape," which Bellodi, the detective, associates with "the struggle and defeat of God in the human heart."

The history of Sicily in the twenty years or so since Sciascia published *The Day of the Owl* has only confirmed this view of it. The *mafia* began as an agrarian phenomenon, but increasing industrialization has not killed it off, and it has adapted itself to the modern world—and not only to Sicily and the rest of Italy; its business links with the United States are well known. It has thrived on fear and silence, on *omertà*, a concept for which English has no single word. *Omertà* has to do with a manliness that is expressed by silence, like the schoolboy code that will not allow one to name the thief or bully; but its main support is fear of reprisals. There are, as *The Day of the Owl* tells us in its brilliant opening pages, no witnesses to a *mafia* murder. There has been some change of late; it is no longer true that people in authority will generally deny the very existence of the organization, and there have even been some convictions in Palermo itself, though they might not have happened had the U.S. not been involved. And Sciascia's story will stand as an image of the way things still are. It is not so long since an official sent from Rome—an official of much higher rank and much more power than Bellodi—was murdered in Palermo. And it is certainly no less plausible now than it was then to see in the *mafia* an image of an apparently incurable disease that blights civilization and crushes the few honorable and decent human beings who resist it.

Sciascia once said in an interview, "I've tried to understand why a person is *mafioso*. To this end I've written a book—and I still think it's a good book although I don't like it, in a way I detest it, but I think I've explained why an individual is *mafioso*." To do that, he needed to show that the entire social structure was permeated by the disease; and that is his great, despairing subject, the sickness of human society, of which the *mafia* is only a repulsive symptom.

Sciascia is an intellectual of the Left, with strong attachments to the thought of Gramsci, and in this capacity he has taken part in the political struggles of modern Italy. Like some of his heroes (though he is never to be identified with them), he stands for reason and justice in a corrupt world. A Communist by conviction, though not a party member, he is always at enmity with the powerful Christian Democrats; but he also opposed the Italian Communist Party when it formed an alliance with them, believing that the party should rather function as the opposition to so corrupt a political organization. He made his position very clear at the time of the Moro affair. In 1978 Aldo Moro was kidnapped by the terrorist Red Brigade; the Christian Democrats (with Communist support) refused to negotiate for his release, and Moro was murdered. Sciascia found this refusal to be wrong. The argument in its favor was that dealing with the terrorists would indeed have been corrupt, and weakening to the State; but Sciascia held that those who advanced that argument were corrupt anyway, and intent on making political capital out of Moro's unwilling martyrdom by setting him up as a hero when he was in fact just another crafty southern politician.

Not everybody would agree with him on this particular issue, but Sciascia's position is consistent with his desire always to oppose the powerful and the corrupt, and with his condemnation of the Communist Party for doing a deal with the Christian Democrats. He once took office on the Palermo City Council in the Communist interest, but resigned in disgust. He is now a Radical member of the European Parliament, and lives much of the time in France.

We are obviously dealing with a very unusual crime story writer. And we cannot bracket off these short novels as "entertainments" in the Graham Greene sense; they are not to be thought of as a sort of appendix to a body of more serious and important work. Sciascia is a fairly prolific writer, and his work includes historical novels, plays, diaries, and comments on current affairs; but there is no relaxation in the detective stories, rather a continuous and highly literary attention to his great subject, which is often treated with bitter humor. "Italy," remarks a character in *A Man's Blessing*—a man named Benito, of the same age as Mussolini, who is convinced that the taint of Fascism still lingers—"Italy is a country so blessed that for every weed they destroy, two spring up in its place." In Sciascia irony and humor, like everything else, including those long extraordinary conversations on justice which might seem to have no place in detective stories, are at the service of a project that is never less than serious.

In ordinary detective stories there is always a good deal of disposable material, standard wrapping produced by the simple necessity of having things happen somewhere. There is nothing of the kind in Sciascia. Look, for example, at the scene in *The Day of the Owl* when Bellodi interviews the semi-illiterate brothers of the murdered contractor: the "foreign" policeman confronted by a native Sicilian stiffness, narrowness, *omertà*—remember that these are the victims of the *mafia*. Or take the long conversation between the detective Rogas and the writer Nocio in *Equal Danger*; how much use is an intellectual of Nocio's stamp in the struggle against a corrupt society that has to be defended against itself? Even more remarkable is Rogas's interview with the President of the Supreme Court, who argues that there is no such thing as a judicial error. However unworthy the priest, the mystery of the transubstantiation infallibly occurs whenever the Mass is celebrated; "and so it is with a judge when he celebrates the law: justice cannot *not* be revealed. . . ." As his argument develops, the President can assert that the guilt of the accused is of no moment, and that justice might as well be done by a process of decimation. It is not often that a detective story conveys so strong a sense of nightmarish intellectual exhilaration; we would associate it rather with Kafka, or perhaps Dostoyevsky. Nor are such passages to be thought of as intrusive; they are of the stuff of these extraordinary tales, skillfully assimilated to narratives of which the most obvious characteristic is a sober realism.

Indeed it is this realism that distinguishes the writings of Sciascia from other works apparently of the same genre but in fact more properly thought of as self-indulgent fantasies. "One corollary of all the detective novels to which a goodly share of mankind repairs for refreshment specifies that a crime present its investigators with a picture, the material and, so to speak, stylistic elements of which, if meticulously assembled and analyzed, permit a sure solution. In actuality, however, the situation is different. The coefficients of impunity and error are high not because, or not only or not always because, the investigators are men of small intelligence but because the clues a crime offers are usually utterly inadequate. A crime, that is to say, which is planned or committed by people who have every interest in working to keep the impunity coefficient high. The factors that lead to the solution of seemingly mysterious or gratuitous crimes are what may be called the professional stool pigeon, the anonymous informer, and chance. And to a degree—but only to a degree—the acuteness of the investigators." So Sciascia, explaining why *A Man's Blessing* will remain within the limits of the probable, and why its investigator, an observant but not a wise or street-wise professor, must fail. So must the detectives of *The Day of the Owl* and *Equal Danger*, though they are, each in his own way, more admirable than the professor. The "impunity coefficient" confronting them is just as high.

The Day of the Owl was first published in 1961 as *Il Giorno della Civetta*. The title is derived from some lines in Shakespeare's *Henry VI* (Part III, 5.4.55):

> And he that will not fight for such a hope
> Go home to bed, and like the owl by day
> If he arise, be mocked and wondered at.

The speaker is Somerset, and it may be worth noting that a couple of scenes later we see him defeated and led off to execution. Yet the point seems to be that it is more absurd not to fight than to fight for justice, however slight the chance of victory. The owl recurs in the sinister little dialect rhyme recited by the police officer at the *chiarchiaro*.

Bellodi is used to the daylight of the north but works in the Sicilian dark. The opening scene shows us what he is up against. The hitman fires his shotgun, the belated passenger slumps down on his briefcase; the driver sees nothing, the passengers melt away, the seller of *panelle*—Sicilian fritters—sees everything; but when he is brought back he asks with innocent surprise, "Why, has there been a shooting?" Bellodi, differentiated from Sicilians by speech and manners as well as appearance, patiently questions the bereaved Colasbernas, who are dominated by shame rather than grief and regard the polite police officer as a natural enemy. Soon we see that more polished Sicilians, members of Parliament, owners of sulfur mines, regard him with at least as much suspicion; an ex-partisan, a fighter against fascism, a Communist or no better than one, he is their enemy also. The ill-fated informer Parrinieddu, we are told, would also have been astounded to know that he was speaking to an officer who "regarded the authority vested in him as a surgeon regards the knife"; for him as for his betters the only point of having power is to abuse it. The man from Parma, who speaks a different language, has to learn this truth as he seeks for others.

The power of the Mafia (kindly described by its apologist as a "secret association for mutual aid, no more or less than freemasonry") is everywhere skillfully suggested, and the Captain can no more prevail over it than he can cure the Sicilian obsession with cuckoldry and violence. His investigation is conducted with intelligence and resourcefulness; he can handle a Marchica. But he cannot get past don Mariano, and is himself sufficiently sicilianized to take some pleasure in Mariano's magnanimous tribute to him: "You're a man." Coming from one who is "beyond the pale of morality and the law, incapable of pity," this is still taken by the Captain as a compliment.

Towards the end of *The Day of the Owl* there is a sardonic scene in which two Sicilians attend a session of the Parliament in Rome. Crude, foreign, they murmur the old insult of cuckoldry at the fascist who asserts (with some superficial justice) that in the fascist times

Sicily was better run, the *mafia* better controlled; and they hear, too, the government claim that the so-called *mafia* exists only in the imagination of the Left. Back in Parma, Bellodi decides to go back south and try again, as Sciascia himself will, from a perverse love of Sicily.

But the *mafia* phenomenon, being a product of human evil, spreads everywhere. Five years after *The Day of the Owl* Sciascia published *A Man's Blessing*. Here a death-threat to a pharmacist, and the subsequent murder of this man and a doctor friend, when they are out hunting, turns into a matter of national politics—the sell-out of the Communist Party to the Christian Democrats. The Italian title of the book, *A Ciascun il suo* ("to each his own") is a translation of the Vatican newspaper's Latin motto, *Osservatore Romano, Unicuique suum*; the anonymous letter containing the death-threat had been made up of words cut from that newspaper. The professor who notices this begins an investigation, not because he desires to convict anybody of the murder, but out of curiosity, because he, too, is the product of "the centuries of contempt that an oppressed people, an eternally vanquished people, had heaped on the law." In fact, timid and mother-dominated as he is, he knows less of what is going on than anybody, and becomes a victim of his own sexual frustration. He is very little different from the hoodlums and voyeurs, for all his education and culture, and he ends up dead in an abandoned sulfur mine, having uncovered some small truths but still ignorant of other, larger ones, such as the complicity of the Church in shady political deals.

The professor is not merely a Sicilian, however; he is like all of us who feel uneasy when confronted with the law and the bureaucracy. On his way to get the certificate of a clean police record needed when applying for a driver's license, he "was masochistically mulling over the apprehensions typical of any Italian about to enter the labyrinth of a public office building, especially one that goes by the name of Justice." In such circumstances we are all owls by day. We fear both the power of the law and its possible corruption. Perhaps it was to emphasize this universality that Sciascia set his third detective story, *Equal Danger* (1971), in an imaginary country that is and is not Italy. What was called, in *The Day of the Owl*, the "natural tragic solitude" of the Sicilian may now be seen as a universal condition. And, as the author remarks in his concluding note, the details may be Sicilian or Italian, but the substance of the book "must be that of a fable about power anywhere in the world."

The Italian title of *Equal Danger* is *Il Contesto, The Context*, suggesting the scope of the fable: the investigator Rogas is not dealing with the crimes of individual *mafiosi*, but with the whole system, which of course he cannot beat. When the first lawyer is killed Rogas is told that his inquiries must not prejudice the dead man's reputation. As the killings continue, one judge or prosecutor after another, he is again told to abandon his trail, but "Rogas had principles in a country where almost no one did," and carries on, even when demoted. He refuses to accept the "insurrectional cadre" theory because he will not give up the view that the murderer is avenging a wrongful conviction; he has no great faith in official justice, and no desire to cover up the past by falsifying the present.

Few detective stories contain poems, but this one

does, and it is meant to demonstrate the ineffectiveness of the intellectual—in this case the writer Nocio, who also introduces Pascal's wager into the discussion of revolution. In the spirit of Pascal, Nocio bets on the revolution because he will lose nothing if it doesn't take place, but will win everything if it does. Rogas, however, doesn't want "to risk winning"; moreover, he has "a soft spot for losing, for losers." That is why he can identify himself, up to a point, with the elusive murderer, the wronged Cres, and understand his opposition to the law, especially as it is represented by the President of the Supreme Court. He deals skillfully with the investigation, and patiently with the "blandly iniquitous" men of power; but he is beaten in the end.

As a novel of ideas *Equal Danger* reaches its climax in the long conversation with the President. As a story of action it ends with a situation of strange and potent ironies. Rogas dies with the Communist leader Amar when they meet in secret at the National Gallery. Amar dies in front of a portrait of a modern Mexican revolutionary leader by Velásquez (one of Sciascia's many obscure jokes); Rogas is found under a fifteenth-century Florentine painting of the Madonna of the Chain (another little mystery, perhaps an allusion to the part played by the Church in the business of oppression). For the convenience of the State, but also of Amar's successor as party chief, the record will show that Rogas killed Amar. Meanwhile the President himself has been murdered. As they did in France in 1968, the Communists decide that they cannot risk a revolution "at this moment." Another stranded intellectual, Rogas's friend Cusan, ends the book by hopelessly echoing these words. In his concluding note Sciascia speaks of the "steadily greater degradation" wrought by the concatenated power that "we can roughly term *mafioso*"; perhaps the *catena* of the Madonna refers also to that power. Professing to have begun with an amusing puzzle, a "concatenation of clues," Sciascia says that by the time he had finished, the task he had set himself was no longer amusing; like his hero he sees that the revolution "is already defeated." The victor is concatenated power; against it a just cause has no chance, and is shown in the record as evil. But Rogas would not, though he knew these things, "go home to bed"; and Bellodi does so only to convalesce before returning to the country of the *chiarchiaro* and the society of the *lupara*, where Sciascia locates the symbolic source of the evils that dominate the entire human community.

FRANK KERMODE